"Turn, Hell-Hound, Turn!"

The fight. Leap, clash, sweep; hoarse, snarling voices. Macbeth is beaten backward, Macduff raises his claymore, and they plunge out of sight. A scream. A thud. Silence.

Seyton carries his claidheamh-mor and on it, streaming blood, the head of Macbeth. Real blood drips onto his upturned face.

And being well-trained professional actors, they respond, with stricken faces and shaking lips. *"Hail, King of Scotland!"*

The curtain falls...

Praise for A Masterpiece

"Classic Ngaio Marsh."

—*Chicago Sun-Times*

"Marsh's inimitable style is irresistible."

—*Library Journal*

"A theatrical setting, wonderfully vivid characters, and a mystery that only Chief Superintendent Roderick Alleyn could solve ... Dame Ngaio's last novel is first-rate entertainment."

—*Publishers Weekly*

Mysteries by Ngaio Marsh

NGAIO MARSH

Light Thickens

BERKLEY PRIME CRIME, NEW YORK

For James Laurenson, who played The Thane,
and for Helen Thomas (Holmes), who was his
Lady, in the third production of the play
by The Canterbury University Players.

This Berkley Prime Crime Book contains the complete
text of the original hardcover edition.

LIGHT THICKENS

A Berkley Prime Crime Book / published by arrangement with
Little, Brown and Company

PRINTING HISTORY
Little, Brown and Company edition / July 1982
Jove edition / September 1983
Berkley Prime Crime edition / December 1994

ISBN: 0-425-14529-8

Berkley Prime Crime Books are published
by The Berkley Publishing Group,
200 Madison Avenue, New York, New York 10016.
The name BERKLEY PRIME CRIME and the
BERKLEY PRIME CRIME
design are trademarks belonging to Berkley Publishing Corporation.

PRINTED IN THE UNITED STATES OF AMERICA

10 9 8 7 6 5 4 3 2 1

Contents

Cast of Characters

Peregrine Jay	Director, Dolphin Theatre
Emily Jay	His wife
Crispin, Robin, Richard	Their sons
Annie	Their cook
Jeremy Jones	Designer, Dolphin Theatre
Winter Meyer	Dolphin business manager
Mrs. Abrams	Secretary
Bob Masters	Stage manager
Charlie	Assistant stage manager
Ernie James	Property Master
Nanny	Miss Mannering's dresser
Mrs. Smith	Mother of William
	Lighting manager
	Stage-door keeper
	Restaurateur

SCOTLAND YARD

Roderick Alleyn	Chief Superintendent
Fox	Detective Inspector
Thompson	Detective Sergeant
Bailey	Detective Sergeant
Sir James Curtis	Pathologist

Dolphin Theatre

Macbeth
by
William Shakespeare

Duncan, King of Scotland	Norman King
Malcolm } his sons	Edward King
Donalbain	An Actor
Macbeth } generals of the Kings's army	Dougal Macdougal
Banquo	Bruce Barrabell
Macduff	Simon Morten
Lennox	
Ross	
Menteith } Noblemen of Scotland	Actors
Angus	
Caithness	
Fleance, son to Banquo	An Actor
Siward, Earl of Northumberland }	Actors
Young Siward, his son	
Seyton, an officer attending on Macbeth	Gaston Sears
Boy, son to Macduff }	William Smith
A Bloody Sergeant	
A Porter	Actors
Doctor	
Lady Macbeth	Margaret Mannering
Lady Macduff	Nina Gaythorne
Waiting Women	Actresses
The Weird Sisters {	Rangi Western
	Wendy
	Blondie

Sundry soldiers, servants and apparitions
The Scene: Scotland and England
Directed by Peregrine Jay
Setting and Costumes by Jeremy Jones

PART ONE

Curtain Up

1

FIRST WEEK

I

PEREGRINE JAY heard the stage door at the Dolphin open and shut and the sound of voices. The scene and costume designer and the lighting manager came through to the open stage. They wheeled out three specially built racks, unrolled their drawings, and pinned them up.

They were stunning. A permanent central rough stone stairway curved up to Duncan's chamber. Two turntables articulated with this to represent, on the right, the outer facade of Inverness Castle or the inner courtyard, and on the left, a high stone platform with a gallows and a dangling rag-covered skeleton, or, turned, another wall of the courtyard. The central wall was a dull red arras above the stairway, open to the sky.

The lighting manager showed a dozen big drawings of the various sets with the startling changes brought about by his craft. One of these was quite lovely: an opulent evening in front of the castle with the setting sun bathing everything in splendor. One felt the air to be calm, gentle, and full of the sound of wings. A heavenly evening. And then, next to it, the same scene with the enormous doors opened, a dark interior, torches, a piper, and the Lady in scarlet coming to welcome the fated visitor.

"Jeremy," Peregrine said, "you've done us proud."

"Okay?"

"It's so *right*! It's so bloody *right*. Here! Let's up with the curtain. Jeremy?"

The designer went offstage and pressed a button. With a long-drawn-out sigh the curtain rose. The shrouded house waited.

"Light them, Jeremy! Blackout and lights on them. Can you?"

"It won't be perfect but I'll try."

"Just for the hell of it, Jeremy."

Jeremy laughed, moved the racks, and went to the lights console.

Peregrine walked through a pass-door to the front-of-house. Presently there was a total blackout, and then, after a pause, the drawings were suddenly there, alive in the midst of nothing and looking splendid.

"Only approximate, of course," Jeremy said in the dark.

"Let's keep this for the cast to see. They're due now."

"You don't want to start them off with broken legs, do you?" asked the lighting manager.

There was an awkward pause.

"Well — no. Put on the light in the passage," said Peregrine in a voice that was a shade too offhand. "No," he shouted. "Bring down the curtain again, Jeremy. We'll do it properly."

The stage door was opened and more voices were heard, two women's and a man's. They came in exclaiming at the dark.

"All right, all *right*," Peregrine called out cheerfully. "Stay where you are. Lights, Jeremy, would you? Just while people are coming in. Thank you. Come down in front, everybody. Watch how you go. Splendid."

They came down. Margaret Mannering first, complaining about the stairs, in her wonderful warm voice with little breaks of laughter, saying she knew she was unfashionably punctual. Peregrine hurried to meet her.

"Maggie, *darling*! It's all meant to start us off with a bang, but I do apologize. No more steps. Here we are. Sit down in the front row. Nina! Are you all right? Come and sit down, love. Bruce! Welcome, indeed. I'm so glad you managed to fit us in with television."

I'm putting it on a bit thick, he thought. Nerves! Here they all come. Steady now.

They arrived singly and in pairs, having met at the door. They greeted Peregrine and each other extravagantly or facetiously, and all of them asked why they were sitting in front and not onstage or in the rehearsal room. Peregrine kept count of heads. When they got to seventeen and then to nineteen he knew they were waiting for only one: the Thane.

He began again, counting them off. Simon Morten, Macduff. A magnificent figure, six feet two. Dark. Black eyes with a glitter, thick black hair that sprang in short-clipped curls from his skull. A smooth physique not yet running to fat and a wonderful voice. Almost too good to be true. Bruce Barrabell, the Banquo. Slight. Five feet ten inches tall. Fair to sandy hair. Beautiful voice. And the King? Almost automatic casting — he'd played every Shakespearian king in the canon except Lear and Claudius, and played them all well if a little less than perfectly. The great thing about him was his royalty. He was more royal than any of the remaining crowned heads of Europe and his name actually was King: Norman King. The Malcolm was, in real life, his son — a young man of nineteen — and the relationship was striking.

There was the Lennox, sardonic man. Nina Gaythorne, the Lady Macduff, who was talking very earnestly with the Doctor. And I don't mind betting it's about superstition, thought Peregrine uneasily. He looked at his watch. Twenty minutes late, he thought. I've half a mind to start without him, so I have.

A loud and lovely voice and the bang of the stage door.

Peregrine hurried through the pass-door and up onto the stage.

"Dougal, my dear fellow, welcome," he shouted.

"But I'm so sorry, dear boy. I'm afraid I'm a fraction late. Where is everybody?"

"In front. I'm not having a reading."

"Not?"

"No. A few words about the play. The working drawings, and then away we go."

"Really?"

"Come through. This way. Here we go."

Peregrine led the way. "The Thane, everybody," he announced.

It gave Sir Dougal Macdougal an entrance. He stood for a moment on the steps into the front-of-house, an apologetic grin transforming his face. Such a nice chap, he seemed to be saying, no upstage nonsense about him. Everybody loves everybody. Yes. He saw Margaret Mannering. Delight! Acknowledgment! Outstretched arms and a quick advance. "Maggie! My dear! How too lovely!" Kissing of hands and both cheeks. Everybody felt as if the central heating had been turned up another five points. Suddenly they all began talking.

Peregrine stood with his back to the curtain, facing the company with whom he was about to take a journey. Always it felt like this. They had come aboard: they were about to take on other identities. In doing this something would happen to them all: new ingredients would be tried, accepted, or denied. Alongside them were the characters they must assume. They would come closer and if the casting was accurate, slide together. For the time they were onstage they would be one. So he held. And when the voyage was over they would all be again, as Peregrine thought, a little bit different.

He began talking to them.

"I'm not starting with a reading," he said. "Readings are okay as far as they go for the major roles, but bit-parts are bit-parts and as far as the Gentlewoman and the Doctor are concerned, once they arrive they are bloody important, but their zeal won't be set on fire by sitting around waiting for a couple of hours for their entrance.

"Instead, I'm going to invite you to take a hard look at this play and then get on with it. It's short and it's faulty. That is to say, it's full of errors that crept into whatever script was handed to the printers. Shakespeare didn't write the silly Hecate bits so out she comes. It's compact and drives quickly to its end. It's remorseless. I've directed it, in other theatres, twice — each time, I may say, successfully and without any signs of bad luck — so I don't believe in the bad-luck stories associated with it and I hope none of you do either. Or if you do, you'll keep your ideas to yourselves."

He paused long enough to sense a change of awareness in his audience and a quick, instantly repressed, movement of Nina Gaythorne's hands.

"It's straightforward," he said. "I don't find any major difficulties or contradictions in Macbeth. He is a hypersensitive, morbidly imaginative man beset by an overwhelming ambition. From the moment he commits the murder he starts to disintegrate. Every poetic thought, magnificently expressed, turns sour. His wife knows him better than he knows himself and from the beginning realizes that she must bear the burden, reassure her husband, screw his courage to the sticking-place, jolly him along. In my opinion," Peregrine said, looking directly at Margaret Mannering, "she's not an iron monster who can stand up to any amount of hard usage. On the contrary, she's a sensitive creature who has an iron *will* and has made a deliberate, evil choice. In the end she never breaks, but she talks and walks in her sleep. Disastrously."

Maggie leaned forward, her hands clasped, her eyes brilliantly fixed on his face. She gave him a little series of nods. At the moment, at least, she believed him.

"And she's as sexy as hell," he added. "She uses it. Up to the hilt."

He went on. The witches, he said, must be completely accepted. The play was written in James the First's time at

[7]

his request. James the First believed in witches. In their power and their malignancy. "Let us show you," said Peregrine, "what I mean. Jeremy, can you?"

Blackout, and there were the drawings, needle-sharp in the focused lights.

"You see the first one," Peregrine said. "That's what we'll go up on, my dears. A gallows with its victim, picked clean by the witches. They'll drop down from it and dance clumsy widdershins around it. Thunder and lightning. Caterwauls. The lot. Only a few seconds and then they'll leap up and we'll see them in midair. Blackout. They'll fall behind the high rostrum onto a pile of mattresses. Gallows away. Pipers. Lighted torches and we're off."

Well, he thought, I've got them. For the moment. They're caught. And that's all one can hope for. He went through the rest of the cast, noting how economically the play was written and how completely the inherent difficulty of holding the interest in a character as seemingly weak as Macbeth was overcome.

"Weak?" asked Dougal Macdougal. "You think him *weak*, do you?"

"Weak, in respect of this one monstrous thing he feels himself drawn toward doing. He's a most successful soldier. You may say 'larger than life.' He takes the stage, cuts a superb figure. The King has promised he will continue to shower favors upon him. Everything is as rosy as can be. And yet — and yet —"

"His wife?" Dougal suggested. "And the witches!"

"Yes. That's why I say the witches are enormously important. One has the feeling that they are conjured up by Macbeth's secret thoughts. There's not a character in the play that questions their authority. There have been productions, you know, that bring them on at different points, silent but menacing, watching their work.

"They pull Macbeth along the path to that one definitive action. And then, having killed the King, he's left — a Murderer. Forever. Unable to change. His morbid imagination takes charge. The only thing he can think of is to kill again. And again. Notice the imagery. The play closes in on him. And on us. Everything thickens. His clothes are too big, too heavy. He's a man in a nightmare.

"There's the break, the breather for the leading actor, that comes in all the tragedies. We see Macbeth once again with the witches and then comes the English scene with the boy Malcolm taking his oddly contorted way of finding out if Macduff is to be trusted, his subsequent advance into Scotland, the scene of Lady Macbeth speaking of horrors with the strange, dead voice of the sleepwalker.

"And then we see him again; greatly changed; aged, desperate, unkempt; his cumbersome royal robes in disarray, always attended by Seyton, who had grown in size. And so to the end."

He waited for a moment. Nobody spoke.

"I would like," said Peregrine, "before we block the opening scenes, to say a brief word about the secondary parts. It's the fashion to say they're uninteresting. I don't agree. About Lennox, in particular. He's likable, down to earth, quick-witted but slow to make the final break. There's evidence in the imperfect script of some doubt about who says what. We will make Lennox the messenger to Lady Macduff. When next we see him he's marching with Malcolm. His scene with an unnamed thane (we'll give the lines to Ross), when their suspicion of Macbeth, their nosing out of each other's attitudes, develops into a tacit understanding, is 'modern' in treatment, almost black comedy in tone."

"And the Seyton?" asked a voice from the rear. A very deep voice.

"Ah, Seyton. Obviously, he's 'Sirrah,' the unnamed servant who accompanies Macbeth like a shadow, who carries his great claymore, who joins the two murderers and later in the play emerges with a name — Seyton. He has hardly any lines but he's ominous. A big, silent, ever-present amoral fellow who only leaves his master at the end. The very end. We're casting Gaston Sears for the part. Mr. Sears, as you all know, in addition to being an actor is an authority on medieval arms and is already working for us in that capacity." There was an awkward silence followed by an acquiescent murmur.

The saturnine person, sitting alone, cleared his throat, folded his arms, and spoke. "I shall carry," he announced, basso-profundo, "a claidheamh-mor."

"Quite so," said Peregrine. "You are the sword-bearer. As for the —"

"— which has been vulgarized into 'claymore.' I prefer 'claidheamh-mor,' meaning 'great sword'; it being —"

"Quite so, Gaston. And now —"

For a time the voices mingled, the bass one coming through with disjointed phrases: ". . . Magnus's leg-biter . . . quillons formed by turbulent protuberances . . ."

"To continue!" Peregrine shouted. The sword-bearer fell silent.

"And the witches?" asked a helpful witch.

"Entirely evil," answered the relieved Peregrine. "Dressed like fantastic parodies of Meg Merrilies but with terrible faces. We don't see their faces until *look not like th' inhabitants o' the earth, and yet are on 't*, when they are suddenly revealed."

"And speak?"

"Braid Scots."

"What about me, Perry? Braid Scots, too?" suggested the Porter.

"Yes. You enter through the central trap, having been collecting fuel in the basement. And," Peregrine said with ill-concealed pride, "the fuel is bleached driftwood and *most* improperly shaped. You address each piece in turn as a farmer, as an equivocator, and as an English tailor, and you consign them all to the fire."

"I'm a funny man?"

"We hope so."

"Aye. Aweel, it's a fine idea, I'll gie it that. Och, aye. A bonny notion," said the Porter.

He chuckled and mouthed and Peregrine wished he wouldn't but he was a good Scots actor.

He waited for a moment, wondering how much he had gained of their confidence. Then he turned to the designs and explained how they would work and then to the costumes.

"I'd like to say here and now that these drawings and those for the sets — Jeremy has done both — are, to my mind, exactly right. Notice the suggestion of the clan tartans: a sort of primitive pre-tartan. The cloak has a distinctive check affair. All Macbeth's servitors and the murderers wear it. We're in the days when the servitors of royal personages wear their badges and the livery of their masters. Lennox, Angus, Ross, Seyton, wear the distinctive cloaks with the family plaid. Banquo and Fleance have particularly brilliant ones, blood-red with black and silver borders. For the rest, trousers, fur jerkins, and thonged sheepskin chaps. Massive jewelry. Great jeweled bosses, heavy necklets, and heavy bracelets, in Macbeth's case reaching up to the elbow and above it. The general effect is heavy, primitive, but incidentally extremely sexy. Gauntlets, fringed and ornamented. And the crowns! Macbeth's in particular. Huge and heavy, it must look."

" 'Look,' " said Macdougal, "being the operative word, I hope."

"Yes, of course. We'll have it made of plastic. And Maggie . . . do you like what you see, darling?"

What she saw was a skin-tight gown of dull metallic material, slit up one side to allow her to walk. A crimson, heavily furred garment was worn over it, open down the front. She had only one jewel, a great clasp.

"I hope I'll fit it," said Maggie.

"You'll do that," he said. "And now" — he was conscious of a tightness in his chest — "we'll clear stage and get down to business. Oh! There's one point I've missed. You will see that for our first week some of the rehearsals are at night. This is to accommodate Sir Dougal, who is shooting the finals of his new film. The theatre is dark, the current production being on tour. It's a bit out of the ordinary, I know, and I hope nobody finds it too awkward?"

There was a silence during which Sir Dougal with spread arms mimed a helpless apology.

"I can't forbear saying it's very inconvenient," said Banquo.

"Are you filming?"

"Not precisely. But it might arise."

"We'll hope it doesn't," Peregrine said. "Right? Good. Clear stage, please, everyone. Scene One. The Witches."

II

"It's going very smoothly," said Peregrine, three days later. "Almost *too* smoothly."

"Keep your fingers crossed," said his wife, Emily. "It's early days yet."

"True." He looked curiously at her. "I've never asked you," he said. "Do you believe in it? The superstitious legend?"

"No," she said quickly.

"Not the least tiny bit? Really?"

Emily looked steadily at him. "Truly?" she asked.

"Yes."

"My mother was a one-hundred-percent Highlander."

"So?"

"So it's not easy to give you a direct answer. Some superstitions — most, I think — are silly little matters of habit. A pinch of spilt salt over the left shoulder. One may do it without thinking but if one doesn't it's no great matter. That sort of thing. But . . . there are other ones. Not silly. I don't *believe* in them. No. But I think I avoid them."

"Like the *Macbeth* ones?"

"Like them. Yes. But I didn't mind you doing it. Or not enough to try to stop you. Because I don't *really* believe," said Emily very firmly.

"I don't believe at all. Not at any level. I've done two

productions of the play and they both were accident-free and very successful. As for the instances they drag up — Macbeth's sword breaking and a bit of it hitting someone in the audience or a dropped weight narrowly missing an actor's head — if they'd happened in any other play nobody would have said it was an unlucky one. How about Rex Harrison's hairpiece being caught in a chandelier and whisked up into the flies? Nobody said *My Fair Lady* was unlucky."

"Nobody dared to mention it, I should think."

"There is that, of course," Peregrine agreed.

"All the same, it's not a fair example."

"Why isn't it?"

"Well, it's not serious. I mean . . . well . . ."

"You wouldn't say that if you'd been there, I daresay," said Peregrine.

He walked over to the window and looked at the Thames: at the punctual late-afternoon traffic. It congealed on the south bank, piled up, broke out into a viscous stream, and crossed by bridge to the north bank. Above it, caught by the sun, shone the theatre: not very big but conspicuous in its whiteness and, because of the squat mass of little riverside buildings that surrounded it, appearing tall, even majestic.

"You can tell which of them's bothered about the bad-luck stories," he said. "They won't say his name. They talk about the 'Thane' and the 'Scots play' and 'The Lady.' It's catching. Lady Macduff — Nina Gaythorne — silly little ass, is steeped up to the eyebrows in it. And talks about it. Stops if she sees I'm about but she does, all right, and they listen to her."

"Don't let it worry you, darling. It's not affecting their work, is it?" Emily asked.

"No."

"Well, then."

"I know, I know."

Emily joined him and they both looked out, over the Thames, to where the Dolphin shone so brightly. She took his arm. "It's easy to say, I know," she said, "but if you *could* just *not*. Don't brood. It's not like you. Tell me how the great Scot is making out as Macbeth."

"Fine. Fine. He's uncannily lamblike and everyone told me he was a Frankenstein's Monster to work with."

"It's his biggest role so far, isn't it?" Emily asked.

"Yes. He was a good Benedick, but that's the only other Shakespeare part he's played. Out of Scotland. He had a bash at Othello in his repertory days. He was a fantastic Anatomist in Bridie's play when they engaged him for the revival at the Haymarket. That started him off in the West End. Now, of course, he's way up there."

"How's his love life going?"

"I don't really know. He's making a great play for Lady Macbeth at the moment but Maggie Mannering takes it with a tidy load of salt, don't worry."

"Dear Maggie!"

"And dear you!" he said. "You've lightened the load no end. Shall I tackle Nina and tell her not to? Or go on pretending I haven't noticed?"

"What would you say? 'Oh, by the way, Nina darling, *could* you leave off the bad-luck business, scaring the pants off the cast? Just a thought!' "

Peregrine burst out laughing and gave her a pat. "I tell you what," he said, "you're so bloody sharp you can have a go yourself. I'll ask her for a drink, here, and you can choose your moment and then lay into her."

"Are you serious?"

"No. Yes, I believe I am. It might work."

"I don't think it would. She's never been here before. She'd rumble."

"Would that matter? Oh, I don't know. Shall we leave it a bit longer? I think so."

"And so do I," said Emily. "With any luck they'll get sick of it and it'll die a natural death."

"So it may," he agreed and hoped he sounded convincing. "That's a comforting thought. I must return to the blasted heath."

III

HE wouldn't have taken much comfort from the lady in question if he could have seen her at that moment. Nina Gaythorne came into her minute flat in Westminster and began a sort of delousing ritual. Without waiting to take off her hat or her gloves, she scuffled in her handbag and produced a crucifix, which she kissed and laid on the table near a clove of garlic and her prayerbook. She opened the letter, put on her spectacles, crossed herself, and read aloud the ninety-first Psalm.

" 'Whoso dwelleth under the defence of the Most High,' " read Nina in the well-trained, beautifully modulated tones of a professional actress. When she reached the end, she kissed her prayerbook, crossed herself again, laid her marked-up part on the table, the prayerbook on top of it, the crucifix on the prayerbook, and, after a slight hesitation, the clove of garlic at the foot of the crucifix.

"*That* ought to settle their hash," she said and took off her gloves.

Her belief in curses and things being lucky or unlucky was based not on any serious study but merely on the odds and ends of gossip and behavior accumulated by four generations of theatre people. In that most hazardous profession where so many mischances can occur, when so much hangs in the precarious balance on opening night, when five weeks' preparation may turn to ashes or blaze for years, there is a fertile soil indeed for superstition to take root and flourish.

Nina was forty years old, a good dependable actress, happy to strike a long run and play the same part eight times a week for year after year, being very careful not to let it become an entirely mechanical exercise. The last part of this kind had come to an end six months ago and nothing followed it, so that this little plum, Lady Macduff, uncut for once, had been a relief. And the child might be a nice boy. Not the precocious little horror that could emerge from an in-different school. And the house! The Dolphin! The enormous prestige attached to an engagement there. Its phenomenal run of good luck and, above all, its practice of using the same people when they had gained an entry, whenever a suitable role occurred: a happy engagement. Touch wood!

So, really, she must *not*, really *not*, talk about the Scots play to other people in the cast. It just kept slipping out. Peregrine Jay had noticed and didn't like it. I'll make a resolution, Nina thought. She shut her large, faded eyes tight and said aloud:

"I promise on my word of honor and upon this prayerbook *not* to talk about you-know-what. Amen."

"Maggie," shouted Simon Morten. "Hold on, wait a moment."

Margaret Mannering stopped at the top of Wharfingers Lane where it joined the main highway. A procession of four enormous lorries thundered past. Morten hurried up the last steep bit. "I got trapped by Gaston Sears," he panted. "Couldn't get rid of him. How about coming to the George for a meal? It won't take long in a taxi."

"Simon! My dear, I'm sorry. I've said I'll dine with Dougal."

"But — where *is* Dougal?"

"Fetching his car. I said I'd come up to the corner and wait for him. It's a chance to talk about our first encounter. In the play, I mean."

"Oh. I see. All right, then."

"Sorry, darling."

"Not a bit. I quite understand."

"Well," she said. "I hope you do."

"I've said I do, haven't I? Here comes your Thane in his scarlet chariot."

He made as if to go and then stopped. Dougal Macdougal pulled up to the curb. "Here I am, sweetie," he declared. "Hullo, Simon. Just the man to open the door for the lovely lady and save me a bash on the bottom from oncoming traffic."

Morten removed his beret, pulled on his forelock, and opened the door with exaggerated humility. Margaret got into the car without looking at him and said, "Thank you, darling."

He banged the door.

"Can we drop you somewhere?" Dougal asked, as an afterthought.

"No, thank you. I don't know where you're going but it's not in my direction." Dougal pulled a long face, nodded, and moved out into the traffic. Simon Morten stood looking after them, six feet two of handsome disgruntlement, his black curls still uncovered. He said: "Well, shit off and be damned to you," crammed his beret on, turned into the lane, and entered the little restaurant known as the Junior Dolphin.

"What's upset the Thane of Fife?" asked Dougal casually.

"Nothing. He's being silly."

"Not, by any chance, a teeny-weeny bit jealous?"

"Maybe. He'll recover."

"Hope so. Before we get round to bashing away at each other with Gaston's claymores."

"Indeed, yes. Gaston really is more than a bit dotty, don't you think? All that talk about armory. And he wouldn't *stop.*"

"I'm told he did spend a short holiday in a sort of halfway house. A long time ago, though, and he was quite harmless. Just wore a sword and spoke middle English. He's a sweet man, really. He's been asked by Perry to teach us the fight. He wants us to practice duels in slow motion every day for five weeks building up muscle and getting a bit faster very slowly. To the Anvil Chorus from *Trovatore.*"

"Not really?"

"Of course not, when it comes to performance. Just at rehearsals to get the rhythm. They are frightfully heavy, claymores are."

"Rather you than me," said Maggie and burst out laughing.

Dougal began to sing very slowly. "*Bang*. Wait for it. *Bang*. Wait again. And bangle-bangle *bang*. Wait. *Bang*."

"With two hands, of course."

"Of .course, I can't lift the thing off the floor without puffing and blowing. Gaston brought one down for us to try."

"He's actually *making* the ones you're going to use, isn't he? Couldn't he cheat and use lighter material or papier-mâché for the hilt or something?"

"My dear, no good at all. It would upset the balance."

"Well, do be careful," said Maggie vaguely.

"Of course. The thing is that the blades won't be sharp at all. Blunt as blunt. But if one of us was simply hit, it would merely break his bones."

"Really?"

"To smithereens," said Dougal. "I promise you."

"I think you're going to look very silly, the two of you, floundering about. You'll get laughs. I can think of all sorts of things that might go wrong."

"Such as?"

"Well! One of you making a swipe and missing and the claymore getting stuck in the scenery."

"It's going to be *very* short. In time. Only a minute or so. He backs away into the O.P. corner and I roar after him. Simon's a very powerful man, by the by. He picked the claymore up in a dégagé manner and then he spun round and couldn't stop and hung on to it, looking absolutely terrified. That *was* funny," said Dougal. "I laughed like anything at old Si."

"Well, don't, Dougal. He's very sensitive."

"Oh, pooh. Listen, sweetie. We're called for eight-thirty, aren't we? I suggest we go to my restaurant on the Embankment for a light meal and settle our relationship and then we'll be ready for the blood and thunder. How does that strike you? With a dull thud or pleasurably?"

"Not a large, sinking dinner before work? And nothing to drink?"

"A dozen oysters and some thin brown bread and butter?"

"Delicious."

"Good," said Dougal.

"By 'settle our relationship' you refer exclusively to the Macbeths, of course."

"Do I? Well, so be it. For the time being," he said coolly, and drove on without further comment until they crossed the river, turned into a tangle of little streets emerging finally in Savoy Minor, and stopped.

"I've taken the flat for the duration. It belongs to Teddy Somerset, who's in the States for a year," said Dougal.

"It's a smashing facade."

"Very Regency, isn't it? Let's go inside. Come on."

So they went in.

It was a sumptuous interior presided over by a larger-than-life nude efficiently painted in an extreme of realism. Maggie gave it a quick look, sat down underneath it, and said: "There are just one or two things I'd like to get sorted out. They've discussed the murder of Duncan before the play opens. That's clear enough. But always it's been 'if' and 'suppose,' never until now, 'He's coming here. It's now or never.' Agreed?"

"Yes."

"It's only been something to talk about. Never calling for a decision. Or for anything real."

"No. And now it does, and he's face to face with it, he's appalled."

"As she knows he will be. She knows that without her egging him on he'd never do it. So what has she got that will send him into it? Plans. Marvelous plans. Yes. But he won't go beyond talking about plans. Sex. Perry said so, the first day. Shakespeare had to be careful about sex because of the boy actor. But we don't."

"We certainly do not," he said. He moved behind her and put a hand on her shoulder.

"Do you realize," Maggie said, "how short their appearances together are? And how *beaten* she is after the banquet scene and they are alone. She makes a superb effort during the scene, but I think, once she's rid of those damned thanes and is left with her mumbling, shattered lion of a husband and they go dragging upstairs to the bed they cannot sleep in, she knows all that's left for her to do is shut up. The next and last time we see her she's talking disastrously in her sleep. Really, it's quite a short part, you know."

"How far am I affected by her collapse, do you think?" he asked. "Do I notice it? Or by that time am I so determined to give myself over to idiotic killing?"

"I think you are." She turned to look at him, and something in her manner of doing this made him withdraw his already possessive hand. She stood up and moved away.

"I think I'll just ring up the Wig and Piglet for a table," he said abruptly.

"Yes, do."

When he had done this she said: "I've been looking at the imagery. There's an awful lot about clothes being too big and heavy. I see Jeremy's emphasizing that and I'm glad. Great walloping cloaks that can't be contained by a belt. Heavy crowns. We have to consciously fill them. You much more than I, of course. I fade out. But the whole picture is nightmarish."

"How do you see *me*, Maggie?"

"My dear! As a falling star. A magnificent, violently ambitious being, destroyed by his own imagination. It's a cosmic collapse. Monstrous events attend it. The heavens themselves are in revolt. Horses eat each other."

Dougal breathed in deeply. Up went his chin. His eyes, startlingly blue, flashed under his tawny brows. He was six feet one inch in height and looked more.

"That's the stuff," said Maggie. "I think you'll want to make it very, *very* Scots, Highland Scots. They'll call you The Red Macbeth," she added, a little hurriedly. "It *is* your very own name, sweetie, isn't it — Dougal Macdougal?"

"Oh, aye, it's ma given name."

"That's the ticket, then."

They fell into a discussion on whether he should, in fact, use the dialect, and decided against it as it would entail all the other lairds doing so too.

"Just porters and murderers, then," said Maggie. "If Perry says so, of course. You won't catch me doing it." She tried it out. "*Come tae ma wumman's breasts and tak' ma milk for gall.* Really, it doesn't sound too bad."

"Let's have one tiny little drink to it. Do say yes, Maggie."

"All right. Yes. The merest suggestion, though."

"Okay. Whiskey? Wait a moment."

He went to the end of the room and pressed a button. Two doors rolled apart, revealing a little bar.

"Good heavens!" Maggie exclaimed.

"I know. Rather much, isn't it? But that's Teddy's taste."

She went over to the bar and perched on a high stool. He found the whiskey and soda and talked about his part. "I hadn't thought 'big' enough," he said. "A great, faulty giant. Yes. Yes, you're right about it, of course. *Of course.*"

"Steady. If that's mine."

"Oh! All right. Here you are, lovey. What shall we drink to?"

"Obviously. *Macbeth.*"

He raised his glass. Maggie thought: He's a splendid figure. He'll make a good job of the part, I'm sure. But he said in a deflated voice: "No. No, don't say it. It might be bad luck. No toast," and drank quickly as if she might cut in.

"Are you superstitious?" she asked.

"Not really. It was just a feeling. Well, I suppose I am, a bit. You?"

"Like you. Not really. A bit."

"I don't suppose there's one of us who isn't. Just a bit."

"Peregrine," Maggie said at once.

"He doesn't seem like it, certainly. All that stuff about keeping it under our hats even if we do fancy it."

"Still. Two successful productions and not a thing happening at either of them," said Maggie.

"There is that, of course." He waited for a moment and then in a much too casual manner said: "They were going to do it in the Dolphin, you know. Twenty years or so ago. When it opened."

"Why didn't they?"

"The leading man died or something. Before they'd come together. Not a single rehearsal, I'm told. So it was dropped."

"Really?" said Maggie. "What are the other rooms like? More nudes?"

"Shall I show you?"

"I don't think so, thank you."

She looked at her watch. "Shouldn't we be going to your Wig and Piglet?"

"Perry's taking the witches first. We've lots of time."

"Still, I'm obsessively punctual and shan't enjoy my oysters if we're cutting it short."

"If you insist."

"Well, I do. Sorry. I'll just tidy up. Where's your bathroom?"

He opened a door. "At the end of the passage," he said.

She walked past him, hunting in her bag as she went, and thought, If he pounces I'll be in for a scene and a bore.

He didn't pounce but nor did he move. Unavoidably she brushed against him and thought: He's got more of what it takes, Highland or Lowland, than is decent.

She did her hair, powdered her face, used her lipstick, and put on her gloves in a bathroom full of mechanical weight-reducers, potted plants, and a framed rhyme of considerable indecency.

"Right?" she asked briskly on reentering the sitting room.

"Right." He put on his overcoat and they left the flat. It was dark outside now. He took her arm. "The steps are slippery," he said. "You don't want to start off with a sprained ankle, do you?"

"No. That I don't."

He was right. The steps glimmered with untimely frost and

she was glad of his support. His overcoat was Harris tweed and smelled of peat fires.

As she got into the car, Maggie caught sight of a tall man wearing a short overcoat and a red scarf. He was standing about sixty feet away.

"Hullo," she exclaimed. "That's Simon. Hi!" She raised her hand but he had turned away and was walking quickly into a side street.

"I thought that was Simon Morten," she said.

"Where?"

"I made a mistake. He's gone."

They drove back over the river and along the Embankment to the Wig and Piglet. The street lights were brilliant: snapping and sparkling in the cold air and broken into sequins on the outflowing Thames. Maggie felt excited and uplifted. When they entered the little restaurant with its huge fire, white tablecloths, and shining glasses, her cheeks flamed and her eyes were brilliant. Suddenly she loved everybody.

"You're fabulous," Dougal said. Some of the people had recognized them and were smiling. The maître d'hôtel made a discreet fuss over them. She was in rehearsal for a superb play and opposite her was her leading man.

She began to talk, easily and well. When champagne was brought she thought; I ought to stop him opening it. I *never* drink before rehearsals. But how dreary and out of tune with the lovely evening that would be.

"Temperamental inexactitude," she said quite loudly. "British Constitution."

"I beg your pardon, Maggie?"

"I was just testing myself to make sure I'm not tiddly."

"You are not tiddly."

"I'm not used to whiskey and you gave me a big one."

"No, I didn't. You are not tiddly. You're just suddenly elevated. Here come our oysters."

"Well, if you say so, I suppose I'm all right."

"Of course you are. Wade in."

So she did wade in and she was not tiddly. In the days to

come she was to remember this evening, from the time when she left the flat until the end of their rehearsal, as something apart. Something between her and London, with Dougal Macdougal as a sort of necessary ingredient. But no more.

IV

GASTON SEARS inhabited a large old two-story house in a tiny cul-de-sac opening off Alleyn Road in Dulwich. It was called Alleyn's Surprise and the house and grounds occupied the whole of one side. The opposite side was filled with neglected trees and an unused pumping house.

The rental of such a large building must have been high, and among the Dulwich College boys there was a legend that Mr. Sears was an eccentric foreign millionaire who lived there, surrounded by fabulous pieces of armor, and made swords and practiced black magic. Like most legends this was founded on highly distorted fact. He *did* live amongst his armor and he did very occasionally make swords. And his collection of armor was the most prestigious, outside the walls of a museum, in Europe. And certainly he *was* eccentric.

Moreover, he was comfortably off. He had started as an actor, a good one in far-out, eccentric parts, but so inclined to extremes of argumentative temperament that nobody cared to employ him. A legacy enabled him to develop his flair for historic arms and accoutrements. His expertise was recognized by all the European collectors and he was the possessor of honorary degrees from various universities. He made lecture tours in America for which he charged astronomical fees, and extorted frightening amounts from greedy, ignorant, and unscrupulous buyers which more than compensated for the opinions he gave freely to those he decided to respect. Of these Peregrine Jay was one.

The unexpected invitation to appear as sword-bearer to Macbeth had been accepted with complacency. "I shall be able to watch the contest," he had observed. "And afterward correct any errors that may creep in. I do not altogether trust tne Macbeth. Dougal Macdougal! Indeed!" he sneered. "No. He is not to be trusted."

He was engaged upon making molds for the weapons. From a mold of the genuine, historical claidheamh-mor a replica would be cast in molten steel, which Macbeth would wear. Gaston himself would carry the real claidheamh-mor throughout the performance. A second claymore, less elaborate, would make the mold for the weapon Macduff would wear.

His workshop was a formidable background. Suits of armor stood ominously about the room, swords of various ages and countries hung on the walls with drawings of details in ornamentation. A life-size effigy of a Japanese warrior in an ecstasy of the utmost ferocity, clad in full armor, crouched in warlike attitude, his face contorted with rage and his sword poised to strike.

Gaston hummed and occasionally muttered as he made the long wooden trough that was to contain clay from which the matrix would be formed. He made a good figure for a Vulcan, being hugely tall with a shock of black hair and heavily muscled arms.

"*Double, double toil and trouble,*" he hummed in time with his hammering. And then:

"*Her husband's to Aleppo gone, master o' the Tiger*
But in a sieve I'll thither sail
And, like a rat without a tail,
I'll do and I'll do and I'll do —
And on the final *I'll do* he tapped home his nail.

V

BRUCE BARRABELL, who played Banquo, was not on call for the current rehearsal. He stayed at home and learned his part and dwelt upon his grievances. His newest agent was getting him quite a bit of work but nothing that was likely to do him any lasting good. A rather dim supporting role in another police series for Grenada. And now, Banquo. He'd asked to be tried for Macbeth and been told the part was already cast. Macduff: same thing. He was leaving the theatre when some whippersnapper came after him and said would he come to read Banquo. There'd been some kind of a slipup. So he did and he'd got it. Small part, actually. Lot of standing round with one foot up and the other down on those bloody steps. But there was one little bit. He flipped his part over and began to read it.

"*There's husbandry in heaven; Their candles are all out.*"

He read it aloud. Quietly. The slightest touch of whimsicality. Feel the time of night and the great empty courtyard. He had to admit it was good. "There's *housekeeping* in Heaven." The homely touch that somehow made you want to cry. Would a modern audience understand that housekeeping was what was meant by husbandry? Nobody else could write about the small empty hours as this man did. The young actor they'd produced for Fleance, his son, was nice: unbroken, clear voice. And then Macbeth's entrance and Banquo's reaction. Good stuff. *His* scene, but of course the Macbeth would overact and Perry would let him get away with it. Look at the earlier scene. Although Perry, fair's fair, put a stop to that little caper. But the intention was there for all to see.

He set himself to memorize, but it wasn't easy. Incidents out of the past kept coming in. Conversations . . .

"Actually, we are not quite strangers. There was a *Macbeth* up in Dundee, sir. I won't say how many years ago."

"Oh?"

"We were witches." Whispering it. Looking coy.

"Really? Sorry. Excuse me. I want to — Perry, Perry, dear boy, just a word —"

Swine! Of course he remembered.

VI

IT WAS the Angus's birthday. He, the Ross, and the rest of the lairds and the three witches were not called for the evening's rehearsal. They arranged with other free members of the cast to meet at the Swan in Southwark and drink Angus's health.

They arrived in twos and threes and it was quite late by the time the witches, who had been rehearsing in the afternoon, came in. Two girls and a man. The man (First Witch) was a part Maori called Rangi Western, not very dark but with the distinctive short upper lip and flashing eyes. He had a beautiful voice and was a prize student from the London Academy of Music and Dramatic Art. The second witch was a nondescript thin girl called Wendy, possessed of a remarkable voice: harsh, with strange, unexpected intervals. The third was a lovely child, a white-blonde, delicate, with enormous eyes and a babyish high-pitched voice. She was called Blondie.

Their rehearsal had excited them. They came in talking loudly. "Rangi, you were *marvelous*. You sent cold shivers down my spine. Truly. And that movement! I thought Perry would stop you but he didn't. The stamp. It was super. We've got to do it, Wendy, along with Rangi. His tongue. And his eyes. Everything."

"I thought it was fabulous giving us the parts. I mean the *difference*! Usually they all look alike and are too boring for words — all masks and mumbles. But we're *really* evil. I mean *really*!"

"Angus!" they shouted. "Happy birthday, love. Bless you."

Now they had all arrived. The witches were the center of attention. Rangi was not very talkative, but the two girls excitedly described his performance at rehearsal.

"He was standing with us, listening to Perry's description, weren't you, Rangi? Perry was saying we have to be the *incarnation* of evil. Not a drop of goodness anywhere about us.

"It's got to be *there*. You know? In every move we make. How did he put it, Wendy?"

" 'Trembling with animosity,' " said Wendy.

"Yes. And I was standing by Rangi and I *felt* him tremble, I swear I did."

[27]

"You did, didn't you, Rangi? Tremble?"

"Sort of," Rangi mumbled. "Don't make such a thing about it."

"No, but you were marvelous. You sort of grunted and bent your knees. And your *face*! Your tongue! And eyes!"

"Anyway, Perry was completely taken with it and asked him to repeat it and asked us to do it — not too much. Just a kind of ripple of hatred. It's going to work, you know."

"Putting a curse on him. That's what it is, Rangi, isn't it?"

"Have a drink, Rangi, and show us."

Rangi made a brusque, dismissive gesture and turned away to greet the Angus.

The men closed around him. They were none of them quite drunk, but they were noisy. The members of the company now far outnumbered the other patrons, who had taken their drinks to a table in the corner of the room and looked on with ill-concealed interest.

"It's my round," Angus shouted. "I'm paying, all of you. No arguments. Yes, I insist. *That which hath made them drunk hath made me bold*," he shouted.

His voice faded out and so, raggedly, did all the others. Blondie's giggle persisted and died. A single voice — Angus's — asked uncertainly: "What's up? Oh. Oh, I see. Oh, hell! Never mind. Sorry everybody. Drink up."

They drank in silence. Rangi drained his pint of light and bitter. Angus nodded to the barman, who replaced it with another. Angus mimed pouring in something else and laid an uncertain finger on his lips. The barman winked and added a tot of gin. He pushed the drink over toward Rangi's hand. Rangi's back was turned but he felt the glass, looked around, and saw it.

"Is that mine?" he asked, puzzled.

They all seized on this. They said confusedly that of course it was his drink. "Go on, have it. Drink it up. No heeltaps."

It was something to make a fuss about, something that would make them all forget about Angus's blunder. They bet Rangi wouldn't drink it down then and there. So Rangi did. There was a round of applause.

"Show us, Rangi. Show us what you did. Don't *say* anything, just show."

"E-e-e-*ah!*" he shouted suddenly. He slapped his knees and stamped. He grimaced, his eyes glittered, and his tongue whipped in and out. He held his umbrella before him like a spear and it was not funny.

It lasted only a few seconds.

They applauded and asked him what it meant and was he "weaving a spell." He said no, nothing like that. His eyes were glazed. "I've had a little too much to drink," he said. "I'll go now. Good-night, all of you."

They objected. Some of them hung on to him but they did it halfheartedly. He brushed them off. "Sorry," he said, "I shouldn't have taken that drink. I'm no good with drinking." He pulled some notes out of his pocket and shoved them across the bar. "My round," he said. "Good-night, all."

He walked quickly to the swing doors, lost his balance, and regained it.

"You all right?" Angus asked.

"No," he answered. "Far from it."

He walked into the doors. They swung out and he went with them. They saw him pull up, look stiffly to right and left, raise his umbrella in a magnificent gesture, get into the taxi that responded, and disappear.

"He's all right," said one of the lairds. "He's got a room round here."

"Nice chap."

"Very nice."

"I've heard, I don't know who told me, mark you," said Angus, "that drink has a funny effect on Maori people. Goes straight to their heads and they revert to their savage condition."

"Rangi hasn't," said Ross. "He's gone grand."

[29]

"He did when he performed that dance or whatever it was," said the actor who played Menteith.

"You know what I think?" said Ross. "I think he was upset when you quoted."

"It's all a load of old bullshit, anyway," said a profound voice in the background.

This provoked a confused expostulation that came to its climax when the Menteith roared out: "Thass all very fine but I bet you wouldn't call the play by its right name. Would you do that?"

Silence.

"There you are!"

"Only because it'd upset the rest of you."

"Yah!" they all said.

The Ross, an older man who was sober, said: "I think it's silly to talk about it. We feel as we do in different ways. Why not just accept that and stop nattering?"

"Somebody ought to write a book about it," said Wendy.

"There *is* a chapter about it in a book called *Supernatural on Stage*, by Richard Huggett."

They finished their drinks. The party had gone flat.

"Call it a day, chaps?" asked Ross.

"That's about the strength of it," Menteith agreed.

The nameless and lineless thanes noisily concurred and gradually they drifted out.

Ross said to the Angus, "Come on, old boy, I'll see you home."

"I'm afraid I've overstepped the mark. Sorry. *We were carousing till the second cock.* Oh, dear, there I go again."

"Come on, old boy."

"All right." He made a shaky attempt to cross himself. "I'm okay," he said.

"Of course you are."

"Right you are, then. Good-night, Porter," he said to the barman.

"Good-night, sir."

They went out.

"Actors," said one of the guests.

"That's right, sir," the barman agreed, collecting their glasses.

"What was that they were saying about some superstition? I couldn't make head or tail of it."

"They make out it's unlucky to quote from this play. They don't use the title either."

"Silly sods," remarked another.

"They take it for gospel."

"Probably some publicity stunt by the author."

The barman grunted.

"What is the name of the play, then?"

"*Macbeth*."

VII

REHEARSALS for the duel had begun and were persisted in remorselessly. At 9:30 every morning Dougal Macdougal and Simon Morten, armed with weighted wooden claymores, slashed and banged away at each other in a slow dance superintended by a merciless Gaston.

The whole affair, step by step, blow by blow, had been planned down to the last inch. Both men suffered agonies from the strain on muscles unaccustomed to such exercise. They sweated profusely. Gaston had found an ancient 45-rpm record of the Anvil Chorus, which when played at a lower speed ground out a lugubrious, laborious, nightmarelike accompaniment, made more hateful by Gaston humming, also out of tune.

The relationship among the three men was, from the first, uneasy. Dougal tended to be facetious. "What ho, varlet. Have at thee, miscreant," he would cry.

Morten — Macduff — did not respond to these sallies. He was ominously polite and glum to a degree. When Dougal swung at him, lost his balance, and ran, as it were, after his own weapon, wild-eyed, an expression of great concern upon his face, Morten allowed himself a faint sneer. When Dougal finally tripped and fell in a sitting position with a sickening thud, the sneer deepened.

"The balance!" Gaston screamed. "How many times must I insist? If you lose the balance of your weapon you lose your own balance and end up looking foolish. As now."

Dougal rose. With some difficulty and using his claymore as a prop.

"No!" chided Gaston. "It is to be handled with respect, not dug into the floor and climbed up."

"This is merely a dummy. Why should I respect it?"

"It weighs exactly the same as the claidheamh-mor."

"What's that got to do with it?"

"Again! We begin at the beginning. Again! Up! Weakling!"

"I'm not accustomed," said Dougal magnificently, "to being treated in this manner."

"No? Forgive me, Sir Dougal. And, let me tell you, Sir Dougal, that I, Gaston Sears, am not accustomed to conducting myself like a mincing dancing master, Sir Dougal. It is only because this fight is to be performed before audiences of discrimination, with weapons that are the precise replicas of the original claidheamh-mor, that I have consented to teach you."

"If you ask me, we'd get on a lot better if we faked the whole show. The whole bloody show. Oh, all right, all right," Dougal amended, answering the really alarming expression that contorted Gaston's face. "I give in. Let's get on with it. Come on."

"Come on," echoed Morten. "*Thou bloodier villain than terms can give thee out!*"

Whack. Bang. Down came his claymore, caught on Macbeth's shield. "Te-*tum*. Te-*tum-te* — disengage," shouted Gaston. "Macbeth sweeps across. Macduff leaps over the blade. Te-tum-tum. That is better. That is an improvement. You have achieved the rhythm. Now we shall take it a little faster."

"Faster! My God, you're killing us."

"You handle your weapon like a peasant. Look. I shall show you. Here, give it to me."

Dougal, using both hands, threw the claymore at him. With great dexterity, Gaston caught it by the hilt, twirled it, and held it before him, pointed at Dougal.

"Hah!" he shouted. "Hah and hah again." He lunged, changed his grip, and swept the weapon up — and down.

Dougal leaped to one side. "Christ Almighty!" he cried. "What are you doing?"

Grimacing abominably, Gaston brought the heavy claymore up in a conventional salute.

"Handling my weapon, Sir Dougal. And you will do so before I have finished with you."

Dougal whispered.

"I beg your pardon?"

"You've got the strength of the devil, Gaston."

"No. It is a matter of balance and rhythm more than strength. Come, take the first exchange a tempo. Yes, a tempo. Come."

He offered the claymore ceremoniously to Dougal, who took it and heaved it up into the salute.

"Good! We progress. One moment."

He went to the phonograph and altered the timing. "Listen," he said and switched it on. Out came the Anvil Chorus, remorselessly truthful as if rejoicing in its own restoration. Gaston switched it off. "That is our timing." He turned to Simon Morten. "Ready, Mr. Morten?"

"Quite ready."

"The cue, if you please."

"*Thou bloodier villain than terms can give thee out.*"

And the fight was a fight. There was rhythm and there was timing. For a minute and a quarter all went well and at the end the two men, pouring sweat, leaning on their weapons, breathless, waited for his comment.

"Good. There were mistakes but they were comparatively small. Now, while we are warm and limbered up we shall do it once more, but without the music. Yes. Are you recovered? Good."

"We are not recovered," Dougal panted.

"This is the last effort for today. Come. I shall count the beats. Without music. From the cue."

"*Thou bloodier villain than terms can give thee out.*"

"*Bang*. Pause. *Bang*. Pause. And *bangle — bangle — bang*. Pause."

They got through it but only just, and they were really cooked at the end.

"Good," said Gaston. "Tomorrow. Same time. Thank you, gentlemen."

He bowed and left.

Morten, his black curls damp and the tangled mat of hair on his chest gleaming, vigorously toweled himself. Sir Dougal, tawny, fair-skinned, drenched in sweat and breathing hard, reached for his own towel and feebly dabbed at his chest.

"We did it," he said. "I'm flattened but we did it."

Morten grunted and pulled on his shirt and sweater.

"You'd better get something warm on," he said. "Way to catch cold."

"Night after night after night. Have you thought of that?"

"Yes."

"Why do I do it! Why do I submit myself! I ask myself, why?"

Morten grunted.

"I'll speak to Perry about it. I'll demand insurance."

"For which bit of you?"

"For all of me. The thing's ridiculous. A good fake and we'd have them breathless."

"Instead of which we're breathless ourselves," said Morten and took himself off. It was the nearest approach to a conversation that they had enjoyed.

So ended the first week of rehearsals.

2

SECOND WEEK

PEREGRINE had blocked the play up to the aftermath following the assassination of King Duncan. The only break in the performance would come here.

Rehearsals went well. The short opening scene with the witches scavenging on the gallows worked. Rangi, perched on the arm, was terribly busy with the head of the corpse. Blondie, on Wendy's back, ravaged its feet. A flash of lightning. Pause. Thunder. They hop down, like birds of prey. Dialogue. Then their leap. The flash catches them. In the air. Blackout and down.

"Well," said Peregrine. "The actions are spot-on. Thank you. It's now up to the lights: an absolute cue. Catch them in a flash before they fall. You witches must remember to keep flat and then scurry off in the blackout. Okay?"

"Can we keep well apart?" asked Rangi. "Before we take off? Otherwise we may fall on each other."

"Yes. Get in position when you answer the caterwauls. Wendy, you take the point farthest away when you hear them. Blondie, you stay where you are, and Rangi, you answer from under the gallows. Think of birds — ravens. That's it. Splendid. Next scene."

It was their first rehearsal in semicontinuity. It would be

terribly rough but Peregrine liked his cast to get the feeling of the whole as early as possible. Here came the King. Superb bearing. Lovely entrance. Pause on steps. Thanes move on below him. Bloody Sergeant on ground-level, back to audience. The King — magnificent.

Up to his tricks again, thought Peregrine and stopped them.

"Sorry, old boy," he said. "There's an extra move from you here. Remember? Come down. The thanes wheel round behind you. Bloody Sergeant moves up and we'll all focus on him for the speech. Okay?"

The King raised a hand and slightly shook his head. "So sorry. Of course." He graciously complied. The Bloody Sergeant, facing front and determined to wring the last syllable from his minute part, embarked upon it with many pauses and gasps.

When it was over, Peregrine said: "Dear boy, you are determined *not* to faint or *not* to gasp. You can't quite manage it but you do your best. You keep going. Your voice fades out but you master it. You even manage your little joke, *As sparrows eagle or the hare the lion*, and we cut to: *But I am faint, my gashes cry for help*. You make a final effort. You salute. Your hand falls to your side and we see the blood on it. You are helped off. Don't *do* so much, dear boy. *Be!* I'll take you through it afterward. On."

The King returned to his place of vantage. Ross made an excitable entrance with news of the defeat of the faithless Cawdor. The King established his execution and the bestowal of his title upon Macbeth. Peregrine had cut the scene down to its bones. He made a few notes and went straight on to the witches again.

Now came the moment for the first witch and the long speech about the sailor to Aleppo gone. Then the dance. Legs bent. Faces distorted. Eyes. Tongues. It works, thought Peregrine. The drums and pipes, offstage, with retreating soldiers. Very ominous. Enter Macbeth and Banquo. Witches in a cluster, floor-level. Motionless.

Macbeth was superb. The triumphant soldier — a glorious figure: ruddy, assured, glowing with his victories. Now, face to face with evil itself and hailed by the title. The hidden dream suddenly made actual; the unwholesome pretense, a tangible reality. He writes to his wife and sends the letter ahead of his own arrival.

Enter the Lady. Maggie was still feeling her way with the part, but there were no doubts about her intention. She had deliberately faced the facts and made her choice, rejected the right and fiercely embraced the wrong. She now braces herself for the monstrous task of screwing her husband to the sticking-place. She knows very well that there was no substance in their previous talks although his morbidly vivid imagination gave them a nightmarish reality.

The play hurried on: the festive air, Macbeth's piper, servants scurrying with dishes of food and flagons of wine, and all the time Macbeth is crumbling. The great barbaric chieftain who should outshine all the rest makes dismal mistakes. He was not there to welcome the King, is not in his place now. His wife has to leave the feast, find him, tell him the King is asking for him, only to have him say he will proceed no further in the business and offer conventional reasons.

There is no time to lose. For the last assault she lays the plot before her husband (and the audience) — quickly, urgently, and clearly. He catches fire, says he is *"settled,"* and commits himself to damnation.

Seyton, with the claymore, appears in the shadows. He follows them off.

The lights will be extinguished by a servant who leaves only the torch in a wall-bracket outside the King's door. A pause, during which the stealthy sounds of the night will be established. Cricket and owl. The sudden crack of expanding wood. A ghostly figure, who would scarcely be seen when the lighting was established, appears on the upper level, enters the King's room, waits there for a heartbeat or two, reenters, and slips away into the shadows. . . . The Lady.

Ngaio Marsh

An inner door at ground-level opens to admit Banquo and Fleance and the exquisite little night scene follows.

Bruce Barrabell had a wonderful voice and he knew how to use it, which is not to say he turned on "the Voice Beautiful." It was there, a gift of nature, an arrangement of vocal chords and resonators that stirred the blood in the listener. He looked up and one knew it was at the night sky where husbandry was practiced and the candles were all out. He felt the nervous, emaciated tension of the small hours and was startled by the appearance of Macbeth attended by the tall shadow of Seyton.

He says he dreamed of the three weird sisters. Macbeth replies that he thinks not of them and then goes on, against every nerve in the listener's body, to ask Banquo to have a little talk about the sisters when he has time. Talk? What about? He goes on, with sickening ineptitude, to say the talk will "*make honour*" for Banquo, who at once replies that as long as he loses none he will be "*counsell'd*," and they say good-night.

Peregrine thought: *Right*. That was *right*. And when Banquo and Fleance went off he clapped his hands softly but not so softly that Banquo didn't hear him.

Now Macbeth is alone. The ascent to the murder is begun. Up and up the steps, following the dagger that he knows is a hallucination. A bell rings. *Hear it not, Duncan.*

Dougal was not firm in his lines. He started off without the book but depended more and more on the prompter, couldn't pick it up, shouted "*What*!," flew into a temper, and finally started off again with his book in his hand.

"I'm not ready," he shouted to Peregrine.

"All right. Take it quietly and read."

"I'm *not ready*."

Peregrine said: "All right, Dougal. Cut to the end of the speech and keep your hair on. Give your exit line and off."

"*Summons thee to heaven or to hell,*" Dougal snapped and stamped off through the mock-up exit at the top of the stair.

Reenter the Lady at stage-level.

Maggie was word-perfect. She was flushed with wine, overstrung, ready to start at the slightest sound but with the iron will to rule herself and Macbeth. When his cue for reentry came Dougal was back inside his part. His return at stage-level was all Peregrine hoped for.

"I have done the deed. Didst thou not hear a noise?"

"I heard the owl scream and the crickets cry. Did not you speak?"

"When?"

"Now."

"As I descended?"

"Ay."

"Hark! Who lies i' the second chamber?"

"Donalbain."

"This is a sorry sight."

"A foolish thought to say a sorry sight."

She glances at him. He stands there, blood-bedabbled and speaks of sleep. She sees the two grooms' daggers in his hands and is horrified. He refuses to return them. She takes them from him and climbs up to the room.

Macbeth is alone. The cosmic terrors of the play roll in like breakers. At the touch of his hands the multitudinous seas are incarnadined, making the green one red.

The Lady returns.

Maggie and Dougal had worked together on this scene and it was beginning to take shape. The characters were the absolute antitheses of each other: he, every nerve twanging, lost to everything but the nightmarish reality of murder, horrified by what he has done. She, self-disciplined, self-schooled, logical, aware of the frightful dangers of his unleashed imagination. *"These deeds must not be thought after these ways: so it will make us mad."*

She says a little water will clear them of the deed, and takes him off, God save the mark, to wash himself.

"We'll stop here," said Peregrine. "I've a lot of notes, but it's shaping up well. Settle down, please, everybody."

They were in the theatre. The stage was lit by working

lights, and the shrouded house waited, empty, expectant, for whatever was to be poured into it.

The stage manager and his assistant shifted chairs onstage for the principals and the rest sat on the stairs. Peregrine laid his notes on the prompter's table, switched on the lamp, and sat down.

He took a minute or two, reading his notes and seeing they were in order.

"It's awfully stuffy in here," said Maggie suddenly. "Breathless, sort of. Does anybody else think so?"

"The weather's changed," said Dougal. "It's got much warmer."

Blondie said: "I hope it's not a beastly thunderstorm."

"Why?"

"They give me the jimjams."

"That comes well from a witch!"

"It's electrical. I get pins and needles. I can't help it."

Ascendant thunder, startling, close, everywhere, rolled up to a sharp, definitive crack. Blondie screamed.

"Sorry!" she said. "I'm sorry." She put her fingers in her ears. "I can't help it. Truly. Sorry."

"Never mind, child. Come over here," said Maggie.

She held out her hand. Blondie, answering the gesture rather than the words, ran across and crouched beside her chair.

Rangi said: "It's true, she can't help it. It affects some people like that."

Peregrine looked up from his notes. "What's up?" he asked and then, seeing Blondie, said, "Oh. Oh, I see. Never mind, Blondie. We can't see the lightning, can we, and the whole thing'll be over soon. Brace up, there's a good girl."

"Yes. Okay."

She straightened up. Maggie patted her shoulder. Her hand checked and then closed. She looked at the other players, made a long face, and briefly quivered her free hand at them.

"Are you cold, Blondie?" she asked.

"I don't think so. No. I'm all right. Thank you. Ah!" She gave a little cry.

There was another roll of thunder; not so close, less precipitate.

"It's moving away," said Maggie.

It died out in an indeterminate series of three or four thuds and bumps. Then, without warning, the sky opened and the rain crashed down.

" 'Overture and Beginners, please,' " Dougal quoted and got his laugh.

By the time, about an hour later, when Peregrine finished his notes and recapped the faulty passages, the rain stopped almost as abruptly as it had begun, and the actors left the theatre on a calm night with stars shining, brilliant, above the rain-washed air. London glittered. A sense of urgency and excitement was abroad and when Peregrine whistled the opening phrase of a Brandenburg concerto it might have been a whole orchestra giving it out.

"Come back to my flat for an hour, Maggie," said Dougal. "It's too lovely a night to go home on."

"No, thank you, Dougal. I'm tired and hungry and I've ordered a car and here it is. Good-night."

Peregrine saw them all go their ways. Still whistling, he walked toward the car park and only then noticed that a little derelict shed on the waterfront lay in a ramshackle heap of rubble.

"I hadn't realized it's been demolished," he thought.

Next morning a workman operating a scoop-lift pointed to a black scar on one of the stones.

"See that?" he said cheerfully to Peregrine. "That's the mark of the devil's thumb, that is. You don't often see it. Not nowadays, you don't."

"The devil's thumb?"

"That's right, Squire. Lightning."

II

SIMON MORTEN had taken the part of Macduff by storm. His dark good looks and dashing, easy mockery of the Porter on his first entrance with Lennox, his assertion of his hereditary right to wake his King, his cheerful run up the stairs, whistling as he went into the bloodied chamber while Lennox warmed himself at the fire and talked cosily about the wild intemperance of the night, all gave him an easy ascendancy.

Macbeth listened, but not to him.

The door opens. Macduff stumbles, incoherent, ashen-faced, the former man wiped out as if by the sweep of the murderer's hand. The stirred-up havoc, the alarum bell, the place alive, suddenly, with the horror of assassination. The courtyard is filled with men roused from their sleep, nightgowns hastily pulled on, wild and disheveled. The bell jangling madly.

The scene ends with the flight of the King's sons. In a short, final scene Macduff, already suspicious, decides not to attend Macbeth's coronation at Scone but to retire to his own headquarters at Fife. It is here that he will make his fatal decision to turn south to England, where he will learn of the murder of his wife and children. From then on he will be a man with a single object: to return to Scotland, find Macbeth, and kill him.

When Banquo has been murdered, Macduff moves forward and the end is now inevitable.

Morten had become enamored of the fight, which he continued to rehearse with Dougal. At Gaston's suggestion they both began to exercise vigorously, apart from the actual combat, and became expert in the handling of their weapons: twirling and slashing with alarming dexterity. The steel replicas were now ready and they used them.

Peregrine came down to the theatre early on the morning after the storm and found them hard at it. Blue sparks flew, the claymores whistled. The actors leaped nimbly from spot to spot. Occasionally they grunted. Their shields were tightly strapped to their left forearms, leaving the hands free for the double-handed weapons. Peregrine gazed upon them with considerable alarm.

"Nimble, aren't they?" asked Gaston, looming up behind him.

"Very," Peregrine nervously agreed. "I haven't seen them for a week. I — I suppose they are safe. By and large. *Safe*," he repeated on a shriller note as Macduff executed a downward sweep, which Macbeth deflected and dodged by the narrowest of margins.

"Absolutely," Gaston said. "I stake my reputation upon it. Ah. Excuse me. Very well, gentlemen. Call it a morning. Thank you. Don't go, Mr. Jay. Your remark about safety has reminded me. There will, of course, be no change in the size and position of the rostra? They are precisely where they will be for the performance?"

"Yes."

"Good. To the fraction of an inch, I hope? Their footwork has been rehearsed with the greatest care, you know. Like a dance. Let me show you."

He produced a plan of the stage. It was extremely elaborate and was broken up into innumerable squares.

"The stage is marked — I daresay you have noticed — in exactly the same way. Let us say I am asking the Macduff to deliver a downward sweep from right to left and the Macbeth is to parry it and lean to the lower level. I shall say" — and here he raised his voice to a shriek — "Macduff! Right foot at thirteen-B. Raise claidheamh-mor — move ninety degrees. Sweep to twelve. Er — one. Er — two. Er — three. Meanwhile . . ."

He continued in this baffling manner for some seconds and then resumed in his normal bass: "So you will understand, Mr. Jay, that the least inaccuracy in the squares might well lead to — shall we say — to the bisection of the opponent's foot. No. I exaggerate. Crushing would be more appropriate. And we would not want that to happen, would we?"

"Certainly not. But, my dear Gaston, please don't misunderstand me. I think the plan is most ingenious and the result — er — breathtaking, but would it not be just as effective, for instance —"

He got no further. He saw the crimson flush rise in Gaston's face.

"Are you about to suggest that we employ a 'fake'?" Gaston demanded, and before Peregrine could reply said, "In which case I leave this theatre. For good. Taking with me the weapons and writing to *The Times*, to point out the ludicrous aspects of the charade that will inevitably be foisted upon the audience. Well? Yes or no?"

"Yes. No. I don't know which I mean, but I implore you not to go waltzing out on us, Gaston. You tell me it's safe and I accept your authority. I'll get the insurance people to cover us," he added hurriedly. "You've no objection to that, I hope?"

Gaston waved his hand grandly and ambiguously. He went up onstage and collected the weapons, which the users had put into felt containers. "I keep charge of the claidheamh-mors," he explained. "And return with them each day. And now, if you will excuse me —"

"Thank you, Gaston," Peregrine said with relief.

III

PEREGRINE had to admit, strictly to himself, that a slight change had come over the atmosphere in the theatre. It was not that rehearsals went badly. They went, on the whole, very well, with no more than the expected clashes of temperament among the actors. Barrabell was the most prominent when these were in question. He had only to appear on stage for an argument to begin about the various movements of the actors. Peregrine was, by and large, a patient and sagacious director, and he never let loose a formidable display of anger without considering that the time had come for it and the result would be salutary. He had never encountered Barrabell before but it didn't take him long to suspect a troublemaker and this morning he had confirmation of it. Barrabell and Nina Gaythorne arrived together. He had dropped his beautifully controlled voice to its lowest level, he had taken her arm, and in her faded, good-natured face there appeared an expression that reminded Peregrine of a schoolchild receiving naughty but absorbing information upon a forbidden ground.

"Most unexpected . . ." the Voice confided. "We were sitting . . ." It sank below the point of audibility. ". . . concentrated . . . *most* extraordinary . . ."

"Really?"

". . . Blondie . . . rigor . . ."

"No!"

"I promise."

At this point they came through the scenic archway and saw Peregrine.

There was a very awkward silence.

"Good morning," said Peregrine happily.

"Good morning. Perry. Er — good morning. Er."

"You were talking about last night's storm."

"Ah. Yes. Yes, we were. I was saying it was a heavy storm."

"I didn't see it," said Nina. "Not really."

"Did you notice that old scrap shed on the waterfront has collapsed?" Peregrine asked.

"Ah!" said Barrabell on a full note. "*That*'s what it is! The difference!"

"It was struck by lightning."

"Fancy!"

"The center of the storm."

"Not the theatre."

"No," they both fervently agreed. "Not our theatre."

"Did you hear about Blondie?"

Nina made noises.

"Blondie has this thing about lightning," said Peregrine. "Electricity in the air. My mother has it. She's seventy and very perky."

"Oh yes?" said Nina. "How lovely."

"Very fit and well but gets electrically disturbed during thunderstorms."

"I see," said Barrabell.

"It's quite a common occurrence. Like cat's fur crackling. Nina darling," said Peregrine, putting his arm around her, "I've got three little boys coming this morning to audition for the Macduff kid. Would you be an angel and go through the scene with them? Here are their photographs. Look."

He opened a copy of *Spotlight* at the child-actor's section. Three infant phenomena were displayed. Two were embarrassingly overdressed and bore an innocent look that only just failed to conceal an awful complacency. The third had sensible clothes and a cheeky face.

"*He's* got something," said Nina. "I would feel I could bear to cuddle him. When was the photo taken, I wonder?"

"Who can tell? He's called William Smith, which attracts one. The others, as you'll see, are called Wayne and Cedric."

"Little horrors."

"Probably. But one never knows."

"We'll have to see, won't we?" said Nina, who had recovered her poise and was determined not to get involved with Barrabell-Banquo again.

A girl from the manager's office came through to say the juveniles had arrived, each with its parent.

"I'll see them one by one in the rehearsal room. Nina, would you come, dear?"

"Yes, of course."

They went together.

For a little while Barrabell was alone. He had offered his services as the obligatory Equity representative for this production. It is not a job that most actors like very much. It is not pleasant to tell a fellow player that his subscription is overdue or to appeal against an infringement, imagined or genuine, by the management, though the Dolphin, in its integrity and strong "family" reputation, was not likely to run into trouble of that sort.

Barrabell belonged to a small, extreme leftist group called the Red Fellowship. Nobody seemed to know what it wanted except that it didn't want anything that was established or that made money in the theatre. Dougal Macdougal was equally far on the right and wanted, or so it was believed, to bring a Jacobite pretender to the throne and restore capital punishment.

Barrabell kept his ideas to himself. Peregrine was vaguely aware of his extremism but being himself hopelessly uncommitted to anything other than the theatre gave it no more consideration than that.

The rest of the cast were equally vague.

So when the business of appointing a representative came up and Barrabell said he'd done it before and if they liked he'd do it again they were glad to let him be their Equity rep. Equity is an apolitical body and takes in all shades of opinion.

But if they were indifferent to him, he was far from being indifferent to them. He had a cast list with little signs against quite a number of names. As rehearsals went on he hoped to add to it. Dougal Macdougal's name was boxed in. Barrabell looked at it for some time with his head on one side. He then put a question mark beside it.

The rest of the cast for the morning's rehearsal arrived. Peregrine and Nina returned with a fresh-faced child in tow.

"Quickest piece of casting in our records," said Peregrine. "This is William Smith, everybody. Young Macduff to you."

The little boy's face broke into a delightful smile. Delighted and delightful. It was transformed.

"Hul-lo, William," said Sir Dougal.

"Hullo, sir," said William. Not a vowel wrong and nothing forced.

"His mama is coming back for him in an hour," said Peregrine. "Sit over there, William, and watch rehearsal."

He sat by Nina.

"This morning we're breaking new ground," said Peregrine. "Banquet scene with ghost of Banquo. I'll explain the business with the ghost. You, Banquo, will wear a mask. A ghastly mask. Open mouth with blood running. You'll have time to change your clothes. You will have a double, also masked, of course. The table will have a completely convincing false side with heavily carved legs and the black space painted between them. You and your double will be hidden behind this side. Your stool is at the head of the table.

"Now. The Macbeths' costumes. The Lady has voluminous sleeves, attached all the way down to her costume. When she says *Meeting were bare without it*, she holds out her hands. She is standing in front of the stool and masks it. Macbeth goes up to her and on his own *Sweet remembrancer* takes and kisses her hands. They form, momentarily, a complete mask to the stool. Banquo, from under the table, slides up onto the stool. The speed with which you do this is all-important. Banquo, you sit on the stool with your back to Macbeth and your head bent down. The Macbeths move off to his right.

"On Macbeth's *Where?* Banquo turns. Recognition. Climax. He's a proper job. Bloody hair, throat cut, chest stabbed, blood all over it. On *feed and regard him not* the thanes obey her but rather self-consciously. They eat and mumble. Keep it quiet. Macbeth shrinks back and to the right. She follows. On Macbeth's *What care I*, Banquo lets his head go back and then fall forward. He rises and exits left. This is going to take a lot of work. You thanes, all of you, cannot see him. Repeat: you can *not* see him. He almost touches you but for you he is *not there*. You all watch Macbeth. Have you all got that? Stop me if I'm going too fast."

"Just a moment," said Banquo.

Here we go, thought Peregrine. "Yes, Bruce?" he asked.

"How much room will there be under this trick-table affair?"

"Plenty. I hope."

"And how do I see?"

Peregrine stopped himself saying: With your eyes. "The mask," he explained, "is being very carefully designed. It is actually an entire head. The eyeholes are big. Your own eyes will be painted out. Gaston has done an excellent drawing for us. He will take a mold of your face and make the masks."

"Oh, my God."

"A bloodied cloak will be firmly fixed to the neck and ripped up in several places."

"I'll want to see all these things, Perry. I'll want to rehearse in them."

"So you shall. Till the cows come home."

"Thank you very much," said the beautiful voice silkily.

"Any more questions? No? Well, let's try it."

They tried it slowly and then faster. Many times.

"I think it'll work," Peregrine said at last to Nina, who was sitting behind him.

"Oh, *yes*, Perry. Yes."

"We'll move on to the next 'appearance.' Sir Dougal, you have this distraught, confused, self-betraying speech. You pull yourself together and propose a health. You stand in front of the stool, masking it, holding out the cup in your left hand. Ross fills it. The understudy is in position. Under the table. Is he here? Yes, Toby. You've moved up to the end. You can see when Macbeth's arm and hand, holding the goblet, are in place and you slip up on the stool. Macbeth proposes the toast. He moves away, facing front. He does, what we all hope he will not do: he names Banquo. The thanes drink. He turns to go upstage and there is the ghost. On *unreal mockery, hence!* the ghost rises. He moves to the stairs, passing between Menteith and Gaston and past the soldiers on guard, up into the murder chamber. Everyone watches Macbeth, who raves on. Now, inch by inch, we'll walk it."

They did so, marking what they did in their scripts, gradually working through the whole scene, taking notes, walking the moves, fitting the pieces together. Peregrine said: "If ever there was a scene that could be ruined by a bit-part actor, this is it. It's all very well to say you must completely ignore the ghost, that for you it's not there; it's hellishly difficult to do it. If you can actually look at it without focusing your eyes, that's fine, but again it calls for a damn good actor to achieve it. We've got to make the audience accept the reality of the ghost and be frightened by it. The most intelligent of you all, Lennox, has the line: *Good-night; and better health attend his majesty*. When next we see Lennox he's speaking of his suspicions to Ross. The actor will, ever so slightly, not a fraction too much, make us aware of this. A hair's-breadth pause after he says *Good-night*, perhaps. You've got your moves. Take them once more to make sure and go away and think through the whole scene, step by step, and then decide absolutely what you are feeling and doing at every moment."

When they had gone Peregrine took Macbeth's scene with the murderers. Then the actual murder of Banquo.

"Listen!" Peregrine said. "Just listen to the gift this golden hand offers you. It's got everything. The last glint of sunset, the beat of hooves, the near approach of disaster:

The West yet glimmers with some streaks of day.
Now spurs the lated traveller apace
To gain the timely inn

And now we hear the thud of horses' hooves. Louder and louder. They stop. A pause. Then the horses go away. Enter Banquo with a lanthorn. I do want a profoundly deep voice for this speech. I'm sorry," he said to the First Murderer. "I'm going to give it to Gaston. It's a matter of voice, dear boy, not of talent. Believe me, it's a matter of voice."

"Yes. All right," said the stricken Murderer.

They read the scene.

"That's exactly what I want. You will see that Seyton is present in both these scenes and indeed is never far from Macbeth's business from this time on. We are very lucky to have Mr. Sears to take the part. He is the sword-bearer. He looms over the play and so does his tremendous weapon."

"It is," Gaston boomingly explained, "the symbol of coming death. Its shadow grows more menacing as the play draws inexorably towards its close. I am reminded —"

"Exactly," Peregrine interrupted. "The play grows darker. Always darker. The relief is in the English scene. And now . . ." He hurried on, while Gaston also continued in his pronouncements of doom. For a short time they spoke together and then Gaston, having attained his indistinguishable climax, stopped as suddenly as a turned-off tap, said, "Good morning," and left the theatre.

Peregrine opened his arms and let them flop. "One puts up with the unbelievable," he said. "He's an actor. He's a paid-up member of Equity. He spoke that little speech in a way that sent quivers up and down my spine and he's got Sir Dougal Macdougal and Simon Morten banging away at each other with a zeal that makes you sweat. I suppose I'm meant to put up with other bits of eccentricity as they recur."

"Is he certifiable?" asked Maggie.

"Probably."

"I wouldn't put up with it," said Bruce Barrabell. "Get him back."

"What do I say when he comes? He's perfect for the part. Perfect."

Nina said: "Just a quiet word in private? Ask him not to?"

"Not to what?"

"Go on talking while you are talking?" she said doubtfully.

"He hasn't done it since the first day until now. I'll leave it for this time."

"Of course, if one's afraid of him —" sneered Barrabell and was heard.

"I *am* afraid. I'm afraid he'll walk out and I don't mind admitting it. He's irreplaceable," said Peregrine.

"I agree with you, dear boy," said Sir Dougal.

"So do I," said Maggie. "He's too valuable."

"So be it," said Peregrine. "Now, William, let's see how you shape up. Come on, Nina. And Lennox. And the murderers."

They shaped up well. William was quick and unobjectionable. The boy was cheeky and he showed spirit and breeding. His mama returned, a quietly dressed woman from whom he had inherited his vowels. They completed the financial arrangements and left. Nina, delighted with him, also left. Peregrine said to Dougal and Maggie: "And now, my dears, the rest of the day is ours. Let's consolidate."

They did. They, too, went well. Very well. And yet there was something about the rehearsal that made Peregrine almost wish for ructions. For an argument. He had insisted upon the Lady using the sexual attributes she had savagely wrenched away from herself. Maggie agreed. Dougal responded. He actually shivered under her touch. When they broke for discussion, she did so absolutely and was at once the professional actress tackling a professional detail. He was slower, almost resentful. Only for a second or two and then all attention. Too much so. As if he was playing to an audience; in a way, as if he showed himself off to Maggie — "I'm putting on an act for you."

Peregrine told himself he was being fanciful. It's this play, he thought. It's a volcano. Overflowing. Thickening. And then: Perhaps that's why all these damn superstitions have grown up round it.

"Any questions?" he asked them.

"It's about her feeling for Macbeth," said Maggie. "I take it that from the beginning she has none. She simply uses her body as an incentive."

"Absolutely. She turns him on like a tap and turns him off when she gets her response. From the beginning she sees his weakness. He wants to keep his cake and eat it."

"Yes. She, on the other hand, dedicates herself to evil. She's not an insensitive creature but she shuts herself off completely from any thought of remorse. Before the murder she takes enough wine to see her through and notes, with satisfaction, that it has made her bold," said Maggie.

"She asks too much of herself. And pays the penalty. After the disastrous dinner party, she almost gives up," Peregrine said. "Macbeth speaks disjointedly of more crimes. She hardly listens. Always the realist, she says they want sleep! When next we see her she *is* asleep and saying those things that she would not say if she were awake. She's driven herself too hard. Now, the horror finds its way out in her sleep."

"And what about her old man all this time?" asked Dougal loudly. "Is she thinking about him, for God's sake?"

"We're not told but — no. I imagine she still goes on for a time, stopping up the awful holes he makes in the facade but with no pretense of affection or even much interest. He's behaving as she feared he might. She has no sympathy or fondness for him. When next we see him, Dougal, he's half-mad."

"Thank you very much!"

"Well, distracted. But what words! They pour out of him. Despair itself. *To the last syllable of recorded time.* You know," Peregrine said, "it always amazes me that the play never becomes a bore. The leading man is a hopeless character in terms of heroic images. It's the soliloquies that work the magic, Dougal."

"I suppose so."

"You know so," said Maggie, cheerfully. "You know exactly what you're doing. Doesn't he, Perry?"

"Of course he does," Peregrine said heartily.

They were standing onstage. There were no lights on in the auditorium, but a voice out there said: "Oh, don't make any mistake about it, Maggie, he knows what he's doing." And laughed.

It was Morten, the Macduff.

"Simon!" Maggie said. "What are you doing down there? Have you been watching?"

"I've only just come in. Sorry I interrupted, Perry. I wanted to see the office about something."

The door at the back of the stalls let in an oblong of daylight and shut it out again.

"What's the matter with *him*?" Dougal asked at large.

"Lord knows," said Peregrine. "Pay no attention."

"It's nothing," Maggie said. "He's being silly."

"It's not exactly silly, seeing that baleful face scowling at one and him whirling his claymore within inches of one's own face," Dougal pointed out. "And, if I catch your meaning, Maggie love, all for nothing. I'm as blameless as the Bloody Child. Though not, I may add, from choice."

"I'll have a word with him."

"Choose your words, darling. You may inflame him."

"Maggie dear," Peregrine begged her, "calm him down if you can. We're doing the English scene this week and I *would* like him to be normal."

"I'll do my best. He's so *silly*," Maggie crossly reiterated. "And I'm so busy."

Her opportunity occurred the next afternoon. She had stayed in the theatre after working at the sleepwalking scene, while Peregrine worked with Simon on the English scene.

When they had finished and Morten was about to leave, she crossed her fingers and stopped him.

"Simon, that's a *wonderful* beginning. Come home with me, will you, and talk about it? We'll have a drink and a modest dinner. Don't say no. Please."

He was taken aback. He looked hard at her, muttered sulkily, and then said, "Thank you, I'd like that."

"Good. Put on your overcoat. It's cold outside. Have you got your part? Come on, then. Good-night, Perry dear."

"Good-night, lovely lady."

They went out by the stage door. When he heard it bang, Peregrine crossed himself and said, "God bless her." He turned off the working lights, locked the doors, and used his torch to find his way out by the front-of-house.

They took a taxi to Maggie's flat. She rang the bell and an elderly woman opened the door. "Nanny," said Maggie, "can you give the two of us dinner? No hurry. Two hours."

"Soup. Grilled chops."

"Splendid."

"Good evening, Mr. Morten."

"Good evening, Nanny."

They came in, to a bright fire and comfortable chairs. Maggie took his coat and hat and hung them in the hall. She gave him a pretty robust drink and sat him down. "I'm breaking my own rule," she said, pouring a small one for herself. "During rehearsal period, no alcohol, no parties, and no nice gentlemen's nonsense. But you've seen that for yourself, of course."

"Have I?"

"Of course. Even supposing Dougal was a world-beater sex-wise, which I ain't supposing, it'd be a disaster to fall for him when we're playing The Tartans. Some people could do it. Most, I daresay, but not this lady. Luckily, I'm not tempted."

"Maggie?"

"No."

"Promise?"

"Of course."

"*He* doesn't share your views?"

"I don't know how he feels about it. Nothing serious," said Maggie, lightly. She added, "My dear Si, you can see what he's like. Easy come, easy go."

"Have you —" He took a pull at his drink. "Have you discussed it?"

"Certainly not. It hasn't been necessary."

"You had dinner with him. The night there was a rehearsal."

"I can have dinner with someone without falling like an overripe apple for him."

"What about *him*, though?"

"Simon! You're being childish. He did not make a pass at me and if he had I'd have been perfectly well able to cope. I told you. During rehearsals I don't have affairs. You're pathologically jealous about nothing. Nothing at all."

"Maggie, I'm sorry. I'm terribly sorry. Truly. Forgive me, Maggie darling."

"All right. But no bedroom scenes. I told you, I'm as pure as untrodden snow while I'm rehearsing. Honestly."

"I believe you. Of course."

"Well, then, do stop prowling and prowling around like the hosts of whoever-they-were in the hymn book. 'Lor',' as Mrs. Boffin said, 'let's be comfortable.' "

"All right," he said and a beguiling grin transformed his face. "Let's."

"And clean as a whistle?"

"So be it."

"Give yourself another drink and tell me what you think about the young Malcolm."

"The young Malcolm? It's a difficult one, isn't it? I think he'll get there but it'll take a lot of work."

And they discussed the English scene happily and excitedly until dinner was ready.

Maggie produced a bottle of wine, the soup was real, and the chops were excellent.

"How nice this is," said Maggie when they had finished.

"It's perfect."

"So what a Silly Simon you were to cut off your nose to spite your face, weren't you? We'll sit by the fire for half an hour and then you must go."

"If you say so."

"I do, most emphatically. I'm going to work on the sleep-walking scene. I want to get a sleepwalking voice. Dead. No inflections. Metallic. Will it work?"

"Yes."

She looked at him and thought how pleasant and romantic he seemed with his rich black curls and fair skin and what a pity it was that he was so stupidly jealous. It showed in his mouth. Nothing could cure it.

When he got up to go she said, "Good-night, my dear. You won't take it out on Dougal, will you? It would be so silly. There's nothing to take."

"If you say so."

He held her by her arms. She gave him a quick kiss and withdrew.

"Good-night, Simon."

"Good-night."

When she had shut the door and he was alone outside, he said: "All the same, to hell with Sir Dougal Macdougal."

On Thursday morning there was a further and a marked change in the atmosphere. It wasn't gloomy. It was oppressive and nervous. Rather like the thunderstorm, Peregrine thought. Claustrophobic. Expectant. Stifling.

Peregrine finished blocking. By Friday they had covered the whole play and took it through in continuity.

There were noticeable changes in the behavior of the company. As a rule, the actor would finish a scene and come off with a sense of anxiety or release. He or she would think back through the dialogue, note the points of difficulty, and re-rehearse them in the mind or, as it were, put a tick against them as having come off successfully. The actors would disappear into the shadows, or watch for a time with professional interest or read a newspaper or book — each according to temperament and inclination.

This morning it was different. Without exception they sat together and watched and listened with a new intensity. It was as though each actor continued in an assumed character, and no other reality existed. Even in the scenes that had been blocked but not yet developed there was a nervous tension that knew the truth would emerge and the characters march to their appointed end.

The company were to see the fight for the first time. Macduff now had something of a black angel's air about him, striding through the battle on the hunt for Macbeth. He encounters men in the Macbeth tartan and mistakes them for him, but it must be Macbeth or nobody. Then Macduff sees him, armored, helmeted, masked, and cries out: *"Turn, hell-hound, turn!"*

Macbeth turns.

Peregrine's palms were wet. The thanes, waiting offstage now, stood aghast. Steel clashed on steel or shrieked as one blade slid down another. There was no sound other than the men's hard breathing.

Macduff swung his claymore up and then swiftly down. Macbeth caught it on his shield and lurched forward.

Nina, in the audience, screamed.

The boast while they both fight for breath that no man of woman born will kill Macbeth; Macduff's reply that he was *from his mother's womb untimely ripped*; the final exit, Macduff driving him backward and out. Macbeth's scream, cut short, offstage. An empty stage for seconds, then trumpets and drums and reenter Malcolm, Old Siward, and the thanes in triumph. Big scene. Old Siward on his son's death. Reenter Macduff and Seyton with Macbeth's head on the point of his claymore. *"Behold, where stands the usurper's cursed head,"* shouts Macduff.

Malcolm is hailed King of Scotland and the play is over.

"Thank you, everybody," said Peregrine. "Thank you very much."

And in the sounds of relief that answered him the clearly articulated treble of William Smith spoke the final word.

"He got his comeuppance, didn't he, Miss Gaythorne?"

IV

AFTER Peregrine had taken his notes and the mistakes had been corrected, the cast stayed for a little while as if reluctant to break the bond that united them. Dougal said: "Pleased, Perry?"

"Yes. Very pleased. So pleased, I'm frightened."

"Not melodramatic?"

"There were perhaps three moments when it slid over. None of them involved you, Dougal. I'm not even sure about them."

"Good. *Maggie* darling," Dougal cried as she joined them. "You are wonderful. Satanic and lovely and baleful. I can't begin to tell you. Thank you, thank you." He kissed her hands and her face and seemed unable to stop.

"If I can get a word in," said Simon. He was beside them, his hair damp with sweat stuck to his forehead and a line of it glinting on his upper lip. Maggie pushed herself free of Dougal and held Simon by his woolen jacket. "Si!" she said and kissed him. "You're *fantastic*."

They'll run out of adjectives, Peregrine thought, and then we'll all go to lunch.

Simon looked over the top of Maggie's head at Dougal. "I seem to have won," he said. "Or do I?"

"We've all won or hope we all have in three weeks. It's too early for these raptures," said Peregrine.

Maggie said: "I've got someone in a car waiting for me and I'm late." She patted Simon's face and freed herself. "I'm not wanted this afternoon, Perry?"

"No. Thank you, lovey."

" 'Bye, everyone," she cried and made for the stage door. William Smith ran ahead of her and opened it.

"Ten marks for manners, William," she said.

There was nobody waiting for her. She hailed a taxi. That's settled *their* hashes, she thought as she gave her address. And the metallic voice will work wonders if I get it right. She made an arrangement in her vocal cords and spoke.

"Who would have thought the old man to have had so much blood in him?"

"What's that, lady?" asked the startled driver.

"Nothing, nothing. I'm an actress. It's my part."

"Oh. One of them. Takes all sorts, don' it?" he replied.

"It certainly does."

Ross, Lennox, Menteith, Caithness, and Angus were called for three o'clock and had time to get a good tuck-in at the Swan. They walked along the Embankment and the sun shone upon them: four young men with a fifth, the Ross, who was older. They had a certain air about them. They walked well. They spoke freely and clearly and they laughed loudly. Their faces had a pale smoothness as if seldom exposed to the sun. When they were separated by other pedestrians they raised their voices and continued their conversation without self-consciousness. Lennox, when not involved, sang tunefully: *"Not a flower, not a flower sweet on my black coffin let there be strown."*

"Wrong play, dear boy," said Ross. "That's from *Twelfth Night*."

"Bloody funny choice for a comedy."

"Strange, isn't it?"

Lennox said: "Do any of you find this play . . . I don't know . . . oppressive? Almost too much. I mean, we can't escape it. Do you?"

"I do," Ross confessed. "I've been in it before. Same part. It does rather stick with one, doesn't it?"

"Well," Menteith said reasonably, "what's it *about*? Four murders. Three witches. A fiendish lady. A homicidal husband. A ghost. And the death of the name-part with his severed head on the end of a claymore. Rather a bellyful to shake off, isn't it?"

"It's melodrama pure and simple," said Angus. "It just happens to be written by a man with a knack for words."

Lennox said: "What a knack! No. That doesn't really account for the thing I mean. We don't get it in the other tragedies, do we? Not in *Hamlet* or *Lear*. Or even in *Othello*, grim as it is."

"Perhaps it's the reason for all the superstitions."

"I wonder," Ross said. "It may be. They all say the same thing, don't they? Don't speak his name. Don't quote from it. Don't call it by its title. Keep off."

They turned into a narrow side street.

"I tell you what," Caithness said. "I don't mind betting anyone who's prepared to take me up that Perry's the only one of the whole company who *really* doesn't believe a word of it. I mean that — *really*. He doesn't *do* anything, but that's so that our apple-carts won't be upset."

"You sound bloody sure of yourself, little man, but how do you know?" asked Menteith.

"You can tell," said Caithness loftily.

"No, you can't. You just kid yourself you can."

"Oh, do shut up."

"Okay, okay. Look, there's Rangi. What's *he* think of it all?"

"Ask him."

"Hullo! Rangi!"

He turned, waved at the Swan, and pointed to himself.

"So are we," Angus shouted. "Join us."

They caught up with him and all entered the barroom together.

"Look, there's a table for six. Come on."

They slipped into the seats. "I'll get the beer," Ross offered. Everybody want one?"

"Not for me," said Rangi.

"Oh! Why not?"

"Because I do better without. Tomato juice. A double and nothing stronger with it."

Menteith said: "I'll have that too."

"Two double tomatoes. Four beers," Ross stated and went to the bar.

"Rangi," Lennox said, "we've been arguing."

"Oh? What about?"

Lennox looked at his mates. "I don't know exactly. About the play."

"Yes?"

Menteith said: "We were trying to get to the bottom of its power. On the face of it, it's simply what a magical hand can do with a dose of blood-and-thunder. But that doesn't explain the atmosphere it churns up. Or does it?"

"Suppose . . ." Caithness began. "You won't mind, Rangi, will you?"

"I've not the faintest idea what you're going to ask but I don't suppose I will."

"Well, suppose we were to offer a performance of the play on your — what do you call it —"

"The *marai*?"

"Yes. How would you react?"

"To the invitation or to the performance?"

"Well — to the performance, I suppose. Both, really."

"It would depend upon the elders. If they were sticklers, really orthodox people, you would be given formal greetings, the challenge and the presentation of the weapon. It is possible —" He stopped.

"Yes?"

"It would have been possible, I believe, that the *ta-*

hunga — that's what you'd call a wise man — would have been asked, because of the nature of the play, to lay a *tapu* on the performance. He would do this. And then you would go away and dress and the performance would take place."

"You don't mind about using — well, you know — eyes, tongue, and everything in the play?"

"I am not entirely orthodox. And we take the play seriously. My great-grandfather was a cannibal," said Rangi in his exquisite voice. "He believed he absorbed the attributes of his victims."

A complete silence fell upon the table. Perhaps because they had been rather a noisy party before, their silence affected other patrons, and Rangi's declaration, quite loudly made, was generally heard. The silence lasted only for a second or two.

"Four beers and two tomato juices," said Ross, returning with the drinks. He laid the tray on the table.

3

THIRD WEEK

I

In the third week the play began to consolidate. The parts that were clearly spurious had of course been taken out — the structure fully revealed. It was written with economy: the remorseless destiny of the Macbeths, the certainty from the beginning that they were irrevocably cursed, their progress, at first clinging to each other, then separated and swept away downstream to their damnation: these elements declared themselves in every phase of this destructive play.

Why, then, was it not dreary? Why did it excite rather than distress?

"I don't know why," Peregrine said to his wife. "Well, I do, really. It's because it's wonderfully well written. Simple as that. It's the atmosphere that it generates."

"When you directed it before, did you feel the same way about it?"

"I think so. Not so marked, though. It's a much better company, of course. Really, it's a perfect company. If you heard Simon Morten in the English scene, Emily, saying, *My wife kill'd too?* Then when Malcolm offers his silly conventional bit of advice, Simon looks at Ross and says, *He has no children*."

"I know."

"Come down to rehearsal one of these days and see."

"Shall I?"

"Yes. Do. At the end of next week."

"All right. How about the superstitions? Is Nina Gaythorne behaving herself?"

"She's trying to, at least. I don't mind betting she's taking all sorts of precautions on the side *but* as long as she doesn't *talk* about it . . . Barrabell — he's the Banquo, you know — feeds her stories, I'm quite sure. I caught him at it last week. The scrap shed down by the river was struck by lightning, you know."

"No! You never told me."

"Didn't I? I suppose I've clapped locks on anything that looks like superstition and don't unfasten them even for you. I caught Barrabell nicely and gave poor old Nina the shock of her life."

"What were they saying?"

"He was going on about one of the witches — Blondie — making a scene and getting the jimjams during the storm. Some people do get upset, you know — it's electrical. They always say they're sorry and they can't help it."

"Was Blondie all right?"

"Right as rain when the lightning stopped."

"How unfortunate."

"What?"

"That there should be a thunderstorm."

"You don't mean —?"

"Oh, you know how I feel about all the nonsense. I just thought how unfortunate from the point of view of the people who do."

"The silly fatheads have got over it. The theatre wasn't struck by lightning. Being fixed up with a good conductor, it wouldn't have felt it anyway."

"No." After a short silence, Emily said: "How's the little boy behaving?"

"William Smith? Very well. He's a good actor. It'll be interesting to see what happens to him after adolescence.

He may not go on with the theatre but I hope he does. He's doubling."

"The Bloody Child?"

"And the Crowned Child. They're one and the same. You should hear him wail out his *Great Birnam Wood to high Dunsinane Hi-i-ill shall come against him.*"

"Golly!"

"Yes, my girl. That's the word for it."

"How are you working the scene? The apparitions?"

"The usual things. Dry ice. A trapdoor. A lift. Background of many whispering voices: *Double, double.* Strong rhythm. The show of Kings is all Banquo's descendants. Each wears a Banquo head — Gaston's handiwork, of course. The scene ends with *And points at them for his.* The next bit in the script is somebody's incredibly silly addition. I should think the stage manager's for a fourth-rate company in the sticks. It's a wonder he didn't give the witches red noses and slap-sticks."

"So you go on with — what?"

"There's a blackout and great confusion. Crescendo. Noises. Macbeth's voice. Sounds, possibly drums. I'm not sure. Foot-falls, maybe. Lights dim up with Lennox at the door. Macbeth comes out. Rest of scene as written."

"Smashing."

"Well, I hope so. It's going to need handling."

"Yes. Of course."

"It's the only tricky one left from the staging point of view."

"Could Gaston be a help? About witchcraft?"

"I daren't risk asking him. He could, of course, but he does so — so go off at the deep end. He is a teeny bit mad, you know. Only on his own lay, but he is. He's God's gift when it comes to swords. What will you think of the fight? It terrifies me."

"Is it *really* dangerous, Perry?"

He waited for a minute.

"Not according to Gaston, always making sure the stage

is right. He'll keep a nightly watch on it. The two men have reached an absolute perfection of movement. They're getting on together, man to man, a bit better, too. Maggie had a go at Simon, bless her, and he's less crissy-crossy when they are not fighting, thank God."

"Well," said Emily, "nobody can accuse you of being superstitious, I'll say that for you."

"Will you? And you'll come next week when we'll take it in continuity with props?"

"You bet I will," said Emily.

"I don't know what you'll think of Gaston. I mean, of what I'm doing with him. He's the bearer of the great ceremonial sword — the claidheamh-mor. We're making a harness and heavy belt for him to take the hilt. It's the real weapon and it weighs a ton. He's as strong as a bull. He follows Macbeth everywhere like a sort of judgment. And at the end he'll carry the head on it. He is watching Jeremy's drawings for his costume with the eye of a hawk."

"What's it like?"

"Like all the other Macbeth menage. Embryo tartan, black woolen tights, thonged sheepskin leggings. A mask for the fights. In his final appearance with the head on the sword, he — er — he suggested a scarlet tabard."

"Oh, for heaven's sake, Perry!"

"I know. Where would he change and why? With fighting thanes milling all around. I pointed this out and for once he hadn't an answer. He took refuge in huffy grandeur, said it was merely an idea, and went into a long thing about color and symbolism."

"I feel I must meet him."

"Shall I invite him for tea?"

"Do you *like* him?" she asked incredulously.

"Oh, one couldn't exactly do that. Or, I don't think one could. *Collect* him, perhaps. No, he might just turn into a bore and not go home."

"In that case we won't ask him here."

"Or bring the Macbeth's head with him to show you. He did that to me. When we'd finished afternoon rehearsal. It was in the shadows of the wardrobe room. I nearly fainted."

"Frightful?"

"Terrifying. It's sheet-white and so *like* Dougal. With a bloody gash, you know. He wondered if I had any suggestions to make."

"Had you?"

"Just to cover it up quickly. Fortunately, the audience only sees it momentarily. He turns it to face Malcolm, who is up on the steps at the back. It'll be back to audience."

"They'll laugh," said Emily.

"If they laugh at that they'll laugh at anything."

"What do you bet?"

"Well, of course they have in the past always laughed at a head and the management always says it's a nervous reaction. So it may be but I don't think so. I think they know it isn't, and can't be, Macbeth's or anybody else's head and they laugh. It's as if they said: 'This is a bit too thick. Come off it.' All the same, I'm going to risk it."

"You jolly well do and more power to your elbow."

"The final words are cut. The play ends with the thanes all shouting *Hail, King of Scotland!* and pointing their swords at Malcolm. He's in a strong light. I hope the audience will go away feeling, well — relieved, uplifted, as if Scotland stands free of a nightmare."

"I hope so, too. I think they will."

"May you think so when you've seen it."

"I bet I will," said Emily.

"I'll push off. So long, Em, wish me luck."

"With all my heart," she said and gave him a kiss and a packet and a thermos. "Your snack," she said.

"Thanks, love. I don't know when I'll be home."

"Okay. Always welcome."

She watched him get into his car. He gave her a toot and was off.

II

HE was taking the witches' scenes. Mattresses had been placed on the stage behind the gallows rostrum. The body on the scaffold moved slightly in its noose, turned by one of the mysterious drafts that steal about backstage regions. When Peregrine walked in, Rangi was standing beside it, peering into the void beneath.

"Okay," Rangi called. "If you can't see the back of the gallery they can't see you."

"Can't see nuffink," came a muffled voice from the void.

"Fair enough," said Rangi. "You can come up from down there."

"Morning, Rangi," said Peregrine. "Joined the Scene-shifters' Union?"

Rangi grinned. "We wanted to make sure we were masked from down there."

"You want to watch it. The right way is to ask me and I'll check with the stage manager." He put his arm across Rangi's shoulders. "You're not in the land of do-it-yourself, now," he said.

"I'm sorry. I didn't *do* anything. Just yelled."

"All right. You do need to watch it. We might have the whole stage staff going out on strike. Is Bruce Barrabell here?"

"I don't think so."

"Good. Your part's shaping up nicely. Do you like it?"

"Oh, sure. Sure."

"We'll give you a skirt for rehearsals."

"A sort of lady-*tohunga*, uh? Except that *tohungas* are always men."

"You'll look like three disreputable old women until Macbeth sees your faces and they are terrible and know everything. In the opening scene we see them, birdlike, as they are — almost ravens. Busy on the gallows collecting from the corpse what's left of the *grease that's sweaten from the murderer's gibbet*. In the third scene when Macbeth first meets them they've put on a sort of caricature of respectability: filthy aprons, dirty mutches that come under their chins like grave-cloths. Blondie is the sexy one. One breast hangs out. Brown and stringy. They are *not* like female *tohungas*, really."

"Not in the least," said Rangi cheerfully.

Dougal Macdougal arrived. He never "came in." There was always the element of an event. He could be heard loudly greeting the more important members of the company who had now assembled, and not forgetting to say "Morning, morning" to the bit-parts. He arrived onstage, hailed Peregrine as if they hadn't encountered each other for at least a month, saw the witch girls — "Good morning, dear. Good morning, dear" — and fetched up face to face with Rangi. "Oh. Good morning — er — Rainy," he said loftily.

"Settle down, everyone," said Peregrine. "We are taking the witches' scenes. I've got the lights manager to come down and the effects man; I'd like them to sit beside me, take notes, and go away after this rehearsal to nut out their plots. The message I plan to convey depends very much upon dead cues for effects and I hope that between us we'll cook up something that'll raise the pimples on the backs of the audience's necks. Right."

He waited while the witches took up their positions and the others sat in the front-of-house.

"No overture," he said, "in the usual sense. The house darkens and there's a muffled drumbeat. Thud, thud, thud. Like a heart. Curtain up, flash of lightning. We get a fleeting look at the witches. Dry ice."

Rangi on the arm of the gibbet reached down at the head. Wendy doubled up, and Blondie, on Wendy's back, clawed the feet. Busy. Hold for five seconds. Blackout. Thunder. Fade up to half-light concentrated on the witches, who were now all on the ground. Dialogue.

"When shall we three meet again?"

Blondie's voice was a high treble, Wendy's gritty and broken, Rangi's full and quivering.

"*There to meet with* —" A pause. Silence. Then they all whisper, "*Macbeth*."

"Flash of lightning," said Peregrine. "And two caterwauls. Fog, lots of it."

". . . *hover through the fog and filthy air*."

"*Blackout*! Catch them in midair still going up. Split-second cue. Hold blackout for scene change. *Witches*! Ask them to come on, will you, someone?"

"We heard you," said a voice, Rangi's. "We're coming." He and the two girls came on from behind the rostrum.

"There'll have to be means for a quick exit from behind in the blackout. Okay? Charlie there?"

"Okay," said the assistant stage manager, coming onstage.

"Got it?"

"Got it."

"Good. Any questions? Rangi, are the mattresses all right?"

"I was all right. What about you two?"

"All right that time," said Wendy. "We *might* sprain an ankle."

"Fall soft, lie flat, and crawl off," said Peregrine. "Wait a bit." He used his makeshift steps to the stage and ran up onto the rostrum. "Like this," he said, and jumped high. He fell out of sight with a soft thud.

"We'll have to deal with that," said the effects man. "How about the muffled drum again?"

There followed a complete silence. Wendy on the edge of the rostrum looked over. Perry looked up at her.

"All right?" she asked.

"Perfectly," he said in a strange voice. "I won't be a moment. Next scene. Clear stage."

They moved away. Peregrine gingerly explored his left side, swearing under his breath. Below the ribs. Around the hip. Nothing broken but a hellishly sore bruise. He crept up into a kneeling position on the tarpaulin-covered mattress and from there saw what had happened. Under the tarpaulin was an unmistakable shape, cruciform, bumpy, with the hilt tailing out into the long blade. He felt it: undoubtedly a

[70]

claymore. A wooden claymore, discarded since they had begun using the steel replicas of the original.

He got painfully to his feet and, holding his bruise, stumbled onto the clear area behind the scenery. "Charlie?"

"Here, sir."

"Charlie, come here. There's a dummy claymore under the cover. Don't say anything about it. I don't want anyone to know it's there. Mark the position with chalk and then move it out and tuck the cover back in position. Understand?"

"I got you."

"If they know it's there, they'll start talking a lot of nonsense."

"Are you all right, sir?"

"Perfectly," said Peregrine. "Just a jolt."

He straightened up and drew in his breath. "Right," he said and walked onstage and down to his improvised desk in the auditorium.

"Call Scene Three," he said and sank into his seat.

"Scene Three," called the assistant stage manager. "Witches. Macbeth. Banquo."

III

SCENE THREE was pretty thoroughly rehearsed. The witches came in from separate spots and met onstage. Rangi contrived an excretion of venom in voice and face, egged on by moans of pleasure from his sisters. Enter Macbeth and Banquo. Trouble. Banquo's position. He felt he should be on a higher level. He could not see Macbeth's face. On and on in his beautiful voice. Peregrine, exquisitely uncomfortable and feeling rather sick, dealt with him, only just keeping his temper.

"The ladies will vanish as they did before. They get up to position on their *Banquo and Macbeth, all hail*."

"May I interrupt?" fluted Banquo.

"No," said Peregrine over a vicious stab of pain. "You may not. Later, dear boy. On, please."

The scene continued with Banquo disconcerted, silver-voiced, and ominously well behaved.

Macbeth was halfway through his soliloquy. "*Present fears*," he said, "*are less than horrible imaginings* and if the gentleman with the fetching laugh would be good enough to shut his silly trap *my thought whose murder yet is but fantastical* will probably remain so."

He was removed by the total width and much of the depth of the stage from Banquo, who had been placed in a tactful conversation with the other lairds as far away as possible from the soliloquist and had burst into a peal of jolly laughter and slapped the disconcerted Ross on his shoulders.

"Cut the laugh, Bruce," said Peregrine. "It distracts. Pipe down. On."

The scene ended as written by the author and with the barely concealed merriment of Ross and Angus.

Dougal went into the auditorium to apologize to Peregrine. Banquo affected innocence. "Cauldron Scene," Peregrine called.

Afterward he wondered how he got through the rest of the rehearsal. Luckily the actors and apparitions were pretty solid and it was a matter of making the lighting manager and the effects man acquainted with what would be expected of them.

The cauldron would be in the passage under the steps up to what had been Duncan's room. A door, indistinguishable when shut, *would* shut at the disappearance of the cauldron and witches amidst noise, blackout, and a great display of dry-ice fog and galloping hooves. Full lighting and Lennox tapping with his sword hilt at the door.

"You've seen our side of it," Peregrine said to the effects man. "It's up to you to interpret. Go home, have a think. Then come and tell me. Right?"

"Right. I say," said the effects man, "that kid's good, isn't he?"

"Yes, isn't he?" said Peregrine. "If you'll excuse me, I

want a word with Charlie. Thank you so much. Good-bye till we three meet again. Sooner the better."

"Yes, indeed."

The men left. Peregrine mopped his face. I'd better get out of this, he thought, and wondered if he could drive.

It was not yet four-thirty. Banquo was not in sight and the traffic had not thickened. His car was in the yard. To hell with everything, thought Peregrine. He said to the assistant stage manager: "I want to get off, Charlie. Have you fixed it up? The sword?"

"It's okay. Are you all right?"

"It's just a bruise. No breakages. You'll lock up?"

"Sure!"

He went out with Peregrine, opened the car door, and watched him in.

"Are you all right? Can you drive?"

"Yes."

"Saturday tomorrow."

"That's the story, Charlie. Thank you. Don't talk about this, will you? It's their silly superstition."

"I don't talk," said Charlie. "*Are* you all right?"

He was, or nearly so, when he settled. He could manage. Charlie watched him out of the yard. Along the Embankment, over the bridge, and then turn right and right again.

When he got there he was going to sound his horn. To his surprise, Emily came out of their house and ran down the steps to the car. "I thought you'd never get here," she cried. And then: "Darling, what's wrong?"

"Give me a bit of a prop. I've bruised myself. Nothing serious."

"Right you are. Here we go, then. Which is the side?"

"The other. Here we go."

He clung to her, slid out, and stood holding onto the car. She shut and locked the door.

"Shall I get a stick or will you use me?"

"I'll use you, love, if you don't mind."

"Away we go, then."

They staggered up the steps. Emily got the giggles. "If Mrs. Sleigh next door sees us she'll think we're tight," she said.

"You needn't help me, after all. Once I've straightened up I'm okay. My legs are absolutely right. Let go."

"Are you sure?"

"Of course," he said. He straightened up and gave a short howl. "Absolutely all right," he said and walked rather quickly up the steps into the house and fell into an armchair. Emily went to the telephone.

"What are you doing, Em?"

"Ringing up the doctor."

"I don't think —"

"I do," said Emily. She had an incisive conversation. "How did it happen?" she broke off.

"I fell on a sword. On the wooden hilt."

She repeated this into the telephone and hung up. "He's looking in on his way home," she said.

"I'd like a drink."

"I suppose it won't do you any harm?"

"It certainly will not."

She fetched him a drink. "I'm not sure about this," she said.

"I am," said Peregrine. He swallowed it. "Better," he said. "Why did you come running out of the house?"

"I've got something to show you but I don't know that you're in a fit state to see it."

"Bad news?"

"Not directly."

"Then show me."

"Here, then. Look at this."

She fetched an envelope from the table and pulled out a cutting from one of the more lurid Sunday tabloids. It was a photograph of a woman and a small boy. They were in a street and had obviously been caught unaware. She was white-faced and stricken. The little boy looked frightened. "Mrs.

Geoffrey Harcourt-Smith and William," the caption read. "After the verdict."

"It's three years old," said Emily. "It came in the post this morning."

"My God," Peregrine said. "I remember. It was a murder. Decapitation. The last of five, I think. The husband was found guilty but insane and he got a life sentence." Peregrine looked at the cutting for a minute and then held it out. "Burn it?" he said.

"Gladly." She lit a match and he held the cutting over an ashtray. It turned black and disintegrated. He let it drop.

"This too?" Emily asked, holding up the envelope. It was addressed in capital letters.

"Yes. No. No, not that. Not yet," said Peregrine. "Put it in my desk."

Emily did so. "You're quite sure? It is your little William?"

"Three years younger. Absolutely sure. And his mother. Damn."

"Perry, you've never seen the thing. Put it out of your mind."

"I can't do that. But it makes no difference. The father was a schizophrenic monster. Lifetime in Broadmoor. They called him the Hampstead Chopper."

"You don't think — it's — anybody in the theatre who sent this?"

"No."

Emily was silent.

"They've no cause. None."

After a pause he said: "I suppose it might be a sort of warning."

"You haven't told me how you came to fall on the claymore."

"I was showing the girls and Rangi how to fall soft. They don't know what happened. They've each got a special place. The sword was halfway between two places, under the tarp covering the mattresses they fall on."

"It was there when they fell?"

"Must have been."

"Wouldn't they have seen it? Seen the shape under the cover?"

"No. I didn't. It's very dark down there."

They were silent for a moment. The sound of London swelled into the gap. On the river a solitary craft gave out its lonely call.

"Nobody knew," Emily ventured, "that you were going to make that jump?"

"Of course not. I didn't know myself, did I?"

"So it being you that got the jab in the wind was just bad luck."

"Must have been."

"Well, thank God for that, at least."

"Yes."

"Where was it? Before someone hid it?"

"I don't know. Wait a sec. Yes, I do. The two wooden claymores were hung up on nails, on the back wall. They were somewhat the worse for wear, in spite of having cloth shields on the blades. One was split. Being Gaston's work they were carefully made: the right weight and balance and grip but they were really only makeshift. They were no good for anything except playing soldiers." He stopped and then hurriedly said: "I won't elaborate on the sword to the doctor. I'll just say it'd been left lying there and nobody cleared it up."

"Yes. All right. True enough as far as it goes."

"And as for William, beyond taking care what we talk about, we ignore the whole thing."

"The play being what it is —" Emily began and stopped.

"It's all right. He shouted out, 'He got his comeuppance, didn't he?' last week, just like any other small boy. At rehearsal, I mean."

"How old was he when it happened?"

"Six."

"He's nine now?"

"Yes. He looks younger. He's a nice boy."

"Yes. Does it hurt much? Your side?"

"If I move it's unpleasant. I wonder if for the cast there's some chronic affliction I could have had at odd times? The result of something that happened long before *Macbeth*."

"Diverticulitis?"

"Why diverticulitis?"

"I don't know why," said Emily, "but it seems to me it's something American husbands have. Their wives say mysteriously to one: 'My dear! He has diverticulitis.' And one nods and looks solemn."

"I think I'd be safer with a gimpy leg. Perhaps I wrenched it years ago?"

"We can ask the doctor."

"So we can."

"Shall I have a look at you?"

"No, we'd better leave well enough alone."

"What a dotty remark that is. After all," said Emily, "the bit in question is a bit of you that is *not* well, so how can we leave it alone? I'll get our dinner instead. It'll be a proper onion soup and then an omelet. Okay?"

"Lovely," said Peregrine.

Emily made up their fire, gave Peregrine a book to read, and went to the kitchen. The onion soup was prepared and only needed heating. She cut up bread into snippets and heated butter in a frying-pan. She opened a bottle of Burgundy and left it to breathe.

"Emily!" called Peregrine.

She hurried back to the study. "What's up?"

"I'm all right. I've been thinking. Nina. She won't be satisfied with the chronic gallstones or whatever. She'll just think my chronic thing coming back now is another stroke of bad luck."

They had their dinner on trays. Emily tidied them away and they sat with modest glasses of Burgundy over their fire.

Peregrine said: "The sword and the photograph? Are they connected?"

"Why should they be?"

"I don't know."

The doctor came. He made a careful examination and said there were no bones broken but there was severe bruising. He made Peregrine do painful things.

"You'll survive," he said facetiously. "I'm leaving something to help you sleep."

"Good."

"Don't go prancing about showing actors what to do."

"I'm incapable of even the smallest prance."

"Jolly good. I'll look in again tomorrow evening."

"Thank you."

Emily went to the front door with the doctor. "He'll be down at the theatre on Monday come hell or high water," she said. "He doesn't want the cast to know he fell on a sword. What could he have? Something chronic."

"I really don't know. Stomach cramp? Hardly." He thought for a moment. "Diverticulitis?" he suggested. And then: "Why on earth are you laughing?"

"Because it's a joke word." Emily put on a grave face, raised her eyebrows, and nodded meaningfully. "*Diverticulitis*," she said in a sepulchral voice.

"I don't know what you're on about," said the doctor, and then, "Is it something to do with superstitions?"

"That's *very* clever of you. Yes. It is. In a way."

"Good-night, me dear," said the doctor and left.

4

FOURTH WEEK

I

REHEARSALS went well during the first four days of the next week. The play had now been completely covered and Peregrine began to polish, dig deeper, and make discoveries. His bruises grew less painful. He had taken a high hand and talked about his "bad leg" in a vague, brief, and lofty manner and, as far as he could make out, the cast did not pay an enormous amount of attention to it. Perhaps they were too busy.

Macbeth, in particular, made a splendid advance. He gained in stature. His nightmarish descent into horror and blind, idiotic killing was exactly what Peregrine asked of him. Maggie, after they had worked at their scenes, said to him, "Dougal, you are playing like the devil possessed. I didn't know you had it in you."

He thought for a moment and then said: "To tell you the truth, nor did I." And burst out laughing. "Unlucky in love, lucky in war," he said. "Something like that, eh, Maggie?"

"Something like that," she agreed lightly.

"I suppose," he said, turning to Peregrine, "it is absolutely necessary to have Marley's Ghost haunting me? What's he meant to signify?"

"Marley's Ghost?"

"Well — whoever he is. Seyton. Gaston Sears. What's he meant to be, silly old fool?"

"Fate."

"Come off it. You're being indulgent."

"I honestly don't think so. I think he's valid. He's not intrusive, Dougal. He's just — there."

Sir Dougal said: "That's what I mean," and drew himself up, holding his claymore in front of him. "His tummy rumbles are positively deafening," he said. "Gurgle, gurgle. Rumble. Crash. A one-man band. One can hardly hear oneself speak."

"Nonsense," said Peregrine and laughed. Maggie laughed with him.

"You're very naughty," she said to Dougal.

"You've heard him, Maggie. In the banquet scene. Standing up by your throne rumbling away. You do know he's a bit off-pitch in the upper register, Perry, don't you?" He touched his own head.

"You're simply repeating a piece of stage gossip. Stop it."

"Barrabell told me."

"And who told him? And what about your fight?" Peregrine made a wide gesture and swept his notes to the floor. "Damn," he said. "Nothing dotty about that fight, is there?"

"We'd have been just as good if we'd faked it," Dougal muttered.

"No, you wouldn't, and you know it."

"Oh, well. But he does rumble. Admit."

"I haven't heard him."

"Come on, Maggie. I'm wasting my time with this chap," Dougal said cheerfully. Peregrine heard the stage door shut behind him.

He had begun painfully to pick up pages of the notes he had dropped when he heard someone come onstage and cross it. He tried to get up but the movement caught him. By the time he had hauled himself up the door had opened and closed and he did not see who had crossed the stage and gone out of the theatre.

Charlie had hung the claymore with its fellow on the back wall. Peregrine, having put his papers in order, labored up onto the stage and made his way through pieces of scenery and book wings that had been set up as temporary backing. Only the working light had been left on and it was dark enough in this no-man's-land for him to go carefully. He was quite startled to see the figure of a small boy, its back toward him. Looking up at the claymore.

"William!" he said. William turned. His face was white but he said, "Hullo, sir," loudly.

"What are you doing here? You weren't called."

"I wanted to see you, sir."

"You did? Well, here I am."

"You hurt yourself on the wooden claymore," the treble voice stated.

"What makes you think that?"

"I was there. Backstage. When you jumped, I saw you."

"You had no business to be there, William. You come only when you are called and stay in front when you are not working. What were you doing backstage?"

"Looking at my claymore. Mr. Sears said I could have one of them after we opened. I wanted to choose the one that was least knocked about."

"I see. Come here. Where I can see you properly."

William came at once. He stood to attention and clenched his hands.

"Go on," said Peregrine.

"I took it down; it was very dark. I brought it into the better light. It was still pretty dark but I examined it. Before I could get back there and hang it up, the witches came and started rehearsing. Down on the main stage. I hid it under the canvas. I was very careful to hide it where I thought nobody would fall. I hid, too. I saw you fall. I heard you say you were all right."

"You did?"

"Yes."

After a considerable pause, William went on. "I knew you weren't really all right because I heard you swear. But you got up. So I sneaked off and waited till there was only Charlie left and he was whistling. So I bolted."

"And why did you want to see me today?"

"To tell you."

"Has something else happened?"

"In a way."

"Let's have it, then."

"It's Miss Gaythorne. She keeps on about the curse."

"The curse?"

"On the play. Now she's on about things happening. She makes out the sword under the cover is mixed up with all the things that go wrong with *Macbeth*, with" — William corrected himself — "the Scots play. She reckons she wants to sprinkle holy water or something and say things. I dunno. It sounds like a lot of hogwash to me but she goes on and on, and of course the claymore's all my doing, isn't it? Nothing to do with this other stuff."

"Nothing in the wide world."

"Anyway, I'm sorry you've copped one, sir. I am, really."

"So you ought to be. It's much better. Look here, William. Have you spoken to anyone else about this?"

"No, sir."

"Word of a gentleman?" said Peregrine and wondered if it was comically snobbish.

"No, I haven't, not a word."

"Then don't. Except to me, if you want to. If they know I'm hurt because of the claymore they'll go weaving all sorts of superstitious rotgut about the play and it'll get about and be bad for business. Mum's the word. Okay? But I may say something. I'm not sure."

"Okay."

"And you'll get your claymore but no funny business with it."

William looked blankly at him.

"No swiping it around. Ceremonial use only. Understood?"

"I've understood, all right."

"Agreed?"

"I suppose so," William muttered.

Peregrine reminded himself that William was certainly unable to raise the weapon more than waist-high, if that, and decided not to insist. They shook hands and paid a visit to the Junior Dolphin at a quarter to six, where William consumed an unbelievable quantity of crumpets and fizzy drink. He seemed to have recovered his sangfroid.

Peregrine drove him home to a minute house in a tidy little street in Lambeth. The curtains were not yet drawn but the room was lit and he could see a pleasant picture, a fully stocked bookcase, and a good armchair. Mrs. Smith came to the window and looked out before shutting the room away.

William invited him in.

"I'll deliver you but I won't come in, thank you. I'm due at home. Overdue, in fact."

A brisk knock brought his mother to the door. A woman who was worn down to the least common denominator. She was dressed in a good but not new jacket and skirt and spoke incisively. "Yes?"

"Hullo, Mrs. Smith," said Peregrine. "I've got a call to make in this part of the world so I've brought William home. He's doing very well, may I add."

"Thank you, Mr. Jay." She smiled briefly at him and ushered William in as all three said good-bye in chorus.

Peregrine drove home in a state of some confusion. He was glad the hidden-sword mystery was solved, of course, but uncertain about how much, if anything, of the explanation should be passed on to the company. In the end he decided to say something publicly to Gaston about his promising to give the wooden sword to William and William hiding it. But what about Nina Gaythorne and the others? According to William, Nina knew about the sword. How the hell did the silly old trout find out? Peregrine asked himself. Charlie? Perhaps he let it out. No. No. I've got it. Banquo. He was there, probably lurking around before his entrance. He could have seen. And pretty well satisfied that this was the truth, he arrived home.

Emily heard the story of William. "Do you think he'll keep his word?" she asked.

"Yes, I do. I'm quite persuaded he will."

"What was it like? The house. And his mother?"

"All right. I didn't go in. Tiny house. Their own furniture. She's as thin as a lath and definitely upper-class. I don't remember if her circumstances came out at the trial but my guess would be that after the legal expenses were settled there was enough to buy the house or pay the rent and furnish it from what they had. He had been a well-heeled stock-broker. Mad as a hatter."

"And William's at a drama school?"

"The Royal Southwark Drama School. It's good. They get the whole works, all school subjects. Registered as a private school. There must have been enough for William's fees. And she's got some secretarial job, I fancy."

"I've been trying to remember what it was like when I was six. What was he told and how much does he retain?"

"At a guess, I'd say he was told his father was mentally very ill and committed to an asylum. No more."

"Poor little man," said Emily.

"He'll be a good actor. You'll see."

"Yes. How's your bruise?"

"Better every day."

"Good."

"In fact, everything in the garden is —" He pulled up. Emily saw that he had crossed his first and second fingers.

The next day shone brightly. Peregrine and Emily drove happily along the river, over Blackfriars Bridge, and turned right for Wharfingers Lane and the theatre. The entire company had been called and had nearly all arrived and were assembling in the auditorium.

It was to be a complete run-through of the play, with props. This would be the last one entirely for the actors. After that would come the mechanical, effects, and lights rehearsals with endless stops, adjustments, and repositionings. And then, finally, two dress rehearsals.

Emily knew a lot of the company. Sir Dougal was delighted that she had come down to rehearsal. Why did they not see more of her in these days? Sons? How many? Three? All at school? Wonderful!

It struck her that he was excited. Keyed up. Not attending to the answers she gave him. She was relieved when he strolled away.

Maggie came up to her and gave her a squeeze. "I'll want to know what you think," she said. "Really. What you think and feel."

"Perry says you're wonderful."

"Does he? Does he, really?"

"Really and truly. Without qualifications."

"Too good. Too soon. I don't know," she muttered.

"All's well."

"I hope so. This *play,* Emmy, my dear."

"I know."

She wandered away and sat down, her eyes closed, her lips moving. Nina Gaythorne came in, draped in a multiplicity of hand-woven scarves. She saw Emily and waved the end of one of them, at the same time making a strange grimace and raising her faded eyes to contemplate the dome. It was impossible to interpret; some kind of despair? Emily wondered. She waved back conservatively.

The man with Nina Gaythorne was unknown to Emily. Straw-colored. Tight mouth, light eyes. She guessed he was the Banquo. Bruce Barrabell. They sat together, apart from the others. Emily had the uncomfortable feeling that Nina was telling him who she was. She found herself momentarily looking into his eyes, which startled her by their sharpness and the quick furtive withdrawal of his gaze.

Macduff, Simon Morten, she recognized from Peregrine's description. He was physically exactly right; dark, handsome, and reckless, and, at the moment, nervous and withdrawn. A swashbuckler nevertheless.

Here came the three witches, two girls gabbling nervously and Rangi: aloof, indrawn, anxious. Then the Royals: King Duncan, magnificent, portentous, and his two sons, to whom he seemed to lend a condescending ear. Two Murderers. The Gentlewoman and the Doctor. Lennox and Ross. Menteith. Angus. Caithness. And, coming over to Nina Gaythorne, a small boy. So that's William, she thought. Last: huge, brooding, his claymore held upright in its harness, Gaston, the sword-bearer.

I'm thinking about them as they are in the play, mused Emily. And they are behaving as they do in the play. No. Not behaving. How absurd of me. But they are keeping together in their groups.

The front curtains parted and Peregrine came through.

"This," he said, "is an uninterrupted run-through, with props and effects. It will be timed. I'll take notes at the end of the first half. There has been a slight tendency to drag. We'll watch that, if you please. Right. Act One, Scene One. The Witches."

They went up through the box.

Peregrine came down the temporary steps into the house and to his desk. His secretary was beside him and the mechanical people behind.

Emily's heart thumped. A faint, wailing cry, a gust of moaning wind, and the curtain rose.

There are times — rare but unmistakable — in the theatre when, at rehearsal, the play flashes up into a life of its own and attains a reality so vivid that everything else fades into threadbare inconsequence. These startling transformations happen when the play is over halfway to achievement: the actors are not in costume, the staging is still in its bare bones.

Nothing intervenes between the characters and their projection into the void. This was such a day.

Emily felt she was seeing *Macbeth* for the first time. She was constantly taken by surprise. Perfect, Wonderful. Terrible, she thought.

Duncan arrives at the castle. The sound of wings fluttering in the evening air. Peaceful. Then the squeal of pipes, the rumble of the great doors, the opening and the assembly of servants. Seyton. Lady Macbeth a scarlet figure at the top of the stairs. *Don't go in, don't go in.*

But she welcomes him. They all go in and the doors rumble and close on them.

Afterward Emily could not remember if the sounds Shakespeare introduces actually were heard: the cricket, the owl, the usual domestic sounds that continue in an old house when the guests are all asleep in bed. Other ambiguous sounds the Macbeths think they hear. . . .

It's accomplished. The terrible imaginings are real, now, and they go to wash the blood from their hands.

Now comes the knocking at the south entry. Enter from below the drunken Porter with his load of obscenely shaped driftwood. He commits it to the fire, piece after piece, staggers to the entry, and admits Macduff and Lennox.

Simon Morten looked fit, his fair skin bright with the flush of health. He and Lennox brought the fresh morning air in with them, and Simon ran swiftly upstairs into Duncan's bedroom. The door shut behind him.

Macbeth stood very still, every nerve in his body listening. Lennox went to the fire, warmed his hands, and gossiped about the wildness of the nights.

The door upstairs opened and Macduff came out.

Extraordinary! His face was totally drained of color. He whispered: "*Horror. Horror. Horror.*"

Now disaster broke: the alarum bell, the disordered guests, Lady Macbeth's "fainting" when her husband's speech threatened to get out of hand, the appearance of the two frightened sons, their decision to flee. The little front scene when Macduff, an old man, and Ross speak an ominous afterword, and the first part closes.

II

PEREGRINE finished his notes. Macbeth and Macduff waited behind. They were onstage.

"Come on," said Peregrine. "What was the matter? You're both good actors but you don't turn sheet-white out of sheer artistry. What went wrong?"

Sir Dougal looked at Simon. "You went up before I did," he said. "You saw it first."

"Some idiot's rigged a bloody mask in the King's chamber. One of those Banquo things of Gaston's. Open mouth, blood running out of it. Bulging eyes. I don't mind telling you it shocked the pants off me."

"You might have warned me," said Sir Dougal.

"I tried, didn't I? Outside the door. You and Lennox. After I said, *Destroy your sight with a new Gorgon.*"

"You muttered something. I didn't know what you were on about."

"I could hardly yell, 'There's a bloody head on the wall,' could I?"

"All right, all right."

"When you went up the first time, Sir Dougal, was it there?"

"Certainly not. Unless —"

"Unless what?"

"What's the color of the cloak attached to it?"

"Dark gray," said Peregrine.

"If it was covered by the cloak I might have missed it. It was dark up there."

"Who could have uncovered it?"

"The grooms?"

"What grooms? There are no grooms," said Simon. "Are you crazy?"

"I was making a joke," said Sir Dougal with dignity.

"Funny sort of joke, I must say."

"There's some perfectly reasonable explanation," Peregrine said. "I'll talk to the Property Master. Don't let a damn silly thing like this upset you. You're going very well indeed. Keep it up."

He slapped them both on the shoulders, waited till they had gone, and climbed the stairs to the room.

It *was* extremely dark: an opening off the head of the stairs with a door facing them. The audience would see only a small inside section of one wall when this door was open. The wall, which would have a stone finish, faced the audience and ran down to stage-level, and the third wall, unseen by the audience, was simply used as a brace for the other two. It was a skeleton. A ladder leading down to the stage was propped against the floor. A ceiling, painted with joists, was nailed to this structure.

And looming in the darkest corner, facing the doorway, the head of murdered Banquo.

Peregrine knew what to expect but even so he got a jolt. The bulging eyes stared into his. The mouth gaped blood. His own mouth was dry and his hands wet. He walked toward it, touched it, and it moved. It was fixed to a coat hanger. The ends of the hanger rested on the corner pieces of the walls. The gray shroud had a hole, like a poncho, for the head. He touched it again and it rocked toward him and, with a whisper, fell.

Peregrine started back with an oath, shut the door behind him, and called out, "Props!"

"Here, guv."

"Come up, will you? Put the working light on."

He picked the head up and returned it to its place. The working light took some of the horror out of it. Props's head came up from below. When he arrived, he turned and saw it.

"Christ!" he said.

"Did you put that thing there?"

"What'd I do that for, Mr. Jay? Gawd, no."

"Did you miss it?"

[89]

"Last I checked, it and its mates were all laid out in the walking gents' room. Gawd, it'd give you the willies, woon't it? Seeing the thing unexpected, like."

"Take it down and put it back, and, Ernie —"

"Guv?"

"Don't mention this. Don't say you've seen it. Not to anyone."

"Okay."

"I mean it. Hope to die."

"Hope to die."

"Cross your heart, Ernie. Go on. Do it. And say it."

"Aw, hell, guv."

"Go on!"

"Cross me 'eart. 'Ope to die."

"That's the style. Now. Take this thing and put it with the other. Half a jiffy."

Peregrine was wrapping the head in the shroud. He turned back the hem and found a thin stick about two feet long slotted into the hem. A string was knotted halfway across into another and very much longer piece. He took it to the edge of the floor and let the loose end fall. It reached to within three feet of the stage.

Peregrine detached it, coiled it up, and put it in his pocket. He pulled out the stick, snapped it into small pieces, and gave Ernie the head, neatly parceled. He looked at the place where the head had rested and, above it, saw a strut of rough wood.

"Preposterous!" he muttered. "Okay," he said aloud. "We push on." He went downstairs.

"Second part," he called. "Settle down, please."

III

THE second part opened with Banquo alone, suspecting the truth yet not daring to cut and run. Next, Macbeth's scene with the murderers and Seyton nearer, ever present, and then the two Macbeths together. This is perhaps the most

moving scene in the play and reveals the most about them.
It opens up, in extraordinary language, the nightmare of
guilt, their sleeplessness, and when at last they sleep the
terrifying dreams that beset them. She fights on but knows
now, without any shadow of doubt, that her power over him
is less than she had bargained for, while he is acting on his
own, hinting at what he plans but not telling. There follows
the coming of darkness and night and the release of night's
creatures. It ends with self-dedication to the dark. Now comes
the murder of Banquo and the escape of Fleance. And now
the great banquet.

It begins as a front scene before the curtains. Macbeth,
crowned and robed, seems for the moment in command as
if he actually thrives on the shedding of blood. He is a little
too loud, too boisterous in his welcome. He is sending his
guests through the curtains and is about to follow when he
sees Seyton in the downstage entrance. He waits for the last
guest to pass through and then goes to him.

"*There's blood upon thy face.*"

"*'Tis Banquo's, then.*"

Nothing is perfect: Fleance has escaped. Macbeth gives
Seyton money and signals for the curtains to be opened. And
they are opened, upon the opulence of the banquet. The
servants are filling glasses. Lady Macbeth is on her throne.
And the ghost of Banquo, hidden, waits.

It was going well. The masking of the stool. The timing.
The nightmarish efforts of Macbeth to recover something of
his royalty. Every cue observed. Thank God! Peregrine
thought. It's working. Yes. Yes.

"*Our duties and the pledge.*"

The servants swept the covers off the main dishes.

The head of Banquo was in pride of place: outrageous and
glaring on the main dish.

"What the bloody hell is this!" Sir Dougal demanded.

IV

THIS was too much. The time for concealment was past Strangely, Peregrine felt a sort of relief. He would no longer be obliged to offer unlikely explanations, beg people not to talk, be certain they would talk.

He said, "Stop!" and stood up. "Cover that thing."

The servant who still had the oval dish-cover in his hand clapped it back over the head. Peregrine walked down the aisle. "You may sit if you want to but remain in your positions. Any staff who are here, onstage, please."

The assistant stage manager, Charlie, two stagehands, and Props came on and stood in a group on the Prompt side. The entire cast drew forward, some sitting onstage, others leaning against the set.

"Somewhere among you," said Peregrine, "there is a funny man. He has been operating intermittently throughout this rehearsal, his object, if he can be said to have one, being to support the superstitious theories that have grown up around this play. This play. *Macbeth.* You hear me, *Macbeth!* This person put a Banquo mask on the wall of Duncan's room. He's put another one in this serving dish. In any other context these silly tricks would be dismissed but here they are reprehensible. They've upset the extremely high standard of performance, and that is lamentable. I ask the perpetrator of these tricks to let me know, by whatever means he chooses, that he is the — comedian.

"For the good of the production I undertake not to reveal the trickster's name. Nor will I sack the man or refer to the matter again. It shall be as if it had never happened. Is this understood?"

He stopped.

They stared at him rather like children, he thought, brought together for a wigging and not knowing what would come next.

It was Bruce Barrabell who came next, the silver-tongued Banquo.

"No doubt I shall be snubbed," he said. "But I really feel I must protest. If this person is among us, I think we should all know who he is. He should be publicly exposed and dismissed. By us. As the Equity representative, I feel I should take this stand."

Peregrine had not the faintest notion of what, if any, stand the Equity representative was entitled to take. He said grandly: "Properties belonging to the theatre have been misused. Rehearsal time interrupted. This is my affair; I propose to continue. The time for Equity to butt in may or may not arise in due course. If it does I shall advise you of it. At this stage I must ask you to sit down, Mr. Barrabell."

If he won't sit down, he wondered, what the hell do I do?

"Hear, hear," said Sir Dougal helpfully.

There was an affirmative murmur. Nina was heard to say she felt faint. Peregrine said: "Props. When did you last look under the lid of that dish?"

"I never looked under it," said Props. "It was in place on the table, which was carried on as soon as the curtains closed. The dish would 'ave a plastic boar's head for performance, but not until the dress rehearsal."

"Was anyone there? A scene-shifter or an actor?"

"The two scene-shifters who carried the table on. They went off on the other side. And 'im," said Props, jerking his head at Barrabell, "and the other ghost. The double. They got down under the table just before the curtains re-opened."

"Familiar business for Banquo," said Sir Dougal and laughed.

"What do you mean by that, may I ask?" said Barrabell.

"Oh, nothing. Nothing."

"I insist on an explanation."

"You won't get one."

"Quiet, *please*," Peregrine shouted. "Go on, Props. When was the dish actually put on the table?"

Props said: "It's stuck down. All the props not used are

stuck down, aren't they? I put the lid on it after I got it ready, like."

"Before the rehearsal started?"

"That's right. And if there's anybody finks I done it with the 'ead, I never. And if there's any doubts about that I appeal to my union."

"There are no doubts about it," said Peregrine hurriedly. "Where *was* the head? Where are all the heads? Together?"

"In the walking gents' dressing-room. All together. Waiting for the dress rehearsal, next week."

"Is the room unlocked?"

"Yes, it is unlocked. And if you arst 'oo 'as the key, I 'as it. The young gents arst me to unlock it and I unlocked it, din' I?"

"Yes. Thank you."

"I got me rights like everybody else."

"Of course you have." Peregrine waited for a second or two and then said: "Anyone else?"

"Certainly," said a sepulchral voice. "I was there. But very briefly. I simply informed Macbeth of the murder. I came off downstage, Prompt. Somebody was there with my claidheamh-mor. I seized it. I ran upstage, engaged it into my harness, and entered near the throne, as the curtains were reopened. The previous scene," reminisced Gaston, "was that of the murder of Banquo. The claidheamh-mor was correctly held. It would never be used for that affair. It is too large and too sacred. An interesting point arises —"

He settled into his narrative style.

"Thank you, Gaston," said Peregrine. "Very interesting," and hurried on. "Now, Banquo. You were there during this scene. At what stage did you actually get under the table, do you remember?"

"When I heard Macbeth say, *Thou art the best o' the cutthroats.* The curtains were shut and the scene between Macbeth and Gaston, the murderer, was played in front of them. The head and cloak were stuffy and awkward and I always delay putting them on and getting down there. They are made in one and it takes only seconds to put them on. Angus and Caithness popped the whole thing over my head. I collected the cloak around my knees and went down."

"And the ghost double? Toby?"

A youth held up his head. "I put my head and cloak on in the dressing-room," he said, "and I got under the table as soon as it was there. The table has no upstage side and there was lots of room, really. I waited at the rear until Bruce got under and crawled forward."

Peregrine looked at the familiar faces of his actors and thought: This is ridiculous. He cleared his throat. "I now ask," he said, "which of you was responsible for these tricks."

Nobody answered.

"Very well," Peregrine said. "I would beg you not to discuss this affair among yourselves but," he added acidly, "I might as well beg you not to talk. One point I do put to you. If you think of linking these silly pranks with the *Macbeth* superstitions you will be doing precisely what the perpetrator wants. My guess is that he or she is an ardent believer. So far no ominous signs have occurred. So he or she has planted some. It's as silly and as simple as that. Any comments?"

"One asks oneself," announced Gaston, "when the rumors began and whether, in fact, they go back to some pre-Christian winter solstice ritual. The play being of an extremely sanguinary nature —"

"Yes, Gaston. Later, dear man."

Gaston rumbled on.

Sir Dougal said: "Oh, for pity's sake, will somebody tell him to forget his claddy-mor and to shut his silly old trap."

"How dare you!" roared Gaston suddenly. "I, who have taught you a fight that is authentic in every detail except the actual shedding of blood! How dare you, sir, refer to my silly old trap?"

"I do. I do dare," Sir Dougal announced petulantly. "I'm still in great pain from the physical strain I've been obliged to suffer and all for something that would be better achieved by a good fake and if you won't shut up, by God, I'll use your precious techniques to make you. I beg your pardon, Perry, dear boy, but *really.*"

Gaston had removed his claidheamh-mor from the harness and now, shouting insults in what may have been early Scots, performed some aggressive and alarming exercises with the weapon. The magnificent Duncan, who was beside him, cried out and backed away. "I say!" he protested, "don't! No! Too much!"

Gaston stamped and rotated his formidable weapon.

"Put that damn silly thing away," said Sir Dougal, "whatever it's called: 'glad-time saw.' You'll hurt yourself."

"Quiet!" Perry shouted. "Gaston! Stop it. At once."

Gaston did stop. He saluted and returned the weapon to its sheath, a leather pouch which hung by straps from his heavy belt-harness and occupied the place where a sporran would have rested. Once sheathed and the hilt in place, the monstrous blade rose in front of his body and was grasped by his gloved paws. It passed within an inch of his nose, causing him to squint. Thus armed, he retired and stood to attention, squinting hideously and rumbling industriously, by Maggie's throne. She gave one terrified look at him and then burst out laughing.

So, after a doubtful glance, did the entire company and the people in the stalls, including Emily.

Gaston stood to attention throughout.

Peregrine wiped the tears from his face, walked up to Gaston, put his arm around his shoulders, and took the risk of his life.

"Gaston, my dear man," he said, "you have taught us how to meet these ridiculous pranks. Thank you."

Gaston rumbled.

"What did you say?"

"Honi soit qui mal y pense."

"Exactly," agreed Peregrine and wondered if it was really an appropriate remark. "Well, everybody," he said. "We don't know who played these tricks and for the time being we'll let them rest. Will you all turn your backs for a moment?"

They did so. He whipped off the lid, wrapped the head in its cloak, took it backstage, and returned.

"Right!" he said. "Places, everybody. Are you ready, Sir Dougal, or would you like to break?"

"I'll go on."

"Good. Thank you. From where we left off, please."

"*Our duties and the pledge,*" said the prompter. And they went on to the end of the play.

When it was all over and he had taken his notes and gone through the bits that needed adjustment, Peregrine made a little speech to his cast.

"I can't thank you enough," he said. "You have behaved in a civilized and proper manner like the professionals you are. If, as I believe, the perpetrator of these jokes is among you, I hope he or she will realize how silly they are and we'll have no more of them. Our play is in good heart and we go forward with confidence, my dears. Tomorrow morning. Everyone at ten, please. In the rehearsal room."

v

PEREGRINE had a session with the effects and lighting people that lasted for an hour, at the end of which they went off, satisfied, to get their work down on paper. The stage was now patched with daylight. Sheets of painted plywood were being carried in from the workshop. Workmen shouted and whistled.

"Come on, Em," he said. "You've had more entertainment than we bargained for, haven't you?"

"I have indeed. You handled them beautifully."

"Did I? Good. Hullo, here's William. What are you doing, young man? Emily, this is William Smith."

"William, I very much enjoyed your performance," said Emily, shaking his hand.

"Did you?" said William. "I'm waiting for my mum, Mr. Jay, but" — a vivid flush mounted on his face — "but . . . I wanted to speak to you about — about —" He looked at Emily.

"About what?" Peregrine asked.

"About the heads. About the person who's done it. About everyone saying it's the sort of thing kids do. I didn't do it. Really, I didn't. I think it's silly. And frightening. Awfully frightening," William whispered. The red receded and a white-faced little boy stared at them. His eyes filled with tears.

"William!" Emily cried out. "Don't worry. They are only plastic mock-ups. Nothing to be afraid of. Pretend ghosts. William, never *mind*. Mr. Sears made them." She held out her arms. He hung back and then walked, shamefaced, into her embrace. She felt his heart beat and his trembling.

"Thank you very much, Mrs. Jay," he muttered and sniffed.

Emily held out her hand to Peregrine. "Hanky," she mouthed. He gave her his handkerchief.

"Here you are. Have a blow." William blew and caught his breath. She waggled her head at Peregrine, who said: "It's all right, William. You didn't do it." And walked away.

"There you are! Now you're in the clear, aren't you?"

"If he means it."

"He never, *ever,* says things he doesn't mean."

"Doesn't he? Super," said William and fetched a dry sob.

"So that's that, isn't it?" He didn't answer. "William," Emily said. "Are you really frightened of the heads? Quite apart from anyone thinking you did it. Just between ourselves."

He nodded. "I can't look at them," he whispered. "Much less touch them. They're awful."

"Would they be if you'd made one? You know. It's a long business. You make a mold in plaster of Mr. Barrabell's face and he makes a fuss and says you're stifling him and he won't keep his mouth open. And at last, when you've got it and it's dried, you pour a thin layer of some plastic stuff into it and wait till that dries, and then the hardest part comes," said Emily, hoping she'd got it vaguely right. "You've got to separate the two and bob's your uncle. Well — something like that. Broadly speaking."

"Yes."

"And you see it in all its stages and finally you've got to paint it and add hair and red paint for blood and so on, and it's rather fun, and *you* made it frightening, but you know it's just *you* being rather clever with plaster and plastic and paint."

"That's like the chorus of a song — 'With plaster and plastic and paint,' " said William.

" 'I'm producing a perfect phenomenon,' " said Emily. "So it is. You go on."

" 'I'm making things look what they ain't,' " said William. "Your turn. I bet you can't get a rhyme for 'phenomenon,' " and gave another dry sob.

"You win. When's your mama coming for you?"

"Pretty soon, I should think. She's buying our supper. It's her afternoon off."

"Well. You can wait here with me. Mr. Jay's got stuck into something up there. Have you heard how he came to restore this theatre?"

"No," said William. "I don't know anything about the theatre except it's meant to be rather grand to get a job in it."

"Well," said Emily, "come sit down and I'll tell you."

And she told him how Peregrine, a struggling young author-director, came into the wrecked Dolphin and fell into a bomb hole on the stage and was rescued from it and got the job of restoring the theatre and being made a member of the board.

"Even now, it's a bit like a fairy tale," she said.

"A nice one."

"Very nice."

They sat in companionable silence, watching the men working onstage.

"You go to a drama school, don't you?" Emily said after a pause.

"The Royal Southwark Drama School. It's a proper school. We learn all the usual things and theatre as well."

"How long have you been going to it?"

"Three years. I was the youngest kid there."

"And you like it?"

"Oh, yes," he said. "It's okay. I'm learning karate and how to fence. I'm going to be an actor, you know."

"Are you?"

"Of course," he said calmly.

The door at front-of-house opened and his mother looked in. He turned and saw her. "Here's my mum," he said. "I'd like you to meet her if that's all right. Would it be all right?"

"I'd like to meet her, William."

"Super," he said. "Excuse me." He edged past her and ran up the aisle. Emily stood up and turned around. "It's all right, Mum," he said. "Mrs. Jay said it is. Come on."

Emily said: "Hullo, Mrs. Smith. Do come in. I am so pleased to meet you," and held out her hand. "I'm Emily Jay," she said.

"I'm afraid my son's rather precipitous," said Mrs. Smith. "I've just called to collect him. I do know outsiders shouldn't walk into theatres as if they were bus stops."

"William's your excuse. He's our rising actor. My husband thinks he's very promising."

"Good. Get your overcoat, William — and what's happened to your face?"

"I don't know. What?" asked William unconvincingly.

"What's the matter with all our faces!" Emily exclaimed. "One of Gaston Sears's dummy heads for the parade of Banquo's successors got onto the banquet table and gave us the fright of our lives. Run and get your coat, William. It's over the back of your seat."

He said: "I'll get it," and wandered down the aisle.

Emily said: "I'm afraid it frightened him and made him jump and he became a very little boy, but he's quite recovered now. It did look *very* macabre."

"I'm sure it did," said Mrs. Smith. She had gone down

the aisle and met William. She put him into his coat with her back turned to Emily.

"Your hands are cold," he said.

"I'm sorry. It's very chilly outdoors." She buttoned him up and said: "Say good-night to Mrs. Jay."

"Good-night, Mrs. Jay."

"Good-night, old boy."

"Good-night," said Mrs. Smith. "Thank you for being so kind."

They shook hands.

Emily watched them go out. A lonely little couple, she thought.

"Come along, love," said Peregrine. He had come up behind her and put his arm around her. "All's settled. We can go home."

"Right."

They went out by the front-of-house. The life-size photographs were there being put into their frames. Sir Dougal Macdougal. Margaret Mannering. Simon Morten. The Three Witches. Out they came, one after another. Only a week left.

Emily and Peregrine stood and looked at them.

"Oh, darling!" she said. "This is your big one, isn't it? So big. So *big*."

"I know."

"Don't let these nonsense things worry you. They're silly."

"Yes. I know. You're talking to me as if I'm William."

"Come along, then. Home."

So they went home.

VI

THE final days were, if anything, less hectic than usual. The production crew had the use of the theatre and the actors worked in the rehearsal room on a chalked-out floor. Gaston insisted on having the stage to rehearse the fight, pointing out the necessity for the different levels and insisting on the daily routine being maintained. "As it will be," he said, "throughout the season."

Macbeth and Macduff made noises of protest but by this time they had become proud of their expertise and had gradually speeded up to an unbelievable pace. The great cumbersome weapons swept about within inches of their persons, sparks literally flew, muffled cries escaped them. The crew, overawed, knocked off and watched them for half an hour.

The end of the fight was a bit of a problem. Macbeth was beaten back to the O.P. exit, which was open but masked from the audience by an individual Stonehenge-like piece, firmly screwed to the floor. Macbeth backed down to it and crouched behind his shield. Macduff raised his claymore and swept it down. Macbeth caught it on his shield. A pause. Then, with an inarticulate, bestial sound, he leaped aside and backward. He was out of sight. Macduff raised his claymore high above his head and plunged offstage. There was a scream cut short by an unmistakable sound: an immense thud.

For three seconds the stage was empty and silent.

"Ratatat-ratatat-ratatat-RATATAT and bugles. Crescendo! Crescendo! And enter Malcolm et al.," roared Gaston.

"How about it?" asked Sir Dougal. "It's a close call, Gaston. He missed the scenery but only by a hair's breadth, you know. These claymores are so bloody long."

"He missed. If you both repeat where you were and what you do to a fraction of an inch, he'll always miss. If not — *not*. We'll take it again, if you please. The final six moves. Places. Er — one. Er — two. Er — three . . ."

"We're at hellishly close quarters at the side, there," said Simon when they had finished. "And it's dark as hell, too. Or will be."

"I'll be there with the head on my claidheamh-mor. Don't go hunting for me, though," said Gaston. "Simply take up your place and I'll fall in behind you. Macbeth will have gone straight out."

"I'll scream and scramble off, don't you worry," said Sir Dougal.

"All right."

"Until tomorrow. Same time. I thank you, gentlemen," said Gaston to the stagehands. He saluted and withdrew.

"Proper caution, in't 'e?" said a stagehand.

"Well, gentlemen," said the foreman, doing a creditable bit of mimicry, "shall we resume?"

They went about nailing the sanded and painted wallboard facing to the set. The stairs curved up to the landing and the door to Duncan's room. The red arras was hung and dropped in above the stairway. Below the landing a tunnel pierced the wall, making a passage to the south entry.

Peregrine, on his way to the rehearsal room, saw this and found it all good. The turntables, right and left, presented outside walls. The fireplace appeared. The gallows came into view and was anchored.

It was all smooth, he thought, and moved on into the rehearsal room. He had called the scene — he thought of it as the Aleppo scene — when the witches greet Macbeth. He was a little early but most of them were there. Banquo was there.

If they had been the crew of a ship, he thought, Barrabell would have been the sea-lawyer. He knew what Barrabell had been like as a schoolboy. Always closeted with other, smaller boys who listened furtively to him, always behind the dubious plan but never answerable. Always the troublemaker but never openly so. A boy to be dreaded.

Peregrine said: "Good morning, everybody."

"Good morning, Perry."

Yes. There he was with two of the witches. Silly little things, listening to his nonsense, whatever it was. The first witch, Rangi, hadn't arrived yet. He would not listen to Barrabell, Peregrine thought. He goes his own way. He too is an actor and a good one. For that I respect him.

Bruce Barrabell detached himself from the witches and made for him.

"Happy, Perry?" he asked, coming close to him. "Sorry! I shouldn't ask, should I? It's not done. Unlucky."

"Very happy, Bruce."

"We haven't got the Boy Beautiful with us this morning?"

"Do you mean William Smith? He'll be here."

"He's dropped the hyphen, of course. Poor little chap."

Peregrine, inside himself, did what actors call a double-take. His heart skipped a beat. He looked at Barrabell, who smiled at him. *Damn,* Peregrine thought. *He knows. Oh, damn, damn, damn.*

Rangi came in and looked at the clock. Just in time.

"Second witches' scene," Peregrine said. "Witches on from the three points of the compass. There will be a rumble of thunder. Just a hint. You arrive at exactly the same time and at dead center. Rangi through the passage. Each with a disheveled marketing bag. Blondie, Prompt. Wendy, O.P. It wasn't together last time. You'll have to get a sign. Rangi's got the farthest to walk. The other two are equal. Perhaps you should all have sticks? I don't want any hesitation. Wait for the thunder and start when it stops. Try that. Ready? Rumble, rumble. Now."

The three figures appeared, hobbled on, met. "Much better," said Peregrine. "Once more. This time greet each other. Rangi center. A smacking kiss on each of his cheeks simultaneously by each of you. In front. Together. Right. Dialogue."

They used their natural, well-contrasted voices. The rhymes were stressed. The long speech about the hapless sailor gone to Aleppo was a curse.

"Though his bark cannot be lost
Yet it shall be tempest-tos't.
Look what I have."

And Rangi scuffled in his market bag.

"Show me, show me," slavered the greedy Wendy.

Rangi's hand in his bag was stilled. He himself was still. Frozen. And then he suddenly opened the bag and peered inside. He withdrew his clenched hand.

"*Here I have a pilot's thumb*
Wrack'd as homeward he did come," said Rangi. He opened his hand very slightly.

"What's wrong?" Peregrine asked. "Haven't they given you something for the thumb?"

Rangi opened his hand. It was empty.

"I'll speak to Props. On you go."

"*A drum! a drum!*" said Wendy. "*Macbeth doth come.*"

And now their dance, about, about, turn and twist, bow, raise their joined hands. All very quick.

"*Peace! The charm's wound up.*"

"Yes," Peregrine said. "That speech has improved enormously. It's *really* alarming now. One feels the wretched sailor in his doomed ship, tossing and turning, not dying and not living. Good. We'll go on. Banquo and Macbeth. One moment, though. Banquo, the whole scene has been very carefully ordered so that Macbeth, the convention of the soliloquy having changed over four centuries, will not seem to be within hearing distance of his brother officers. You and Ross and Angus are talking together. Way upstage. But very quietly and with virtually no movement. Shakespeare himself seems to have felt the usual convention not really good enough. His *I thank you, gentlemen* is a dismissal. They bow and move as far away as they can get. The soliloquy, I needn't tell you, is of great importance. So no loud laughter, if you please. Okay?"

"I took the point the first time you made it," said Banquo.

"Good. That will save me the fatigue of making it a third time. Are you ready? *The earth hath bubbles.*"

The scene went forward. The messages of favors to come were delivered. The golden future opened out. Everything was lovely, and yet . . . and yet . . .

Presently they embarked on the cauldron scene. Peregrine developed the background of whispering. "*Double, double toil and trouble* —" Would it be heard? He tried a murmur; not good. "We'll try it whispered when the whole company is here," Peregrine said. "Six groups, each beginning after *trouble*. I think that'll work."

The witches were splendid. Clear and baleful. Their movements were explicit. They were real. But Peregrine was conscious that Rangi was troubled by something. He did not fumble a cue or muddle a movement or need a prompt, but he was unhappy. Unwell? Sickening for something? Oh, God, please not, thought Peregrine. Why is he looking at me? Am I missing something?

"*And points at them for his.*" Thunder and fog. Blackout, the door shut, and Lennox knocking on it. The scene ends.

"All right," said Peregrine. "I've no notes specifically for you. It will need adjustments, no doubt, when we get the background noise settled. Thank you all very much."

They all left the rehearsal room, except Rangi.

"Is something amiss? What's the matter?"

He held out his market bag. "Will you look in it, sir?" Peregrine took the bag and opened it.

Out of it a malignant head stared up at him. Mouth open, eyes open, teeth bared. Pinkish paws stretched upward.

"Oh, God!" said Peregrine. "Here we go again. Where was this bag?"

"With the other two on the props table. Since yesterday."

"Anyone look in it?"

"I shouldn't think so. Only to put the rat in. There was no means of telling which bag belonged to whom. It might have been Blondie's. She'd have fainted or gone into high-powered hysterics," said Rangi.

"She wouldn't have looked in. Nor would Wendy. Their bags are filled with newspaper and fastened with thongs, tightly knotted. Yours isn't because you are meant to open it and produce the pilot's thumb."

"So I was meant to find it," said Rangi.

"It wouldn't have worked with the other two."

"There's an obvious man to have played all these silly tricks."

"Props?" said Peregrine.

"Ask yourself."

"I do and I don't believe it. Did you hear his outcries and threats to appeal to his union over the Banquo's head business? Was that all my eye? We'd have to say we've got a bloody star-actor on the books. No. We've had him as Props for years. I simply cannot wear him for the job."

"Can't you narrow down the field? Where everyone was at the different times? Who could have gone up to Duncan's room with the head, for instance? As a matter of fact, I ran into him with it. Props. Coming down the ladder from Duncan's chamber. Now I think of it," said Rangi, "his manner was odd. I said: 'What are you doing with that thing?' and he said he was putting it where it ought to be. I'm sorry, Perry. I really think he's your man, you know. He must have put it under the dish-cover, mustn't he?"

"He was taking the one back to the other heads in the walking men's room. I told him to."

"Did you see him do it?"

"No."

"Ask him if he did it."

"Of course I will. But I'm sure he didn't put it in the dish. I admit he doesn't look too good but I'm sure of it."

"This blasted rat. Where did it come from? Have we been using traps?"

"And who sets them? All right. Props. He put one up in a narrow passage where Henry couldn't squeeze in." (Henry was the theatre cat.) "Props told me so himself. He was proud of his cunning."

Rangi said: "We'll have to look at it."

He opened the bag and turned it upside down. The rat's forequarters fell with a soft plop on the floor.

"There's the mark of the bar across its neck. It's deep. And wet. Its neck is broken. It's bled," said Rangi. "It doesn't smell. It's been recently killed."

"We'll have to keep it."

"Why?"

Peregrine was taken aback. "Why?" he said. "Upon my

word I don't know. I'm treating it like evidence for a crime and there's no crime of that sort. Nor any sort, really. All the same . . . wait a bit."

Peregrine went to a rubbish bin, found a discarded brown-paper bag, and turned it inside out. He brought it back and held it open. Rangi picked the rat up by the ear and dropped it in. Peregrine screwed up the neck of the bag tightly.

"Horrible beast," he said.

"We'd better — ssh."

A padded footfall and the swish of a broom sounded in the passage.

"Ernie!" Peregrine called. "Props!"

The door opened and he came in. How many years, Peregrine asked himself, had Ernie been Props at the Dolphin. Ten? Twenty? Dependable always. A cockney with an odd, quirky sense of the ridiculous and an oversensitive reaction to an imagined slight. Thin, sharp face. Quick. Sidelong grin.

"Hullo, guv," he said. "Fought you'd of gawn by now."

"Just going. Caught any rats?"

"I never looked. 'Old on."

He went to the back of the room behind a packing case. A pause and then Props's voice. " 'Ullo! What's this, then?" A scuffling and he appeared with a rattrap on a long string.

"Look at this," he said. "I don't get it. The bait's gone. So's the rat's head. There's *been* a rat. Fur and gore and hindquarters all over it. Killed. Somebody's been and taken it. Must of."

"Henry?" asked Peregrine.

"Nah! Cats don't eat rats. Just kill 'em. And 'Enery couldn't get up that narrer passage. Nah! It's been a man. 'E's pulled out the trap, lifted the bar, and taken the rat's forequarters."

"The caretaker?"

"Not 'im. They give 'im the willies, rats do. It ought to be 'im that sets the trap, not me, but 'e won't."

"When did you set it, then, Ernie?"

"Yesterday morning. They was all collected in 'ere waiting for rehearsal, wasn't they?"

"Yes. We did the crowd scenes," said Peregrine. He looked at Rangi. "You weren't here," he said.

"No. First I've heard of it."

Peregrine saw an alert, doubtful look on Props's face.

"We've been wondering who knew all about the trap. Pretty well the whole company seems to be the answer," said Peregrine.

"That's right," Props said. He was staring at the brown-paper parcel. "What's that?" he asked.

Peregrine said: "What's what?"

"That parcel. Look. It's mucky."

He was right. A horrid wetness seeped through the paper. "It's half your rat, Props," said Peregrine. "Your rat's in the parcel."

" 'Ere! What's the game, eh? You've taken it off of the trap and made a bloody parcel of it. What for? Why didn't you say so instead of letting me turn myself into a blooming exhibition? What's all this about?" Props demanded.

"We didn't remove it. It was in Mr. Western's bag."

Props turned and looked hard at Rangi. "Is that correct?" he asked.

"Perfectly correct. I put my hand in to get the pilot's thumb and" — he grimaced — "I touched it." He picked up his bag and held it out. "Look for yourself," he said. "It'll be marked."

Props took the bag and opened it. He peered inside. "That's right," he said. "There's marks." He stared at Peregrine and Rangi. "It's the same bloody bugger what did the other bloody tricks," he said.

"Looks like it," Peregrine agreed. And after a moment: "Personally, I'm satisfied that it wasn't you, Ernie. You're not capable of such a convincing display of bewilderment. Or of thinking it funny."

"Ta, very much." He jerked his head at Rangi. "What about him?" he asked. "Don't 'e fink I done it?"

"I'm satisfied. Not you," said Rangi.

There was a considerable pause before Props said: "Fair enough."

Peregrine said: "I think we say nothing about this. Props, clear up the wet patch in the witch's bag, would you, and return it to its place on the table with the other two. Drop the rat in the rubbish bin. We've overreacted, which is probably exactly what he wanted us to do. From now on, you keep a tight watch on all the props right up to the time they're used. And not a word to anyone about this. Okay?"

"Okay," they both said.

"Right. Go ahead then. Rangi, can I give you a lift?"

"No, thanks. I'll take a bus."

They went out through the stage door.

Peregrine unlocked his car and got in. Big Ben tolled four o'clock. He sat there, dog-tired suddenly. Drained. Zero hour. This time on Saturday: the opening night and the awful burden of the play. Of lifting the cast. Of hoping for the final miracle. Of being, within himself, sure, and of conveying that security somehow to the cast.

Why, why, *why*, thought Peregrine, do I direct plays? Why do I put myself into this hell? Above all, why *Macbeth*? And then: It's too soon to be feeling like this; five days too soon. Oh, God deliver us all.

He drove home to Emily.

"Do you have to go out again tonight?" she asked.

"I'm not sure. I don't think so."

"How about a bath and a zizz?"

"I ought to be doing something. I can't think."

"I'll answer the telephone and if it's important I swear I'll wake you."

"Will you?" he said helplessly.

"Come on, silly. You haven't slept for two nights."

"Haven't I?"

"Not a wink."

She went upstairs. He heard the bath running and smelled the stuff she used in it. If I sit down, he thought, I won't get up.

He wandered to the window. There was the Dolphin across the river, shining in the late-afternoon sun. Tomorrow they'll put up the big poster. MACBETH! OPENING 23 APRIL! I'll see it from here.

Emily came down. "Come on," she said.

She helped him undress. The bath was heaven. Emily scrubbed his back. His head nodded and his mouth filled with foam.

"Blow!"

He blew and the foam floated about, a mass of iridescent bubbles.

"Stay awake for three minutes longer," said her voice. She had evidently pulled out the plug. "Come on. Out."

He was dried. The sensation was laughable. He woke sufficiently to fumble himself into his pajamas and then into bed.

"*Sleep*," he murmured, "*that knits up the ravell'd sleave of care.*"

"That's right," said Emily, a thousand miles away.

He slept.

VII

ACROSS the river, not very far away as the crow flies, the theatre trembled with the rebirth of the play. The actors were gone but business manager Winter Meyer and his staff worked away in the front-of-house. Telephones rang. Bookings were made. Royalty were coming and someone from Buck House would appear the day before they opened to settle the arrangements. The police and Security people would make decisions. Chief Superintendent Alleyn and his wife were coming. The Security pundits thought it a good idea if he were to be put in the box next to the Royalty. Chief Superintendent Alleyn received the order philosophically if not jubilantly and asked for a seat later in the season when he could watch the play rather than the house.

"Of course, of course, my dear chap," Winty gushed. "Anytime. Anywhere. Management seat. Our pleasure."

Flower shop. Cleaners. Press. Programmes. Biographical notes. Notes on the play. Nothing about superstitions.

Winter Meyer read through the proofs and could find nothing to crack the eggshell sensitivity of any of the actors. Until he came to the piece on Banquo.

"Mr. Bruce Barrabell, too long an absentee from the West End." He won't relish that, thought Winty, and changed it to ". . . makes a welcome return to . . ."

He went through the whole thing again and then rang up the printers and asked if the Royal Programme was ready and when he could see a copy.

Winter Meyer's black curls were now iron gray. He had been business manager at the Dolphin ever since it was restored and remembered the play about Shakespeare by Peregrine Jay that twenty years ago had been accompanied by a murder.

Seems a long time ago now, thought Winty. Things have gone rather smoothly since then. He touched wood with his plump white finger. Of course we're in a nice financial position, permanently endowed by the late Mr. Conducis. Almost *too* secure, you might think. *I* don't, he thought with a fat chuckle. He lit a cigar and returned to his work.

He had dealt with his "In" tray. There was only an advertisement left from a wine merchant. He picked it up and dropped it in his wastebasket, exposing a folded paper at the bottom of his tray.

Winty was an extremely tidy man and liked to say he knew exactly where everything lay on or in his desk and what it was about. He did not recognize this folded sheet. It was, he noted, a follow-up sheet of office letter paper. He frowned and opened it.

The typed message read: "murderers son in your co."

Winter Meyer sat perfectly still, his cigar in his left hand and in his right this outrageous statement.

Presently he turned and observed, on a small table, the typewriter sometimes used by his secretary for taking down dictated letters. He inserted a sheet of paper and typed the statement.

This, he decided, corresponds exactly. The monstrous truth declared itself. It had been executed in his office. Somebody had come in, sat down, and infamously typed it. No apostrophe or full stop and no capital letter. Because the writer was in a hurry? Or ignorant? And the motive?

Winty put both typed messages into an envelope and wrote the date on it. He unlocked his private drawer, dropped the envelope in, and relocked it.

The son of a murderer?

Winty consulted his neatly arranged fabulous memory. Since the casting list was completed he mentally ticked off each player until he came to William Smith. He remembered his mother, her nervous manner, her hesitation, her obvious relief. And diving backward, at last he remembered the Harcourt-Smith case and its outcome. Three years ago, wasn't it? Five victims, and all of them girls! Mutilated, beheaded. Broadmoor for life.

If that's the answer, Winty thought, I've pretty well forgotten the case. But, by God, I'll find out who wrote this message and I won't rest till I've faced him with it. Now then!

He thought very carefully for some time and then rang his secretary's room.

"Mr. Meyer?" said her voice.

"Still here, are you, Mrs. Abrams? Will you come in, please?"

"Certainly."

Seconds later the inner door opened and a middle-aged lady came in, carrying her notebook.

"You just caught me," she said.

"I'm sorry."

"It's all right. I'm in no hurry."

"Sit down. I want to test your memory, Mrs. Abrams." She sat down.

"When," he asked, "did you last see the bottom of my 'In' tray?"

"Yesterday morning, Mr. Meyer. Ten-fifteen. Tea-time. I checked through the contents and added the morning's mail."

"You saw the *bottom*?"

"Certainly. I took everything out. There was a brochure from the wine people. I thought you might like to see it."

"Quite. And nothing else?"

"Nothing." She waited for a moment and then said incredulously: "There's nothing *lost*?"

"No. There's something found. A typed message. It's on our follow-up paper and it's typed on that machine over there. No envelope."

"Oh," she said.

"Yes. Where was I? While you were in here?"

"On the phone. Security people. First-night arrangements."

"Ah yes. Mrs. Abrams, was this room unoccupied at any time, *and* unlocked, between then and now? I lunched at my club."

"It was locked. You locked it."

"Before that?"

"Er. I think you went out for a few minutes. At eleven."

"I did?"

"The toilet," she modestly said. "I heard the door open and close."

"Oh yes. And later?"

"Let me think. No, apart from that it was never unoccupied *and* unlocked. Wait!"

"Yes, Mrs. Abrams?"

"I had put a sheet of our follow-up paper in the little machine here in case you should require a memo."

"Yes?"

"You did not. It is not there now. How peculiar."

"Yes, very." He thought things over for a moment and then said: "Your memory, Mrs. Abrams, is exceptional. Do

I understand that the only time it could have been done was when I left the room for — for at least five minutes — more? Would you not have heard the typewriter?"

"I was using my own machine in my own room, Mr. Meyer. No."

"And the time?"

"I heard Big Ben."

"Thank you. Thank you very much." He hesitated. He contemplated Mrs. Abrams doubtfully. "I'm very much obliged. I — thank you, Mrs. Abrams."

"Thank *you,* Mr. Meyer," she said and withdrew.

She closed the door. I wonder, she thought, why he doesn't tell me what was in the message.

On the other side of the door he thought: I would have liked to tell her but — no. The fewer the better.

He sat before his desk and thought carefully and calmly about this disruptive event. He was unaware of the previous occurrences: Peregrine's accident; the head in the King's room; the head in the meat dish; the rat in Rangi's bag. They were not in his department. So he had nothing to relate the message to. A murderer's son in the cast! he thought. Preposterous! What murderer? What son?

He thought again of the Harcourt-Smith case. He remembered that the sensational papers had made a great thing of the wife's having no inkling of Harcourt-Smith's second "personality" and, yes, of his little son, who was six years old.

It is our William, he thought. Blow me down flat but it's our William that's being got at. And after a further agitation: I'll do nothing. It's awkward, of course, but until the show's been running for some time it's better not to meddle. If then. I don't know who's typed it and I don't want to know. Yet.

He looked at his day-to-day calendar. A red ring neatly encircled April 23. Shakespeare's birthday. Opening night. Less than a week left, he thought.

He was not a pious man, but he caught himself wondering for the moment about the protective comfort of a phylactery and wishing he could experience it.

5

DRESS REHEARSALS AND FIRST NIGHT

I

THE days before the opening night seemed to hurry and to darken. There were no disasters and no untoward happenings, only a rushing immediacy. The actors arrived early for rehearsals. Some who were not called came to the last of the piecemeal sessions and watched closely and with a painful intensity.

The first of the dress rehearsals, really a technical rehearsal, lasted all day with constant stoppages for lights and effects. The management had a meal sent in. It was set up in the rehearsal room: soup, cold meat, potatoes in their skins, salad, coffee. Some members of the cast helped themselves when they had an opportunity. Others, Maggie for one, had nothing.

The props for the banquet were all there: a boar's head with a lemon in its jaws and glass eyes. Plastic chickens. A soup tureen that would exude steam when a servingman removed the lid. Peregrine looked under the covers but the contents were all right: glued down. Loose: wine jugs; goblets; a huge candelabrum in the center of the table.

The pauses for lights were continual. Dialogue. Stop. "Catch them going *up*. Refocus it. Is it fixed? This mustn't happen again."

The witches each had a tiny blue torch concealed in their clothes. They switched these on when Macbeth spoken to them. They had to be firmly sewn and accurately pointed at their faces.

Plain sailing for a bit but still the feeling of pressure and anxiety. But that, after all, was normal. The actors played "within themselves." Or almost. They got an interrupted run. The tension was extreme. The theatre was full of marvelous but ominous sounds. The air was thick with menace.

The arrival at Macbeth's castle in the evening was the last seen of daylight for a long time. Exquisite lighting: a mellow and tranquil scene. Banquo's beautiful voice saying *"the air nimbly and sweetly recommends itself unto our gentle senses."* The sudden change when the doors rolled back and the piper skirled wildly and Lady Macbeth drew the King into the castle.

From now on it is night, for dawn, after the murder, was delayed and hardly declared itself, and before the murder of Banquo it is dusk: *"The west yet glimmers with some streaks of day,"* says the watchful assassin.

Banquo is murdered.

After the banquet the Macbeths are alone together, the last time the audience sees them so, and the night is *"almost at odds with morning, which is which."* Otherwise, torchlight, lamplight, witchlight right on until the English scene, out-of-doors and sunny with a good King on the throne.

When Macbeth reappears he is aged, disheveled, half-demented, deserted by all but a few who cannot escape. Dougal Macdougal would be wonderful. He played these last abysmal scenes now well under their final pitch, but with every wayward change indicated. He was a wounded animal with a snarl or two left in him. *"Tomorrow and tomorrow and tomorrow . . ."* The speech tolled its way to the end like a death knell.

Macduff and Malcolm, the lairds and their troops arrive. Now, at last, Macbeth and Macduff meet. The challenge. The fight. The exit and the scream cut short.

[117]

The brief scene in which Old Siward speaks the final conventional merciless word on his son's death, and then Macduff enters downstage, and behind him Seyton, with Macbeth's head on his claidheamh-mor.

Malcolm, up on the stairway among his soldiers, is caught by the setting sun. They turn their heads and see The Head. And finally:

"*Hail, King of Scotland!*" shout the soldiers.

"Curtain," Peregrine said. "But don't bring it down. Hold it. Thank you. Lights. I think they're a little too juicy at the end. Too pink. Can you give us something a bit less obvious? Straw, perhaps. It's too much 'Exit into sunset.' You know? Right. Settle down, everybody. Bring some chairs on. I won't keep the actors very long. Settle down."

They settled.

He went through the play. "Witches, *all* raise your arms when you jump.

"Details. Nothing of great importance except on the Banquo's ghost exit. You were too close to Lennox. Your cloak moved in the draft."

"Can they leave a wider gap?"

"I can," said Lennox. "Sorry."

"Right. Any more questions?" Predictably, Banquo. His scene with Fleance and Macbeth. The lighting. "It feels false. I have to move into it."

"Come on a bit farther on your entrance. Nothing to stop you, is there?"

"It feels false."

"It doesn't give that impression," said Peregrine very firmly. "Any other questions?"

William piped up. "When I'm stabbed," he said. "I kind of hold the wound and then collapse. Could the murderer catch me before I fall?"

"Certainly," said Peregrine. "He's meant to."

"Sorry," said the murderer. "I missed it. I was too late."

They plowed on. Attention to details. Getting everything right, down to the smallest move, the fractional pause. Changes of pace building toward a line of climax. Peregrine spent three quarters of an hour over the cauldron scene. The entire cast were required to whisper the repeated rhythmic chant as in a round. "*Double, double toil and trouble, fire burn and cauldron bubble.*"

At last they moved on. There were no more questions. Peregrine thanked them. "Same time tomorrow," he said, "and I *hope* no stops. You've been very patient. Bless you all. Good-night."

II

BUT again there were stops, next day. A number of technical hitches cropped up during the final dress rehearsal, mostly to do with the lights. They were all cleared up. Peregrine had said to the cast: "Keep something in the larder. Don't reach the absolute tops. Play within yourselves. Conserve your energy. Save the consummate thing for the performance. We know you can do it, my dears. Don't exhaust yourselves."

They obeyed him but there were one or two horrors.

Lennox missed an entrance and arrived looking as if the Devil himself was after him.

Duncan lost his lines, had to be prompted, and was slow to recover. Nina Gaythorne dried completely and looked terror-stricken. William went straight on with his own lines: "*And must they all be hanged that swear and lie?*" and she answered like an automaton.

"It was a dose of stage fright," she said when they came off. "I didn't know where I was or what I said. Oh, this play. This play."

"Never mind, Miss Gaythorne," said William, taking her hand. "It won't happen again. I'll be with you."

"That's something," she said, half-laughing and half-crying.

At the end they rehearsed the curtain calls. The "dead" characters on the O.P. side and the live ones on the Prompt. Then the Macbeths alone, and finally the man himself. Alone.

Peregrine took his notes and thanked his cast. "Change but don't go," he said.

" 'Bad dress. Good show.' " quoted the stage director cheerfully. "Are we getting them down tomorrow?"

He put this to the company.

"If we get it rotten-perfect now, you can sleep in tomorrow morning. It's just a matter of working straight on from cue to cue with nothing between. All right? Any objections? Banquo?"

"I?" said Banquo, who had been ready to make one. "Objections? Oh no. No."

They finished at five of two in the morning. The management had provided beer, whiskey, and sherry. Some of them left without taking anything. William was dispatched in a taxi with Angus and Menteith, who lived more or less in the same direction. Maggie slipped away as soon as her sleep-walking scene was over and she had seen Peregrine. Fleance went after the murder, Banquo, after the cauldron scene, and Duncan, on his arrival at the castle. There were not many holdups. A slight rearrangement of the company fights at the end. Macbeth and Macduff went like clockwork.

Peregrine waited till they were all gone and the night watchman was on his rounds. The theatre was dark except for the dim working light. Dark, coldly stuffy. Waiting.

He stood for a moment in front of the curtain and saw the caretaker's torch moving about the circle. He felt empty and dead-tired. Nothing untoward had happened.

"Good-night," he called.

"Good-night, guv'nor."

He went through the curtain into backstage and past the menacing shapes of scenery, ill-defined by the faraway working light. Where was his torch? Never mind, he'd got all his papers under his arm fastened to a clipboard and he would go home. Past the masking pieces, cautiously along the Prompt side.

Something caught hold of his foot.

He fell forward and a jolt wrenched at his former injury and made him cry out.

"Are you all right?" asked a scarcely audible voice.

He was all right. He still had hold of his clipboard. He'd caught his foot in one of the light cables. Up he got, cautiously. "All serene," he shouted.

"Are you *quite* sure?" asked an anxious voice close at hand.

"God! Who the hell are you?"

"It's me, guv."

"Props! What the blazes are you doing? Where are you?"

"I'm 'ere. Thought I'd 'ang abaht and make sure no one was up to no tricks. I must of dozed off. Wait a tick."

A scrabbling noise and he came fuzzily into view around the corner of a dark object. A strong smell of whiskey accompanied him. "It's the murdered lady's chair," he said. "I must of dropped off in it. Fancy."

"Fancy."

Props moved forward and a glassy object rolled from under his feet.

"Bottle," he said coyly. "Empty."

"So I supposed."

Peregrine's eyes had adjusted to the gloom. "How drunk are you?" he asked.

"Not so bad. Only a few steps down the primrose parf There wasn't more'n three drinks left in the bottle. Honest And nobody got up to no tricks. They've all vanished. Into thin air."

"You'd better follow them. Come on."

He took Props by the arm, steered him to the stage door, opened it, and shoved him through.

"Ta," said Props. "Goo'night," and made off at a tidy shamble. Peregrine adjusted the self-locking apparatus on the door and banged it. He was in time to see Props being sick at the corner of Wharfingers Lane.

When he had finished he straightened up, saw Peregrine, and waved to him.

"That's done the trick," he shouted, and walked briskly away.

Peregrine went to the car park, unlocked his car, and got in.

"Oh, Lord!" he said, and drove himself home.

Emily in her woolly dressing gown let him in.

"Hullo, love," he said, "You shouldn't have waited up."

"Hullo."

He said: "Just soup," and sank into an armchair.

She gave him strong soup laced with brandy.

"Golly, that's nice," he said. And then: "Pretty bloody awful but nothing in the way of practical jokes."

"Bad dress. Good show."

"Hope so."

And in that hope he finished his soup and went to bed and to sleep.

III

Now they were all in their dressing-rooms, doors shut, telegrams, cards, presents, flowers, the pungent smell of greasepaint and wet white and hand-lotion, the close, electrically charged atmosphere of a working theatre.

Maggie made up her face. Carefully, looking at it from all angles, she drew her eyebrows together, emphasized the determined creases at the corners of her mouth. She pulled back her reddish hair, twisted it into a regal chignon, and secured it with pins and a band.

Nanny, her dresser and housekeeper, stood silently, holding her robe. When she turned there it was, opened, waiting for her. She covered her head with a chiffon scarf; Nanny skillfully dropped the robe over it, not touching it.

The tannoy came to life. "Quarter hour. Quarter hour, please," it said.

"Thank you, Nanny," said Maggie. "That's fine." She kissed a bedraggled bit of fur with a cat's head. "Bless you, Thomasina," she said and propped it against her glass.

A tap on the door. "May I come in?"

"Dougal! Yes."

He came in and put a velvet case on her table. "It was my grandma's," he said. "She was a Highlander. Blessings." He kissed her hand and made the sign of the cross over her.

"My dear, thank you. Thank you."

But he was gone.

She opened the case. It was a brooch: a design of interlaced golden leaves with semiprecious stones making a thistle. "It's benign, I'm sure," she said. "I shall wear it in my cloak. In the fur, Nanny. Fix it, will you?"

Presently she was dressed and ready.

The three witches stood together in front of the looking-glass, Rangi in the middle. He had the face of a skull but his eyelids glittered in his dark face. Around his neck on a flax cord hung a greenstone *tiki,* an embryo child. Blondie's face was made ugly, grossly overpainted: blobs of red on the cheeks and a huge scarlet mouth. Wendy was bearded. They had transformed their hands into claws.

"If I look any longer I'll frighten myself," said Rangi.

"Quarter hour. Quarter hour please."

Gaston Sears dressed alone. He would have been a most uncomfortable companion, singing, muttering, uttering snatches of ancient rhymes, and paying constant visits to the lavatory. He occupied a tiny room that nobody else wanted but that seemed to please him.

When Peregrine called he found him in merry mood. "I congratulate you, dear boy," he cried. "You have undoubtedly hit upon a valid interpretation of the cryptic Seyton."

Peregrine shook hands with him. "I mustn't wish you luck," he said.

"But why not, perceptive boy? We wish each other luck. *À la bonne heure.*"

Peregrine hurried on to Nina Gaythorne's room.

Her dressing-table was crowded with objects of baffling inconsistency and each of them must be fondled and kissed. A plaster Genesius, patron saint of actors, was in pride of place. There were also a number of anti-witchcraft objects and runes. The actress who played the Gentlewoman shared the dressing-room and had very much the worst of the bargain. Not only did Nina take three quarters of the working bench for her various protective objects, she spent a great deal of time muttering prophylactic rhymes and prayers.

These exercises were furtively carried out with one scared eye on the door. When Peregrine knocked she leaped up and cast her makeup towel over her sacred collection. She then stood with her back to the bench, her hands resting negligently upon it, and broke out into peals of unconvincing laughter. There was a strong smell of garlic.

Macduff and Banquo were in the next-door room to Sir Dougal's and were quiet and businesslike. Simon Morten was withdrawn into himself, tense and silent. When he first came he did a quarter of an hour's limbering-up and then took a shower and settled to his makeup. Bruce Barrabell tried a joke or two but getting no response, fell silent. Their dresser attended to them.

Bruce Barrabell whistled two notes, remembered it was considered unlucky, stopped short, and said, "*Shit.*"

"Out," said Simon.

"I didn't know *you* were one of the faithful."

"Go on. Out."

He went out and shut the door. A pause. He turned around three times and then knocked.

"Yes?"

"— humbly apologize. May I come back? Please."

"Come in."

"Quarter hour. Quarter hour, please."

William Smith dressed with Duncan and his sons. He was perfectly quiet and very pale. Malcolm, a pleasant young fellow, helped him make up. Duncan, attended by a dresser, benignly looked on.

"First nights," he groaned comprehensively. "How I hate them." His glance rested upon William. "This is your first First Night, laddie, is it not?"

"There've been school showings, sir," said William nervously.

"School showings, eh? Well, well, well," he said profoundly. "Ah, well." He turned to his ramshackle part propped up against his looking-glass and began to mutter. "*So well thy words become thee as thy wounds.*"

"I'm at your elbow, Father. Back to audience. I'll give it to you if needs be. Don't worry," said Malcolm.

"You will, my boy, won't you? No, I shan't worry. But I can't imagine *why* I dried like that. However."

He caught his cloak up in a practiced hand and turned round: "All right, behind?" he asked.

"Splendid," his son reassured him.

"Good. Good."

". . . Ten minutes, please."

A tap on the door. Peregrine looked in. "Lovely house," he said. "They're simmering. William" — he patted William's head — "you'll remember tonight through all your other nights to come, won't you? Your performance is correct. Don't alter anything, will you?"

"No, sir."

"That's the ticket." He turned to Duncan. "My dear fellow, you're superb. And the boys. Malcolm, you've a long time to wait, haven't you? For your big scene. I've nothing but praise for you."

The witches stood in a tight group. The picture they presented was horrendous. They said, "Thank you," all together and stood close to one another, staring at him.

"You'll do," said Peregrine.

He continued his rounds. It wasn't too easy to find things to say to them all. Some of them hated to be wished well in so many words. They liked you to say facetiously, "Fall down and break your leg." Others enjoyed the squeezed elbow and confident nod. The ladies were kissed — on the hands or in the air because of makeup. Round he went with butterflies busily churning in his own stomach, his throat and mouth dry as sandpaper, and his voice seeming to come from someone else.

Maggie said: "It's your night tonight, Perry dear. All yours. Thank you." And kissed him.

Sir Dougal shook both his hands. "*Angels and ministers of grace defend us,*" he said.

"Amen," Perry answered.

Simon, magnificently dark and exuding a heady vitality, also shook his hands. "Thank you," he said, "I'm no good at this sort of thing but blessings and thank you."

"Where's Banquo?"

"He went out. Having a pee, I suppose."

"Give him my greetings," said Peregrine, relieved.

On and on. The thanes, nervy and polite. The walking gents, much obliged to be visited. Finished at last.

Front-of-house waiting for him: Winty's assistant.

"All right," he said. "We're pushing the whole house in. Bit of a job. There are the Royalty-hunters determined to stay in the foyer but we've herded them all in. Winty's dressed up like a sore thumb and waiting in the entrance. The house is packed with security men and Bob's your uncle. They've rung through to say the cars have left."

"Away we go?"

"Away we go."

"Beginners, please. Beginners," said the tannoy.

The witches appeared in the shadows, came onstage, climbed the rostrum, and grouped around the gallows. Duncan and his sons and the thanes stood offstage, waiting for the short opening scene to end.

An interval of perhaps three interminable minutes. Then trumpets filled the air with their brazen splendor and were followed by the sound of a thousand people getting to their feet. Now the National Anthem. And now they settled in their seats. A peremptory buzzer. The stage director's voice.

"Stand by. House lights. Thunder. Curtain up."

Peregrine began to pace to and fro, to and fro. Listening.

IV

AFTER the fourth scene he knew. It was all right. Their hearts are in it, he thought and he crept into the Prompt-side box. Winty squeezed his arm in the darkness and said, "We'll run for months and months. It's a wow."

"Thank God."

He'd been right. They had left themselves with one more step to the top and now they took it.

You darling creatures, he thought, suddenly in love with all of them. Ah, you treasures. Bless you. Bless you.

The rest of the evening was unreal. The visit to the royal box and the royal visit to the cast. The standing ovation at the end. Everything to excess. A multiple Cinderella story. Sort of.

Emily came and hugged him and cried and said: "Oh, yes, darling. Yes. *Yes*."

The company collected around him and cheered. And finally the critic whose opinion he most valued astonishingly came up to him; he said he was breaking the rule of a lifetime but it had undoubtedly been the best Macbeth since Olivier's and the best Lady Macbeth in living memory and he must do a bolt.

"We'll get out of this," Peregrine said. "I'm hungry."

"Where are we going?"

"The Wig and Piglet. It's only minutes away and they stay open till the papers come in. The manager's getting them for me."

"Come on, then."

They edged through the milling crowd of shouting visitors and out the stage door. The alley was full of people waiting for actors to appear. Nobody recognized the director. They turned into the theatre car park, managed to fiddle their way out and up the lane.

At the corner of the main street stood two lonely figures, a thin and faintly elegant woman and a small boy.

"It's William and his mum," said Emily.

"I want to speak to the boy."

He pulled up beside them. Emily lowered her window. "Hullo, Mrs. Smith. Hullo, William. Are you waiting for a bus?"

"We *hope* we are," said Mrs. Smith.

"You're not doing anything of the sort," said Peregrine. "The management looks after getting you home on the first night," he lied. "Didn't you know? Oh, good luck; there's a taxi coming." Emily waved to it. "William," Peregrine said. William ran around to the driver's side. Peregrine got out. "You can look after your mother, can't you? Here you are." He pushed a note into William's hand. "You gave a thoroughly professional performance. Good luck to you."

The taxi pulled up. "In you get, both of you." He gave the driver the address.

"Yes — but — I mean —" said Mrs. Smith.

"No, you don't." They were bundled in. "Good-night." He slammed the door. The taxi made off.

"Phew! That was quick," Emily said.

"If she'd had a moment to get her second wind she'd have refused. Come on, darling. How hungry I am. You can't think."

The Wig and Piglet was full. The head waiter showed them to a reserved table.

"A wonderful performance, sir," he said. "They are all saying so. My congratulations."

"Thank you. A bottle of your best champagne, Marcello."

"It awaits you." Marcello beamed and waved grandly at the wine bucket on their table.

"Really? Thank you."

"Nothing," said Peregrine when he had gone, "succeeds like success." He looked at Emily's excited face. "I'm sorry," he said gently. "On a night like this one should not think forward or back. I found myself imagining what it would have been like if we'd flopped."

"Don't. I know what you mean but don't put the stars out."

"No husbandry in our Heaven, tonight?" He reached out a hand. "It's a bargain," he said.

"A bargain. It's because you're hungry."

"You may be right."

An hour later he said she was a clever old trout. They had a cognac each to prove it and began to talk about the play.

"Gaston," Peregrine said, "may be dotty but he's pretty good where he is tonight, wouldn't you say?"

"Exactly right. He's like death itself, presiding over its feast."

"You don't think we've gone too far with him?"

"Not an inch."

"Good. Winty says it'll run for as long as Dougal and Maggie can take it."

"That's a matter of temperament, isn't it?"

"I suppose so. For Maggie, certainly. She's rock-calm and perfectly steady. It's Dougal who surprises me. I'd expected a good, even a harrowing, performance but not so deeply frightening a one. He's got that superb golden-reddish appearance and I thought, we must be very clever about makeup so that the audience will see it disintegrate. But, upon my soul, he *does* disintegrate, he *is* bewitched, he *has* become the devil's puppet. I began, even, to wonder if it was all right or if it might be embarrassing, as if he'd discarded his *persona* and we'd come face to face with his naked personal collapse. Which would be dreadful and wrong. But no. It hasn't happened. He's come near the brink in the last scene, but he's still Macbeth. Thanks to Gaston, he fights like a man possessed but always with absolute control. And so — evilly. For Macduff, it's like stamping out some horror that's lain under a stone waiting for him."

"And *his* whole performance?"

"If I could scratch about for something wrong I would. But no, he's going great guns. The straightforward avenger."

"I think he plays the English scene beautifully. I'm sorry," said Emily. "I wish I could find something wrong and out-of-key or wanting readjustment somewhere but I can't. Your problem will be to keep them up to this level."

They talked on. Presently the door into the servery opened and their waiter came in with an armful of Sunday papers.

Peregrine's heart suddenly thumped against his ribs. He took up the top one and flipped over the pages.

At Last!

A Flawless Macbeth!

And two rave columns.

Emily saw his open paper trembling in his hands. She went through the remaining ones, folding them back at the dramatic criticisms.

"This is becoming ridiculous," she said.

He made a strange little sound of agreement. She shoved the little pile of papers over to him. "They're all the same, allowing for stylistic differences."

"We'll go home. We're the only ones left. Poor Marcello!"

He lowered his paper and folded it. Emily saw that his eyes were red. "I can't get over it," he said. "It's too much."

He signed his bill and added an enormous tip. They were bowed out.

The Embankment was being washed down. Great fans of water swept to and fro. In the east, buildings were silhouetted against a kindling sky. London was waking up.

They drove home, let themselves in, and went to bed and a fathomless sleep.

The first member of the company to wake on Sunday was William Smith. He consulted his watch, dragged on his clothes, gave a lick to his face, and let himself out by the front door. Every Sunday at the end of their little lane, a newsman set up his wares on a flight of steps in a major traffic road. He trustfully left his customers to put the right amount in a tin, helping themselves to change when required. He kept an eye on them from the Kaff on the Korner.

William had provided himself with the exact sum. Mr. Barnes, he recollected, had said something about the "quality" papers being the ones that mattered. He purchased the most expensive and turned to the headlines.

At Last!

A Flawless Macbeth!

William read it all the way home. It was glorious. At the end it said: "The smallest parts have been given the same loving attention. A pat on the head is here awarded to Master William Smith for totally avoiding the Infant Phenomenon."

William charged upstairs shouting: "Mum! Are you awake? Hi, Mum! What's an Infant Phenomenon? Because I've avoided one."

By midday they had all read the notices and by evening most of them had rung up somebody else in the company and they were all delighted but feeling a sort of anticlimactic emptiness. The only thing left to say was: "Now we must keep it up, mustn't we?"

Barrabell went to a meeting of the Red Fellowship. He was asked to report on his tasks. He said the actors had been too much occupied to listen to new ideas but now that they were clearly set for a long run he would embark on stage two and hoped to have more to report at the next meeting. It was a case of making haste slowly. They were all, he said, soaked up to their eyebrows in a lot of silly superstitions that had grown up around the play. He had wondered if anything could be made of this circumstance but nothing had emerged other than a highly wrought state of emotional receptivity. The correct treatment would be to attack this unprofitable nonsense.

Shakespeare, he said, was a very confused writer. His bourgeois origins distorted his thought-processes.

Maggie stayed in bed all day and Nanny answered the telephone.

Sir Dougal lunched at the Garrick Club and soaked up congratulations without showing too blatantly his intense gratification.

Simon Morten rang up Maggie and got Nanny.

King Duncan spent the afternoon cutting out notices and pasting them in his fourth book.

Nina Gaythorne got out all her remedies and good-luck objects and kissed them. This took some time as she lost count and had to begin all over again.

Malcolm and Donalbain got blamelessly drunk.

The speaking thanes and the witches all dined with Ross and his wife, bringing their own bottles, and talked shop.

The Doctor and the Gentlewoman were rung up by their friends and were touchingly excited.

The nonspeaking thanes dispersed into various unknown quarters.

And Gaston? He retired to his baleful house in Dulwich and wrote a number of indignant letters to those papers whose critics had referred to the weapons used in the duel as swords or claymores instead of claidheamh-mors.

Emily answered their telephone and, by a system they had perfected, either called Peregrine or said he was out but would be delighted to know they had rung up.

So the day passed by and the evening and on Monday morning they pulled themselves together and got down to the theatre and to the business of facing the second night and a long run of *Macbeth*.

PART TWO

Curtain Call

6

FULL HOUSE

I

It had been running to full houses for two weeks. There had been no more silly tricks and the actors had settled down to the successful run of the play. Peregrine no longer came down to every performance but on this Saturday night he was bringing his two older boys, home for half-term. He had a meeting with the management about how long the season should run and whether, for the actors' sakes, after six months they should make a change and, if so, what that change should be.

"We don't need to worry about it if we decide to have a Shakespeare rep. season: say *Twelfth Night* and *Measure for Measure*. With *Macbeth*," said Peregrine, "We'll just keep it in mind. You never know what may turn up, do you?"

They said no, you didn't, and the discussion ended.

The day turned out to be unseasonably muggy and exhausting. Not a breath of wind, the sky overcast, and a suggestion of thunder. "On the left," said Gaston as he prepared to supervise the morning's fight. "Thunder on the left meant trouble in Roman times. The gods rumbling, you know."

"They ought to have heard *you*," said Dougal rudely. "That would have pulled them up in their tracks."

"Come *on*," said Simon. "Let's press on with it. We've got a matinee, remember."

Wearily, they took their places and fought.

"You are dragging. *Dragging!*" Gaston shouted. "Stop. It is worse than not doing it at all. Again, from the beginning."

"Have a heart, Gaston. It's a deadly day for these capers," said Simon.

"I am merciless. Come. Begin. A tempo. Er — one —"

"No!" Dougal said in an access of irritability. "It's too hot and this is needless and I will — not — do — it." He flung down his claymore and stomped off.

Gaston, for once silent, picked up the claymore.

"Now see what your damn gods have rumbled," said Simon crossly and went off after Dougal.

Peregrine was taking Crispin and Robin, aged fifteen and nine, to the evening performance. Richard, being thought a little young, at seven, for *Macbeth*, was going to a farce with his mother.

"Is it bloody?" Richard asked ruefully.

"Very," Peregrine replied firmly.

"Extra special bloody?"

"It is."

"I'd like that. Is it going to run a long time?"

"Yes."

"Perhaps I'll grow up into it."

"Perhaps you will."

Emily took a taxi and she and Richard sailed off together, looking excited. Peregrine and the two older boys took their car. Crispin's form at school was working on *Macbeth* and he asked a great many questions that Peregrine supposed were necessary and that he answered to the best of his ability. Presently, Crispin said: "Old Perky says you ought to feel a great weight's been shifted off your shoulders at the end. When Macduff sort of actually lifts Macbeth's head off and young Malcolm comes in for king."

"I hope you'll feel like that."

"Does the lights man have to allow an *exact* time lag between cue and performance?" asked Robin, who at the moment wanted to become an electrical engineer.

"Yes."

"How long?"

"I've forgotten. About one second, I think."

"Cripes."

"I'm not sure. We can go round after the play and you can ask our lighting man."

"Right!" said Robin happily.

Peregrine turned into the theatre private car park and they got out and locked the car. The foyer was crowded and the House Full notice displayed.

"We're in a box," said Peregrine. "Come on. Up the stairs."

"Super," said the boys. The usher at the door into the circle said: "Good evening, sir," and smiled at them. He wagged his head. Peregrine and the boys left the queue and slipped behind him into the circle.

They passed around the back of the circle into the middle box. Peregrine bought them a programme each. The programme girl smiled upon them. The house was almost full. A tall man, alone, came down the center aisle and made for a management seat in the stalls. He looked up, saw Peregrine, and waved his programme. Peregrine answered.

"Who are you waving to, Pop?"

"Do you see that very tall man just sitting down, in the third row?"

"Yes. He looks super," said Crispin. "Who is he?"

"Chief Superintendent Alleyn. C.I.D. He was here on our opening night."

"Why's he come again?" asked Robin.

"Presumably because he likes the play."

"Oh."

"Actually he didn't get an uninterrupted view on the first night. There were Royals. He was helping the police look after them."

"So he had to sit watching the audience and not the actors?"

"Yes."

A persistent buzzer began sounding in the foyer. Peregrine looked at his watch. "We're ten minutes over time," he said. "Give them five minutes more and then the latecomers'll have to wait until Scene Two. No. It's okay. Here we go."

The house lights dimmed very slowly and the audience was silent. Now it was dark. The flash of lightning, the distant roll of thunder, the faint sound of wind. The curtain went up and the witches were at their unholy work on the gallows.

The play flowed on. Peregrine, sitting between his sons, glanced at them and wondered what was going on in their heads. He had been careful not to rub their noses into the plays and had left it to them whether or not they would read them. As far as he could make out, Mr. Perkins was not sickening Crispin with overinsistence on notes and disputed passages but had interested him first in the play itself and in the magic and strength of its language.

Robin at six years old had seen a performance of *Midsummer Night's Dream* and enjoyed it for all the wrong reasons. The chief comic character, in his opinion, was Hippolyta, and he laughed very heartily at all her entrances. When Emily asked why, he said: "At her legs." He thought Bottom a very good actor and the "audience" extremely rude to laugh at him. At nine years old he would be less surprising in his judgments.

Now, they were both very still and attentive. When Banquo and Fleance came in for their little night scene, Robin turned and looked at Peregrine. He bent down. "Nice," Robin whispered and they nodded to each other. But later, when Macbeth began to climb the stairs, Robin's hand felt for his father's. Peregrine held it tightly until the end of the scene when the Porter came on. Both the boys laughed loudly at the bawdy-looking pieces of driftwood and the Porter's description of the aggravating effects of drinking too much.

Peregrine had not seen the play for almost a week, having

been in Manchester on business with the touring company. He thought the Thane had begun to cherish his lines and slow up a bit, and reminded himself to speak to him. Otherwise all was well.

In the interval, Robin visited the lavatories. Crispin said he might as well stay with him while their father had a drink with the management. They arranged to meet in the foyer, under the photo of Macbeth.

Winter Meyer came out to welcome him. They went into his office. "Still goes on," Winty said. "Booked solid for the next six months."

"Odd," said Peregrine, "when you think of the superstitions. There's a record of good business and catastrophe going back hand in hand for literally centuries."

"Not for us, old boy."

"Touch wood."

"You too?" asked Winty, giving him his drink.

"No. No way. But it's rife in the company."

"Really?"

"Old Nina's got the bug very badly. Her dressing-table's like a secondhand charm shop."

"No signs of catastrophe, though," Winty said. "Are there?" And when Peregrine didn't answer at once, he said sharply: "Are there?"

"There have been signs of some halfwit planting them. Whoever it is hasn't got the results he may have hoped for. But it's very annoying for all that. Or *was*. They seem to have died out."

Winty said, after a moment: "Something rather odd happened in our office, too. It was a week before we opened. I haven't mentioned it to anybody. Except Mrs. Abrams. And she doesn't know what was typed and anyway she's a clam of clams. But since you've brought it up —"

There was a knock at the door and at the same time the warning buzzer sounded.

"I'm sorry," said Peregrine. "I'll have to go. I promised my younger son. He'll be having kittens. Thank you, Winty.

I'll come in tomorrow morning. I think we'd better have a talk about this and the other things."

"So do I. Tomorrow. Thank you, Perry." Peregrine opened the door, sidestepped Mrs. Abrams, and went back to the foyer.

There he found Robin under the photograph of Macbeth. "Oh, hullo," he said casually when Peregrine reached him. "There's the second buzz."

"Where's Cip?"

Crispin was in the crowd by the bookstall. He was searching his pockets. Peregrine, closely followed by Robin, worked his way over to him.

"I've got it all but twenty p.," said Crispin. He clutched a book called *Macbeth Through Four Centuries*.

Peregrine produced a five-pound note, and handed it to the clerk. "For the book," he said. "Come on, boys," and they returned to their box. The interval ended, the house darkened, and the curtain rose.

On Banquo. Alone and suspicious. Macbeth questions him. He is going out? Riding? He must return. For the party. Does Fleance go with him? Yes to all those questions. There is a terrible smile on Macbeth's face, the lips stretch back. *Farewell.*

Seyton is at once sent for the murderers. He has them ready and stands in the doorway and hears the wooing. Macbeth is easier, almost enjoys himself. They are his sort. He caresses them. The bargain is struck; they go off.

Now Lady Macbeth finds him: full of strange hints and of horror. There is the superb invocation to night and he leads her away. And the scene changes. Seyton joins the murderers and Banquo is dispatched.

The banquet. Seyton tells Macbeth that Fleance has escaped.

The bloodied ghost of Banquo appears among the guests.

The play began its inexorable swell toward the appointed ending. After the witches, the apparitions, the equivocal promises, comes the murder of Macduff's wife and child.

Then Lady Macbeth, asleep and talking in that strange, metallic, nightmare voice. Macbeth again, after a long interval. He has degenerated and shrunk. He beats about him with a kind of hectic frenzy and peers hopelessly into the future. These are the death throes of a monster. Please let Macduff find him and finish it.

Macduff has found him. "*Turn, hell-hound, turn!*"

Robin's hand crept into his father's and held it fast.

The fight. Leap, clash, sweep; hoarse, snarling voices. Macbeth is beaten backward, Macduff raises his claymore, and they plunge out of sight. A scream. A thud. Silence. Then the distant approach of pipe and drums. Malcolm and his thanes come out on the upper landing. The rest of his troops march on at stage-level and up the steps with old Siward, who receives the news of his son's death.

Macduff comes on downstage, O.P., followed by Seyton.

Seyton carries his claidheamh-mor and on it, streaming blood, the head of Macbeth. He turns it upstage, facing Malcolm and the troops.

Macduff has not looked at it. He shouts: "*Behold where stands the usurper's cursed head. Hail, King of Scotland!*"

The blood drips onto Seyton's upturned face.

And being well-trained professional actors, they respond, with stricken faces and shaking lips, "*Hail, King of Scotland!*"

The curtain falls.

II

"Cip," Peregrine said, "you'll have to get a cab home. Here's the cash. Take care of Robin, won't you? Do you know what's happened?"

"It seems — some sort of accident?"

"Yes. To the Macbeth. I've got to stay here. Look, there's a cab. Get it."

Crispin darted out and ran toward the taxi, holding up his hand. He jumped back on the platform and the taxi driver drew up. Peregrine said: "In you get, Rob."

"I thought we were going backstage," Robin said. His face was pale, his eyes bewildered.

"There's been an accident. Next time."

He gave the driver their address and they were gone. Someone tapped his arm. He turned and found it was Roderick Alleyn.

"I'd better come round, hadn't I?" he said.

"You! Yes. . . . You've seen it? It really happened?"

"Yes."

They found a crowd of people milling about in the alley. "My God," said Peregrine. "The bloody public."

"I'll try and cope."

Alleyn was very tall. There was a wooden box at the stage door. He made his way to it and stood on it, facing the crowd. "If you please," he said, and was listened to.

"You are naturally curious. You will learn nothing and you will be very much in the way if you stay here. Nobody of consequence will be leaving the theatre by this door. Please behave reasonably and go."

He stood there, waiting.

"Who does he think he is?" said a man next to Peregrine.

"He's Chief Superintendent Alleyn," said Peregrine. "You'd better do what he says."

There was a general murmur. A voice said: "Aw, come on. What's the use."

They moved away.

The doorkeeper opened the door to the length of the chain, peered out, and saw Peregrine. "Thank Gawd," he said. "Hold on, sir." He disengaged the chain and opened the door wide enough to admit them. Peregrine said: "It's all right. This is Chief Superintendent Alleyn," and they went in.

To a silent place. The stage was lit. Masking pieces rose up; black masses, through which the passage could be seen running under the landing in front of the door to Duncan's chamber. At the far end of this passage, strongly lit, was a shrouded object, a bundle, lying on the stage. A dark red puddle had seeped from under it.

They moved around the set and the stage manager came offstage.

"Perry! Thank God," he said.

"I was in front. So was Superintendent Alleyn. Bob Masters, our stage manager, Mr. Alleyn."

"Have you rung the Yard?" Alleyn asked.

"Charlie's doing it," said Masters, "now. Our A.S.M. He's having some difficulty getting a line out."

"I'll have a word with him," said Alleyn and went into the Prompt Corner.

"I'm a policeman," he told Charlie. "Shall I take over?"

"Ah? Are you? Yes. Hullo? Here's a policeman." He held out the receiver. Alleyn said: "Superintendent Alleyn. At the Dolphin. Homicide. Decapitation. That's what I said. I imagine that as I was here I'll be expected to take it on. Yes. I'll hold on while you do." There was a short interval and he said, "Bailey and Thompson. Yes. Ask Inspector Fox to come down. My case is in my room. He'll bring it. Get the doctor. Right? Good."

He hung up. "I'll take a look," he said and went onstage.

Four stagehands and the Property Master were there, keeping guard.

"Nobody's gone," Bob Masters said. "The company are in their dressing-rooms and Peregrine's gone back to the office. There's a sort of conference."

"Good," said Alleyn.

He walked over to the shrouded bundle. "What happened after the curtain fell?" he asked.

"Scarcely anybody *really* realized it was — not a dummy. The head. The dummy's a very good head. Blood and everything. I didn't realize. The curtain went down. I was getting them ready for the curtain calls. And then Gaston, who carried it on the end of his claidheamh-mor — the great

claymore thing he carries throughout the play — that thing —"
He pointed at the bundle.

"Yes?"

"He noticed the blood on his gloves and he looked at
them. And then he looked up and it dripped on his face and
he screamed. The curtain being down."

"Yes."

"We all saw, of course. He let the — the head — on the
claymore — fall. The house was still applauding. So I —
really, I didn't know what I was doing. I went out through
the center break in the curtain and said there'd been an
accident and I hoped they'd forgive us not taking the usual
calls and would go home. And I came off. By that time,"
said Mr. Masters, "panic had broken out in the cast. I ordered them all to their rooms and I covered the head with
that cloth — it's used on the props table, I think. And Props
sort of tucked it under. And that's all."

"It's very clear indeed. Thank you, Mr. Masters. I think
I'll look at the head now, if you please. I can manage for
myself."

"I'd be glad not to."

"Yes, of course," said Alleyn.

He squatted down, keeping clear of the puddle. He took
hold of the cloth and turned it back.

Sir Dougal stared up at him through the slits in his mask.
The eyes were set and glazed. The steel guard over his mouth
had fallen away and the mouth stretched in a clown's grin.
Alleyn saw that he had been struck from behind: the wound
was clean and the margin turned outward. He covered the
face.

"The weapon?" he said.

"We think it must be this," Masters said. "At least, I do."

"This is the weapon carried by Seyton?"

"Yes."

"It's bloodied, of course."

"Yes. It would be anyway. *And* with false blood too. There's false blood over everything. But" — Masters shuddered — "they're mixed."

"Where's the false head?"

"The false —? I don't know. We haven't looked."

Alleyn walked into the O.P. corner. It was encircled with scenery masking pieces and very dark. He waited for his sight to adapt. In the darkest corner, behind one of the pieces, a man's form slowly assembled itself, its head face-down. Its *head*?

He moved toward it, stooped down, and touched the head. It shifted under his fingers. It was the dummy. He touched the body. It was flesh — and blood. And dead. And headless.

Alleyn moved back and returned to the stage.

There was a loud knocking on the stage door.

"I'll go," said Masters.

It was the Yard. Inspector Fox and Sergeants Bailey and Thompson. Fox was the regular, old-style, plainclothesman: grizzled, amiable and implacable.

He said: "Visiting your old haunts, are you, sir?"

"Over twenty years ago, isn't it, Br'er Fox? And you two. I want you to give the full treatment, photos, prints, the lot, to that head onstage there, covered up, and the headless body in the dark corner over there. They parted company just before the final curtain. All right? And the dummy head in the corner. The assumed weapon is the claymore on which the real head's fixed, so include that in the party. Any more staff coming?"

"Couple of uniformed coppers. Any moment now."

"Good. Front doors and stage door for them. On guard."

He turned to Masters. "We'll need to know whom to inform. Can you help?"

"There's his divorced wife. No children. Winty may know. Mr. Winter Meyer."

"He's still here?" Alleyn exclaimed.

"In the office. With Peregrine Jay discussing what we're to do."

"Ah, yes. You've got tomorrow, Sunday, to make up your minds."

He looked at the stage crew. "You've had a bit of a job. Which of you is responsible for the properties?"

Props made an awkward movement.

"You are? I'm afraid I must ask you to wait a little longer. The foreman? I'm sorry, but you and you three men will have to wait, too. There's no need for you to remain onstage any longer. Thank you." The men moved off into the shadows.

Bailey and Thompson assembled their gear.

"You'll want the lights man, won't you?" Alleyn said. "Is he here?"

"Here," said the lights man, who was with Charlie, the assistant stage manager.

"Right! I'll leave you to it. Don't touch anything." And to Masters: "Where does Mr. Gaston Sears dress?"

"I'll show you," said Masters.

He led Alleyn into the world of dressing-rooms. They walked down a passage with doors on either side and the occupants' names on them. It was very, very quiet.

Gaston's room was not much more than a cubicle at the end of the passage. Masters tapped on the door and the deep voice boomed: "Come in." Masters opened the door.

"These two gentlemen would like a word with you, Gaston," he said and made his way back quickly.

There was only just room for Alleyn and Fox. They edged in and with difficulty shut the door.

Gaston had changed into a black dressing-gown and had removed his makeup. He was sheet-white but perfectly composed. He gave his name and address before being asked to do so.

Alleyn exclaimed: "Ah, I was right. You won't remember me but I called on you several years ago, Mr. Sears, and asked you to give us the date and value of a claidheamh-mor, part of a burglar's haul we had recovered."

"I remember it very well. It was of no great antiquity but it was, as far as that went, not a fake."

"That's the one. Tragically enough, it's about a clai-dheamh-mor that I'd like to ask you a few questions now."

"I shall be glad to offer an opinion, particularly as you use the correct term correctly pronounced. It is my own property and it is a perfectly authentic example of the thir-teenth-century fighting tool of the Scottish nobleman. In our production I carry it on all ceremonial occasions. It weighs . . . "

He sailed off into a catalogue of details and symbolic sig-nificance and from thence into a list of previous owners. The further he retreated into history the murkier did his anec-dotes become. Alleyn and Fox stood jammed together. Fox had with difficulty drawn his notebook from his breast pocket and had opened it in readiness, when Alleyn nudged him, to record anything that seemed to be of interest.

". . . as with many other such tools — Excalibur is one — there has grown up, with the centuries, the belief that the weapon — its name — I translate 'Gut-ravager' — en-graved in a Celtic device on the hilts — is said to be pos-sessed with magic powers. Be that as it may —" He paused to draw breath and take thought.

"You would not wish to let it out of your grasp," Alleyn cut in and nudged Fox. "Naturally."

"Naturally. But also I was obliged to do so. Twice. When I joined the murderers of Banquo and when I came off in the last scene. After Macbeth said, *a time for such a word,* the property man took it from me in order to affix the head on it. I *made* the head. I could be thought to have the ability to place it on the claidheamh-mor but unfortunately when I did so the first time, I made a childish error and the weapon, which is extremely sharp, pierced the top of the head and it swung about in a ludicrous fashion. So it was thought better to mend the hole and let Props fix it. He had to ladle blood on it."

"And he returned it to you?"

"He put it in the O.P. corner, on the left as you go in. Nobody else was allowed to go into the corner because of Macbeth and Macduff coming off after their fight, straight into it. I should have said, perhaps, that it is not *pitch*-dark all the time. It was made so for the end of the fight to guard against anyone in front at the extreme right or in the Prompt boxes seeing Macbeth recover himself. A curtain, upstage of it, was closed by a stagehand as soon as their fight was engaged."

"Yes. I've got that."

"Props put the claidheamh-mor in the corner sometime before the end of the fight. I took it up at the last moment before Macduff and I reentered."

"So Macbeth came off, screamed, and was decapitated by the claidheamh-mor from which the dummy's head had been pulled. The real head now replaced it."

"I — yes, I confess I had not worked it out so carefully but — yes, I suppose so. I *think* there would be time."

"And room? To swing the weapon?"

"There is always room. I invented the fight. I know the moves. Macduff, under my instruction, swung his weapon up while still in view of the audience and brought it down when he was just out of view in the O.P. corner. There was room. I was up at the back talking to the King and Props and others. The little boy, William. I saw Macduff come off. I have grown more and more certain," said Gaston, "that there was a malign influence at work, that the claidheamh-mor has a secret life of its own. It is satisfied now. We hope. We hope."

He gazed at Alleyn. "I am extremely tired," he said. "It has been an alarming experience. Horrifying, really. It must be something I have done. I didn't look up at first. It was dark. I took it and engaged the hilts in my harness and entered behind Macduff. And when I looked up it dropped blood on my face. What have I done? How have I, who bought and treasured it, committed an offense? Is it because I have allowed it to be used in a public display? True, I *have*

done so. I have carried it." His piercing eyes brightened.
He reassumed his commanding posture. "Can it have been
the accolade?" he asked. "Was I being admitted to some
esoteric comradeship and baptized with blood?" He made a
helpless gesture. "I am confused," he said.

"We won't worry you any more just now, Mr. Sears. You've
been very helpful."

They found their way back to the stage, where Bailey and
Thompson squatted, absorbed, over their unspeakable tasks.

"Not much doubt about the weapon, Mr. Alleyn," said
Bailey. "It's this thing it's stuck on. Sharp! Like a razor.
And there's the marks, see. Done from the back when the
victim's bending over. Clean as a whistle."

"Yes, I see. Prints?"

"He was wearing gloves. Gauntlets. Whoever he was. They
all were."

"Thompson, have you got all the shots you want?"

"Yes, thanks. Close-up. All around. The whole thing."

The sound of the stage door being opened and a quick,
incisive voice. "All right. Dark, isn't it. Where's the body?"

"Sir James," Alleyn called. "Here!"

"Hullo, Rory. Up to your old games, are you?"

Sir James Curtis appeared, immaculate in dinner jacket
and black overcoat and carrying his bag. "I was at a party
at Saint Thomas's. What have you got — good God, what
is all this?"

"All yours at the moment," said Alleyn.

Bailey and Thompson had stepped aside. Macdougal's head
on the end of the claidheamh-mor stared up at the pathol-
ogist. "Where's the body?" he asked.

"In the dark corner over there. We haven't touched it."

"What's the story?"

Alleyn told him. "I was in front," he said.

"Extraordinary. I'll look at the body."

It lay on its front as Alleyn had found it. The blood-soaked
Macbeth tartan was wrapped closely around the body. Sir
James pulled it away and looked at the wound. The lip was

turned in and a piece of the collar was sliced across it into the gash.

"One blow," he said. He bent over the body. "Better get the remains to the mortuary," he said. "If your men have finished."

They went back onstage.

"You may separate them," said Alleyn.

Bailey produced a large polyethylene bag. He then took hold of the head. Thompson with both hands on the hilt grasped the claidheamh-mor. They faced each other, their feet apart and the blade parallel with the stage: a parody of artisans sweating it out in hell.

"Right?"

"Right."

"Go."

The sound was the worst part of it. It resembled the drawing of an enormous cork. It was effective. Bailey put the head in the bag, wrote on a label, and tied it up. He put the bag in a canvas container. "I'll stow this away," he said and went out to the police car with it.

"What about the weapon?" asked Thompson.

"Put some cardboard around it," said Alleyn. "It'll lie flat on the back seat or on the floor. Then the body and the dummy head. You'll go straight to the mortuary, I suppose?"

"Yes. And you'll be here for some time to come?" said Sir James.

"Yes."

"I'll ring you if anything turns up."

"Thanks."

The ambulance men came in and put the body into another polyethylene bag and the bag on a stretcher and covered it. They carried it out and drove away. Sir James got into his car and followed them.

Alleyn said, "Come on, Fox. We'll find the property man."

Masters was waiting offstage for them.

"I thought you might use the greenroom as an office," he said. "I'll show you where it is."

"That's very thoughtful. I'll see the property man there."

The greenroom was a comfortable place with armchairs, books, a solid table, and framed photographs and pictures on the walls. They settled themselves at the table.

"Hullo, Props," said Alleyn when he came in. "We don't know your name, I'm afraid. What is it?"

"Ernest James, sir."

"Ernest James. We won't keep you long, I hope. This is a pretty grim business, isn't it?"

"Bloody awful."

"You've been on the staff for a long time, haven't you?"

"Fifteen year."

"Long as that? Sit down, why don't you."

"Aw. Ta," said Ernie and sat.

"We're trying at the moment to sort out when the crime was committed and then when the heads were changed. Macbeth's last words are *Hold, enough*. He and Macduff then fight and a marvelous fight it was. He exits and we assume was killed at once. There's a pause. Then pipe and drums coming nearer and nearer. Then a prolonged entry of everyone left alive in the cast. Then dialogue between Malcolm and Old Siward. Macduff comes in with Gaston Sears following him, the head on his giant weapon."

"Was you in front, then, guv'nor?"

"Yes, as it happened."

"Gawd, it was awful. Awful."

"It was indeed. Tell me, Props. When did you put the dummy head on the claymore and when did you put them in the O.P. corner?"

"Me? Yeah, well. I got hold of the bloody weapon — it's as sharp as hell — off 'is 'Igh-and-Mightiness when he came off after the Chief said, *There'd 'ave been a time for such a word*, whatever that may mean. I took it up to the props table, see, and I put the dummy on it. That took a bit of time and handling, like. What with the sharpness and the length, it was awkward. The 'ead's stuffed full of plaster except for a narrer channel and I had to fit it into the channel and shove it home. It kind of locked. And then I doused it with 'blood' rahnd the neck and put it in the corner."

"When?"

"I got faster with practice. Took me about three minutes, I'd say. Simon Morten was shouting, *Make all our trumpets speak.* Round about then."

"And there it remained until Gaston collected it and took it on — with a different head — at the very end."

"Correct."

"Right. We'll ask you to sign a statement to that effect, later on. Can you think of anything at all that could help us? Anything out of the ordinary? Superstitions, for instance?"

"Nuffink," he said quickly.

"Sure of that?"

"Yer."

"Thank you, Ernie."

"Fanks, guv. Can I go home?"

"Where do you live?"

"Five Jobbins Lane. Five minutes' walk."

"Yes. All right." Alleyn wrote on a card: "Ernest James. Permission to leave. R. Alleyn." "Here you are. Show it to the man at the door."

"You're a gent, guv. Fanks," Ernie repeated and took it. But he did not go. He shuffled toward the door and stood there, looking from Alleyn to Fox, who had put on his steel-rimmed glasses and now contemplated him over the tops.

"Is there something else?" Alleyn asked.

"I don't fink so. No."

"Sure?"

"Yes," said Ernie and was gone.

"There *was* something else," Fox observed tranquilly.

"Yes. We'll leave him to simmer."

There was a sharp rap at the door.

"Come in," Alleyn called. And Simon Morten came in.

III

HE had changed, of course, into his street clothes. Alleyn wondered if he was dramatically and habitually pale or if the shock of the appalling event had whitened him out of all semblance to normality.

"Mr. Morten?" Alleyn said. "I was just going to ask if you would come in. Do sit down. This is Inspector Fox."

"Good evening, sir. May I have your address?" asked Fox, settling his glasses and taking up his pen.

He had not expected this bland reception. He hesitated. He sat down and gave his blameless address as if it was that of an extremely disreputable brothel.

"We are trying to get some sort of pattern into the sequence of events," Alleyn said. "I was in front tonight which may be a bit of a help but not, I'm afraid, very much. Your performance really is wonderful: that fight! I was in a cold sweat. You must be remarkably fit, if I may say so. How long did it take you both to bring it up to this form?"

"Five weeks' hard rehearsal and we've still —" He stopped. "Oh, God!" he said. "I actually forgot what has happened — I mean that —" He put his hands over his face. "It's so incredible. I mean —" He dropped his hands and said: "I'm your prime suspect, aren't I?"

"To be that," said Alleyn, "you would have to have pulled off the dummy head and used the claidheamh-mor to decapitate the victim. *He* would have to have waited there and suffered his own execution without raising a finger to stop you. Indeed, he would have obligingly stooped over so that you could take a fair swipe at him. You would have dragged the body to the extreme corner and put the dummy head on it. Then you would have put the real head on the end of the claidheamh-mor and placed them both in position for Gaston Sears to take them up. Without getting blood all over yourself. All in about three minutes."

Simon stared at him. A faint color crept into his cheeks. "I hadn't thought of it like that," he said.

"No? Well, I may have slipped up somewhere but that's how it seems to me. Now," said Alleyn, "when you've got over your shock, do you mind telling me exactly what did happen when you chased him off?"

"Yes. Certainly. Nothing."

"Nothing?"

"Well, he screamed and fell as usual and I ran out. Then I just hung around with all the others who'd been called until I got my cue and reentered. I said my final speech ending with '*Hail, King of Scotland.*' I didn't turn to look at Seyton carrying — that thing. I just pointed my sword at it while facing upstage. I thought some of them looked and sounded — well — peculiar, but they all shouted and the curtain came down."

"Couldn't be clearer. What sort of man was Macdougal?"

"Macdougal? Sir Dougal? Good-looking if you like the type."

"In himself?"

"Typical leading man, I suppose. He was very good in the part."

"You didn't go much for him?"

He shrugged. "He was all right."

"A bit too much of a good thing?"

"Something like that. But, really, he *was* all right."

"*De mortuis nil nisi bonum*?"

"Yes. Well, I didn't know anything that was *not* good about him. Not really. He was fabulous in the fight. I never felt in danger. Even Gaston said he was good. You couldn't fault him. God! I'm the understudy! If it's decided we go on."

"Will it be so decided, do you think?"

"I don't know. I daren't think."

" 'The show must go on'?"

"Yes, I suppose," Simon said after a pause, "it may depend on the press."

"The *press*?"

"Yes. If they've got a clue as to what happened they could

[154]

make such a hoo-hah we couldn't very well go on as if Macbeth was ill or dying or dead or anything of that sort, could we? But if they only get a secondhand account of there having been an 'accident,' which is what Bob Masters said in his curtain speech, they may decide it's not worth a follow-up and do nothing. Tomorrow. One thing is certain," said Simon, "we don't need a word of publicity."

"No. Has it occurred to you," said Alleyn, "that it might strike someone as a good moment to revive all the superstitious stories about *Macbeth*?"

Simon stared at him. "Good God!" he said. "No. No, it hadn't. But you're dead right. As a matter of fact — well, never mind about all that. But Perry, our director, had been on at us and the idiot superstitions and not to believe any of it and — and — well, all that."

"Really? Why?"

"He doesn't believe in any of it," said Simon, looking extremely ill at ease.

"Has there been an outbreak of superstitious observances in the cast?"

"Well — Nina Gaythorne rather plugs it."

"Yes?"

"Perry thinks it's a bad idea."

"Have there been any occurrences that seemed to bolster up the superstitions?"

"Well — sort of. If you don't mind I'd rather not go into details."

"Why?"

"We said we wouldn't talk about them. We promised Perry."

"I'll ask him to elucidate."

"Yes. But don't let him think I blew the gaff, will you?"

"No."

"If you don't want me any more, may I go home?" Simon asked wearily.

"No more right now. But wait a bit, if you don't mind. We can't let the cast go just yet. Leave your dressing-room key with us. We'll ask you to sign a typed statement later on."

"I see. Thank you," said Simon and got up. "You did mean what you said? About it being impossible for me to have — done it?"

"Yes. Unless some sort of crack appears, I mean it."

"Thank God for *that* at least," said Simon.

He went to the door, hesitated, and spoke.

"If I'd wanted to kill him," he said, "I could have faked it at any time during the fight. Easily. And been 'terribly sorry.' You know?"

"Yes," said Alleyn. "There's that, too, isn't there?"

When he had gone, Fox said: "That's one we can tick off, isn't it?"

"At this point, Fox."

"He doesn't seem to have liked the deceased much, does he?"

"Not madly keen, no. But very honest about it as far as it went. He was on the edge of talking about the superstitions, too."

"That's right. So who do you see next?"

"Obviously, Peregrine Jay."

"He was here twenty years ago, at the time of the former case. Nice young chap he was then."

"Yes. He's in conference. Up in the offices," said Alleyn. "Shall I pluck him out?"

"Would you? Do."

Fox removed his spectacles, put them in his breast pocket, and left the room. Alleyn walked about, muttering to himself.

"It must have been then. After the fight. Say, one minute for the pause and the pipe and drums coming nearer, two at the outside. The general entry: say a quarter of a minute, Siward's dialogue about his son's death. Another two minutes. Say three to four minutes all told. At the end of the fight Macbeth exited and yelled. Did Macduff say something that made him stoop? No — he *did* fall forward to give the thud. The man having removed the dummy head, decapitates him, gathers up the real head, and jams it on the claidheamh-mor. That's what takes the time. Does he wedge the hilt against the scenery and then push the head on? He lugs the body into the darkest corner and stands the claidheamh-mor in its place ready for Gaston to grasp it. He puts the dummy head by the body. Where does he go then? What does he look like?"

He stopped short, closed his eyes, and recalled the fight. The two figures. The exchange of dialogue and Macbeth's hoarse final curse: "*And damn'd be him that first cries, Hold enough!*"

"It *must* have been done after the fight. There's no other way. Or is there? Is there? Nonsense."

The door opened. Fox, Winter Meyer, and Peregrine came in.

"I'm sorry to drag you away," said Alleyn.

"It's all right. We'd come to a deadlock. To go on or not. He — was so *right* in the part."

"A difficult decision."

"Yes. It's hard to imagine the play without him. It's hard to imagine anything, right now," said Peregrine.

"How will the actors feel?"

"About going on? Not very happy but they'll do it."

"And the new casting?"

"There's the rub," said Peregrine. "Simon Morten is Macbeth's understudy and the Ross is Simon's. We'll have to knock up a new, very simple fight, a new Macduff can't possible manage the present one. Simon's good and ready. He'll give a reasonable show, but the whole thing's pretty dicey."

"Yes. What sort of actor is Gaston Sears?"

Peregrine stared at him. "Gaston? *Gaston.*"

"He knows — he invented — the fight. He's an arresting figure. It's a very farfetched notion but I wondered."

"It's — it's a frightening thought. I haven't seen much of his acting but I'm told he was good in an unpredictable sort of way. He's a *very* predictable person. A bit on the dotty side, some of them think. It — it certainly would solve a lot of problems. We'd only need to find a new Seyton and he's a tiny part as far as lines go. He's only got to look impressive. My God, I wonder. . . . No. *No,*" he repeated. And then: "We may decide to cut our losses and rehearse a new play. Probably the best solution."

"Yes. I think I should remind you that — it's a dazzling glimpse of the obvious — the murderer, and who he is I've not the faintest notion, will turn out to be one of your actors or else a stagehand. If the latter, I suppose you can go ahead but if the former — well, the mind boggles, doesn't it?"

"I can feel mine boggling, anyway."

"In the meantime I'd like to know what the story is, about the Macbeth superstitions and why Props and Simon Morten go all peculiar when I ask them."

"It doesn't matter now. I'd asked them not to talk to each other or to anyone else about these — happenings. You've got to consider the general atmosphere."

And he told Alleyn sparingly about the dummy heads and the rat's head in Rangi's marketing bag.

"Have you any idea who the practical joker was?"

"None. Nor do I know if there is or is not any link with the subsequent horror."

"It sounds like an unpleasant schoolboy's nonsense."

"It certainly isn't our young William's nonsense," said Peregrine quickly. "He was scared as hell at the head on the banquet table. He's a very nice small boy."

"He'd have to be an infant Goliath to lift the claidheamh-mor two inches."

"Yes. He would, wouldn't he?"

"Where is he?"

"Bob Masters sent him home. Straight away. He didn't want him to see it. Gaston dropped the claidheamh-mor and head on the stage. The boy was waiting to go on for the curtain call. Bob told him there'd been a hitch and there wasn't a call and to get into his own clothes quick and catch an early bus home."

"Yes. William Smith, Fox. In case we want him. Has he got a telephone number?"

"Yes," said Peregrine. "We've got it. Shall I —?"

"I don't think we want it tonight. We'll ask the King and Props to confirm that Gaston Sears stood with the boy off-stage. And that Macduff came straight off. If this is so, it completely clears Macduff. And Gaston, of course."

"Yes," said Peregrine.

"Now," went on Alleyn, "suppose you tell me how the actors backstage positioned themselves, from the fight scene onward."

"During the fight, Malcolm and Old Siward with Ross and Caithness assembled on the Prompt upper landing, out of sight, waiting for their final entrance. The rest of the forces waited on the O.P. side. The 'dead' characters — the King, Banquo, Lady Macduff, and her son — were also waiting O.P. for the curtain call. The witches were alone upstage."

"Macbeth was alive and speaking up to the fight and through it?" asked Alleyn.

"Yes."

"Therefore he *must* have been decapitated in the interval between his and Macduff's exit, fighting, and Macduff's and Gaston's reentry with his head."

"Yes," said Peregrine wearily. "And it's three and a half minutes at the most."

"We'll now summon the entire company and get them, if they can, to give each other alibis for that period."

"Shall I call them?"

"In here, if you would. I don't want them onstage just yet. Nor, I think, do they want it. Thank you, Jay. It'll be a squash but never mind."

Peregrine went out. Winter Meyer, who had stood inside the door without speaking, came to Alleyn's table and put a folded paper on it.

"I think you should see this," he said. "Perry agrees."

Alleyn opened it.

The tannoy boomed out: "Everyone in the greenroom, please. Company and staff call. Everyone in the greenroom."

Alleyn read the typed message: "murderers son in your co."

"When did you get it? And how?" Winty told him.

"Is it true?"

"Yes," said Winty miserably.

"Does anyone else know?"

"Perry thinks Barrabell does. The Banquo."

"Spiteful character?"

"Yes."

"It refers, I am quite sure, to the little Macduff boy, William Smith. I represented the police in the case," Alleyn said. "He was a little chap of six then, but now I've seen the play twice, I recognize him. He's got a very distinctive face. We didn't call him. One of the victims was named Barrabell. Bank clerk. She was beheaded," said Alleyn. "Here come the actors."

IV

By using a considered routine they managed to extract the information wanted in reasonable time.

Gaston Sears's, Props's, and Macduff's alibis were secured. Alleyn read the names out from his programme and each in turn was remembered as being offstage in the group of waiting actors. The King and Nina Gaythorne were whispering to Gaston. Her dress was caught up.

"I want you to be very sure how you answer the next question. Does anyone remember any movement among you all that could have meant someone had slipped into the O.P. corner after Macduff came out?"

"We were too far upstage to do it," said Barrabell. "All of us."

"And does anyone remember Macbeth *not* coming off?"

There was a pause and then Nina Gaythorne said: "William said, 'Where's Sir Dougal? He's still in there.' Or something like that. Nobody paid much attention. Our cue was coming and we were getting into position to go on for the call."

"Yes," Alleyn said. "Now, I wonder if you would all go to your rooms and come out when you are called, as far as you can remember, exactly in the order you observed tonight. From the final fight scenes until the end I want you all to do *exactly* what you did then. Is that understood?"

"Not very pleasant," said Barrabell.

"Murder and its consequences are never very pleasant, I'm afraid. Mr. Sears, will you read Macbeth's lines, if you please?"

"Certainly. I know them, I think, by heart."

"Good. You had better have a look, though. The timing must be exact."

"Very well."

"Do you know the moves?"

"Certainly. I also," he said loftily, "know the fight."

"Good. Are we ready? Will those of you who were in their dressing-rooms please go to them?"

They trooped off. Alleyn said to Peregrine: "You take over cuing, will you? From: *Blow, wind! come, wrack! At least we'll die with harness on our back.* We'll go out onstage. It's tidied up, I hope."

"I hope so," said Peregrine devoutly.

"Come on, then. Fox, you watch the stage. The O.P. side in particular, will you?"

"Right."

"Is the effects man here? He is. With his assistants? I think mechanical effects were overlaid by live voices. Good. We want the whole thing exactly timed as for performance. Right? Can you manage?"

They walked down the dressing-room passages and suddenly the theatre was alive with the presence of actors waiting behind closed doors for the play to begin. Thompson and Bailey had been tidy. They had left the patch of stage where the bundle had been covered over with a mackintosh sheet weighted down. In the O.P. corner, they had outlined the body in chalk before removing it. There was a bucket of "blood" beside it.

"Right," said Alleyn, who had moved into the house front. Peregrine called: "Macbeth. Macduff. Young Siward. You're on, please. Malcolm, Old Siward, and the Forces. Called and waiting." There was the sound of movements offstage.

Gaston entered and spoke. His fatigue had vanished and he was good.

"*At least we'll die with harness on our back,*" he ended and went off into the O.P. area and through it. He waited offstage.

They played through the battle scenes to the point where Macbeth entered on the platform O.P. and Macduff entered from the Prompt corner.

"*Turn, hell-hound, turn!*"

The fight. Gaston was perfect. Macduff, who looked exhausted and tried to go through it at token speed, was forced to respond fully.

Exeunt. Macbeth's scream, cut off. Macduff ran straight through and out. Alleyn set his stopwatch.

The long triumphant entry and final scene with Old Siward. Macduff reentered from the O.P. corner. Gaston, reverted to Seyton, came on behind him, without the claidheahm-mor. He proclaimed in his natural tones: "I assume my claidheamh-mor is not to be found. I presume it has been seized by the police. I take this opportunity," he went on, pitching his considerable voice into the auditorium, "of warning them that they do so at their peril. There is strength in the weapon."

"The claidheamh-mor is perfectly safe in our keeping," said Alleyn. He had stopped the watch. Three minutes.

"It may be, and doubtless is, safe. It is the police who should be trembling."

Before addressing the actors Alleyn allowed himself a moment to envisage Inspector Fox and himself trembling with fear from head to foot.

"Thank you, gentlemen," Alleyn said. "It was asking a lot of all of you to reenact the last scene but I think I can tell you that you have really helped us. Now, if you will do the same thing again, from *Brandish'd by man that's of a woman born* up to *Enter, sir, the castle*, I think you will then be free to go home. It's Macduff's soliloquy. I want you all in your given places. With offstage action and noises, please. Jay, would you?"

Peregrine said: "It's where the group of Macduff's soldiers run across and upstairs. Right? Simon?"

"Oh, God. Yes. All right," said the exhausted Simon.

"Ready, everybody. *Brandish'd by man that's of a woman born.*"

The speech was broken by offstage entries, excursions, and alarums. Alleyn timed it. Three minutes. Macbeth entered on O.P. rostrum.

"Right. Thank you very much, Mr. Morten. And Mr. Sears. We've not established your own movements, Mr. Sears, as you've been kind enough to impersonate Macbeth's. Can you now tell us where you were over this period?"

"Certainly. On the O.P. side but not in the darkened corner. I remained there throughout, keeping out of the way of the soldiers who entered and exited in some disorder. I may say their attempts at soldierly techniques during these exercises were pitiful. However, I was not consulted and I kept my opinions to myself. I spoke, I believe, to several fellow players during this period. Those who were called for the final curtain. Miss Gaythorne, I recollect, advanced some astonishing claptrap about garlic as a protection against bad luck. Duncan was one. Banquo was another. He complained, I recall, that he was called too soon."

Duncan and Banquo agreed. Several other actors remembered seeing Gaston there, earlier in the action.

"Thank you very much," said Alleyn. "That's all, ladies and gentlemen. You may go home. Leave your dressing-room keys with us. We'd be grateful if you would arrange to be within telephone call. Good-night."

They said good-night and left the theatre in ones and twos. Gaston wore his black cloak clutched histrionically above his chest in an actor's hand. He bowed to Alleyn and said: "Good-night, sir."

"Good-night, Mr. Sears. I'm afraid the fight was a severe ordeal. You are still breathless. You shouldn't have been so enthusiastic."

"No, no! A touch of asthma. It is nothing." He waved his hand and made an exit.

The stagehands went at once and all together. At last there were only Nina Gaythorne and one man left, a pale, faintly ginger, badly dressed man with a beautiful voice.

"Good-night, Superintendent," he said.

"Good-night, Mr. Barrabell," Alleyn returned and became immersed in his notebook.

"A very interesting treatment, if I may say so."

"Thank you."

"If I may say so, there was no need, really, to revive anything before Macbeth's exit and from then up to the appearance of his head. About four minutes, during which time he was decapitated."

"Quite so."

"So I wondered."

"Did you?"

"Poor dotty old Gaston," said the beautiful voice, "having to labor through that fight. Why?"

Alleyn said to Fox: "Just make sure the rooms are all locked, will you, Mr. Fox?"

"Certainly, sir," said Fox. He walked past Barrabell as if he were not there, and disappeared.

"One of the old type," said Barrabell. "We don't see many of them nowadays, do we?"

Alleyn looked up from his notebook. "I'm very busy," he said.

"Of course. Young Macduff is not with us, I see."

"No, Mr. Barrabell. They sent him home. Good-night to you."

"You know who he is, of course."

"Of course."

"Oh? Oh, well, good-night," said Barrabell. He walked away with his head up and a painful smile on his face. Nina went with him.

"Br'er Fox," said Alleyn when that officer returned. "Let us consider. Is it possible for the murder to have been performed after the fight?"

"Just possible. Only just. But it *was*."

"Shall we try? I'll be the murderer. You be Macbeth. Run into the corner. Scream and drop down. Hold on." He went into the dark area O.P. "We'll imagine the Macduff. He runs after you and goes straight on and away. Ready? I'm using my stopwatch. Three, two, one, zero, *go*."

Mr. Fox was surprisingly agile. He imitated sword-play, backed offstage, yelled, and fell at Alleyn's feet. Alleyn had removed the imaginary dummy head from the imaginary claidheamh-mor. He raised the latter above his shoulder. It swept down. Alleyn let go, stooped, and seized the imaginary head. He fixed it on the point of the claymore and rammed it home. He propped it in its corner, dragged the body (Mr. Fox weighing fourteen stone) into the darkest corner, wrapped an imaginary cloak around it, and clapped the dummy head down by it. And looked at his watch.

"Four and a third minutes," he panted. "And the cast made it in three. It's impossible."

"You don't seem as disappointed as I'd of expected," said Fox.

"Don't I? I — I'm not sure. I may be going dotty," Alleyn muttered. "I *am* going dotty. Let's check the possibles, Fox. Which is Number One?"

"Macduff? He killed Macbeth as we were meant to think. Duel. Chased him off. Killed him. Fixed the head on the weapon and came on with Seyton carrying it behind him. Sounds simple."

"But isn't. What was Macbeth doing? Macduff chased him off and then had to dodge about, take the dummy head off the claidheamh-mor, and raise it and do the fell deed."

"Yerse."

"Did Macbeth lie there and allow him to get on with it?" Alleyn asked. "And how about the time? If I couldn't do it in three minutes nobody else could."

"Well, no. No."

"Next?"

"Banquo." Fox suggested.

"He could have done it. He was hanging about in that region after he was called. He could have slipped in and removed the dummy head. Waited there for the end of the duel. Done it. Fixed the head. And walked out in plenty of time for the curtain call. He was wearing his bloodied cloak, which would have accounted for any awkward stains. Next."

"Duncan and/or one of his sons. Well," said Fox apologetically. "It's silly, I know, but they *could* have. If nobody was watching them. And they could have come out just when nobody was there. If it wasn't so beastly it would be funny. The old boy rolling up his sleeves and settling his crown and wading in. *And,* by the way, if there were two of them the time thing vanishes. The King beheads him and drags the body over and puts the dummy by it while his son puts the head on the weapon and places them in the corner. However," said Mr. Fox, "it *is* silly. How about one of the witches? The man-witch?"

"Rangi? Partly Maori. He was wonderful. Those grimaces and the dance. He was possessed. He was also with his girls — and you noted it — all through the crucial time."

"All right, then. The other obvious one. Gaston," said Fox moodily.

"But *why* obvious? Well, because he's a bit dotty — but that's not enough. Or is it? And again: time. We've got to face it, Fox. For all of them. Except for the Royal Family, Banquo, and the witches — time! Rangi could have taken a girl in to do the head on the claidheamh-mor and thus saved about a minute. It's impossible to imagine anybody collaborating with the exuberant Gaston."

"Anyway," said Fox. "We've got to face it. They were all too busy fighting and on-going."

"It's all approximate. Council for the defense, whatever the defense might be, would make mincemeat of it."

"They talked during the fight. Here —" He flattened out his Penguin copy of the play. "I got this out of a dressing-room," he said. "Here. Look. Macbeth gets the last word. *And damn'd,*" quoted Mr. Fox, who read laboriously through his specs, "*be him that first cries, Hold, enough!* and with that they set to again. And within the next three minutes, whoever did it, his head was off his shoulders and on the stick."

"Our case in a nutshell, Br'er Fox."

"Yerse."

"And now, if you will, let us examine what may or may not be the side-kicks in evidence. Where's Peregrine Jay? Has he gone with the others?"

"No," said Peregrine, "I've been here all the time." And he came down the center aisle into the light. "Here I am," he said. "Not as bright as a button, I fear, but here."

"Sit down. Did you hear what I said?"

"Yes. I'm glad you said it. I'm going to break my own rule and tell you more fully of what may be, as you've hinted, side-kicks."

"I'll be glad to hear you."

Peregrine went on. He described the unsettling effect of the tales of ill luck that had grown up around the play of *Macbeth* and his own stern injunctions to the company that they ignore them.

"The ones most committed, of course, like Nina Gaythorne, didn't obey me but I think, though I can't be sure, that on the whole they more or less obeyed. For a time, at any rate. And then it began. With the Banquo mask in the King's room."

He described it. "It was extraordinarily — well, effective.

Glaring there in the shadow. It's like all Gaston's work, extremely macabre. You remember the procession of Banquos in the witches' scene?"

"I do indeed."

"Well, to come upon one suddenly! I was warned, but even then — horrid!"

"Yes."

"I examined it and I found an arrangement of string connected with the slate-colored poncho. The head itself was fixed on a coat hanger and the poncho hung from that. The long end of string reached down to the stage. There is a strut in the wall above the head. The string passed over it and down, to stage-level. Now it seemed to me, it still seems to me, that if I'm on the right track this meant that the cloak was pulled up to cover the head and the cord fastened down below. I've had a look and there's a cross-piece in the back of the scenery in exactly the right place."

"It could be lowered from stage-level?"

"Yes. The intention being that it remained hidden until Macduff went in. Macduff saw it first. He tried to warn Macbeth."

"What did you do with it?"

"I called Props and wrapped it up in its cloak and told him to put it with its mates on the property table."

"And then?"

"The next thing that happened was a servant at the banquet swept off the dish-cover and there, underneath was the man's head again. Grinning at Macbeth. It was — well, *awful*. You know?"

"What did you do?"

"I addressed the actors. All of them. I said — the expected things, I suppose. That these were rather disgusting tricks but as none of them was prepared to own up to being the perpetrator I thought the best thing we could do was to ignore them. Something like that."

"Yes. It must have thrown a spanner in your work, didn't it?"

"Of course. But we rose above. Actors are resilient, you know. They react to something with violence and they talk a great deal but they go on. Nobody walked out on us but there was a nasty feeling in the air. But I really think Rangi's rat's head was the worst."

"Rangi's rat's head?" Alleyn repeated.

"Well, it was the head that mattered. In his marketing bag. That's what we called their bags — a sort of joke. For the things they collected for their spell, you know. Some of them off the corpse on the gallows. Did you know the items they enumerate are really authentic?"

"I didn't know that."

"Well, they are. *For a charm of powerful trouble.* There's no mention of a rat's head, though."

"Have you got your own ideas about the author of these tricks?"

"I have, yes. But they are not supported by any firm evidence. Merely unsecured ideas. They couldn't be vaguer. They arise from a personal distaste."

"Can we hear them? We won't attach too much importance to them. I promise."

Peregrine hesitated. Mr. Fox completed his notes and looked benevolently at him, his vast hand poised over the notebook.

"Have you spoken to Barrabell? The Banquo?"

"Not really," said Alleyn. "Only to get his name and address and a very few bits of information about the other people's positions."

"He's a strange one. Beautiful voice, well managed. A mischief-maker. He belongs to some way-out society, the Red Fellowship, I think it's called. He enjoys making sneaky little underhand jokes about other actors. I find myself thinking of him as a 'sea-lawyer.' He's always making objections to 'business' in the play which doesn't endear him to me, of course."

"Of course not."

"I think he knows about young William."

Alleyn took the folded paper from his pocket, opened it, and showed it to Peregrine.

"This was left in Winter Meyer's office and typed on the machine there?"

Peregrine looked at it. "Yes," he said. "Winty told me."

"Did you guess who did it?"

"Yes. I thought so. Barrabell. It was only a guess but he was about. In the theatre at that time. The sort of thing he'd do, I thought."

"Did you say so to Meyer?"

"I did, yes. Winty says he went to the loo. It was the only time the room was free. About eight minutes. There's a window into the foyer. Anybody there could look in, see it was empty, and — do it."

"One of the Harcourt-Smith victims was called Barrabell. Muriel Barrabell. A bank clerk. She was beheaded."

"Do you think —?"

"We'll have to find out," Alleyn said. "Even so, it doesn't give him a motive to kill Macbeth."

"And there's absolutely no connection that we know of with poor Sir Dougal."

"No."

"Whereas with Simon Morten —" Perry stopped.

"Yes?"

"Nothing. That sounds as if I was hiding something. I was only going to say Simon's got a hot temper and he suspected Dougal of making passes at the Lady. She put that right with him."

"He hadn't got the opportunity to do it. He must have chased Macbeth off with his own blunt weapon raised. He'd have to change his weapon for the claidheamh-mor from which he'd have to remove the dummy head while his victim looked on, did nothing, and then obligingly stooped over to receive the stroke."

"And Gaston?"

"First of all, time. I've just done it in dumb show myself,

all out and way over the time. And what's even more convincing, Gaston was seen by the King and Nina Gaythorne by people going on for the call. He actually spoke to them. This was while the murder was taking place. He went into the O.P. corner and collected the claidheamh-mor at the last moment when Macduff came around and he followed him on."

Peregrine raised his arms and let them drop. "Exit Gaston Sears," he said. "I don't think I ever really thought he'd done it but I'm glad to have it confirmed. Who's left?"

"Without an alibi? Barrabell. The stagehands. Various thanes. Lady Macbeth. Old Uncle Tom Cobbleigh and all."

"I'd better go back to the boys in the office. They're trying to make up their minds."

Alleyn looked at his watch. "It's ten past two," he said. "If they haven't made up their minds I suggest they sleep on it. Are the actors called?"

"For four o'clock this afternoon, poor dears."

"It's none of my business, of course, but I don't think you should go on with *Macbeth*."

"No?"

"It's only a matter of time before the truth is known. A very short time probably. You'll get a sort of horror-reaction, a great deal of morbid speculation, and, I should think, the kind of publicity that will be an insult to a beautiful production."

"Oh."

"There will be a trial. We hope. Your actors will be pestered by the press. Quite possibly the Harcourt-Smith case will be revived and young William cornered by the *News of the World* and awful remarks put into his reactions. He and his mother will be hunted remorselessly."

"This may happen whatever we do," said Peregrine unhappily.

"Certainly. But to nothing like the same extent if you don't do this play."

"No. No, nothing like." Peregrine got up and walked to the door.

"I'll speak to them," he said. "Along those lines. Good-night, Alleyn."

"Good-night, my dear chap."

The stage door closed behind him.

"Br'er Fox, what's emerged definitely from it all?" Alleyn asked.

They opened their notebooks. Alleyn also opened his programme.

"We can wipe out most of the smaller parts," he said. "They were too active. All the fighting men. When they were offstage they were yelling and bashing away at each other like nobody's business."

"I stood over by the dark corner and I'll take my oath none of them got within cooee of it," Fox said.

"Yes. They were very well drilled and supposing one of them got out of step on purpose, the others would have known and been down on him at once. It may have looked like an Irishman's picnic but they were worked out in inches."

"You can scratch the lot," said Fox.

"Gladly," said Alleyn and did so. "And who's left?" he asked.

"Speaking parts. It's easier than it looks. The old Colonel Blimpish chap and his son. Never had a chance. The son was 'dead' and lying on the stage, hidden from the audience, and the old boy was stiff-upper-lipping on the stairs while the murder was done."

"So much for the Siwards. And Malcolm was onstage and speaking. Now I'm going to reiterate. Not for the first and, I'm afraid, not for the last time. Gaston Sears was offstage of the crucial moment and talking in a whisper to the King and Miss Gaythorne. Young William was with them.

"The witches had come on for the curtain call and were waiting upstage on the rostrum. Now, Macduff," said Alleyn. "Let's look a bit closer at Macduff. He's a man with a temper and now we know there's been some sort of trouble between him and Macbeth. He ended the fight by chasing Macbeth off. His story is that Macbeth screamed and fell down as usual and he went straight off and was seen to do so by various actors. Confirmed by the actors. By which time Macbeth was dead. I tried it out with you, Br'er Fox, and I was four and a third minutes. We played the scene with Gaston as Macbeth and the cast and it was three. Moreover, Morton — Macduff — would have had to get the dummy head off the claidheamh-mor before killing Macbeth with it while Macbeth — I've said this ad nauseam — stood or lay there waiting to be beheaded. It does *not*, Br'er Fox, make sense. Moreover, as Macduff himself pointed out, it would have been a whole lot easier for him to have done a Lizzie Borden on Macbeth during their fight and afterward say he didn't know how he'd gone wrong."

"His weapon's as blunt as old boots."

"It weighs enough for a whack on the head to fix Macbeth."

"Yerse. But it didn't."

"No. We'll move on. Banquo. Banquo, we find, is a very rum fellow. He's devious, is Banquo, and he was 'dead' all this long time and free, up to the second curtain call to go wherever he liked. He could have gone into the O.P. corner and waited there in the dark with the claidheamh-mor when Gaston left it there for the stagehand to put the dummy head on it. The stagehand did put it there. Banquo removed it and did the deed. There's no motive that I can see but he's a possibility."

"And are you going to tell me that Banquo is the perpetrator of the funny business with the dummy heads? And the typed message?"

"I rather think so. I'm far from happy with the idea, all the same."

"Humph," said Fox.

"We'll knock off now for a while." He looked into the

dark house. "It was a wonderful production, Fox," he said. "The best I've seen. Almost too good. I don't think they can carry on."

"What do you suppose they'll do in its place?"

"Lord knows. Something quite different. *Getting Gertie's Garter,*" said Alleyn angrily.

7

THE YOUNGER ELEMENT

I

It was a quarter past three when Peregrine let himself into his house and gave himself a drink. A very stiff whiskey and a sandwich and then upstairs softly to bed.

"Hullo," said Emily. "You needn't creep about. I waked when you opened the front door."

He turned on his bedside lamp.

"What's happened?" she said when she saw his face.

"Didn't Cip tell you?"

"Only that there'd been an accident. He said, privately, that Robin didn't understand. Not properly and he wasn't sure that *he* did."

"Is Robin upset?"

"You know what he's like."

"Has he gone silent?"

"Yes."

"I'd better tell you," said Peregrine. And did.

"Oh, Perry," she whispered. "How *awful*."

"Isn't it?"

"What will you do? Go on?"

"I think not. It's not decided. Alleyn pointed out what would happen."

"Not the same Mr. Alleyn?" she exclaimed.

"Yes. The very same. He was in front last night. He's a Chief Superintendent now. Very grand."

"Nice?"

"Yes. There's nobody arrested or anything like that. Shall I take a look at the boys?"

"They were both asleep an hour ago. Have a look."

Peregrine crept along the landing and opened their doors. Steady regular breathing in each room.

He came back to his wife and got into bed.

"Sound asleep," he said.

"Good."

"God, I'm tired," he said. He kissed her and fell asleep.

Maggie Mannering with Nanny had ridden home in her hired car. She was in a state of bewilderment. She had heard the cast go by on their way for the curtain call, the usual storm of applause, and the rest of the company's movement forward when everyone except herself and Macbeth went on. She had heard Gaston cry out: "No! For God's sake, no!" and Masters: "Hold it! Hold everything." There had been a sudden silence and then his voice: "Ladies and gentlemen, I regret to tell you there has been an accident —"

And then the confused sound of the audience leaving and Masters again, saying, "Clear, please. Everybody off and to their dressing-rooms. Please." And hurrying figures stumbling past her and asking each other, "What accident? What's happened?" and Malcolm and the soldiers: "It's him. Did you see? Christ Almighty."

There was a muddle of human beings, Nanny taking her to her dressing-room, and she removing her makeup and Nanny getting her into her street clothes.

"Nanny, what's *happened*? Is it Sir Dougal? *What* accident?"

"Never you mind, dear. We'll be told. All in good time."

"Go out, Nanny. Ask somebody. Ask Mr. Masters. Say I want to *know*."

Nanny went out. She ran into somebody, another woman,

in the passage and there was a gabble of voices. There was no mistaking the high-pitched, nicely articulated wail.

"Nina!" Maggie had called. "Come in. Come in, darling."

Nina was in disarray but had changed and had put on her scarves and a tam-o'-shanter of the kind that needs careful adjustment and had not received it. There were traces of mascara under her eyes.

"Maggie!" she cried. "Oh, Maggie, isn't it awful?"

"Isn't *what* awful? Here. Sit down and pull yourself together, for pity's sake and tell me. Is somebody dead?"

Nina nodded her head a great many times.

"*Who*? Is it Dougal? Yes? For the love of Mike, pull yourself together. Has everybody lost their heads?"

Nina produced a shrill cackle of laughter. "What *is* it?" Maggie demanded.

"He has," shrieked Nina. "Dougal has."

"Has *what*?"

"Lost his head. I'm telling you. *Lost his head.*"

And while Maggie took in the full enormity of this, Nina broke into an extraordinary diatribe.

"I told you. I told lots of you. You wouldn't listen. It's the *Macbeth* curse, I said. If you make nonsense of it it'll strike back. If Perry had listened to me, this wouldn't have happened. You ask Brucie Barrabell, he'll tell you. He knows. Those tricks with heads. They were warnings. And now — look."

Maggie went to her little drinks cupboard. She was an abstemious woman and it was stocked for visitors rather than for herself, but she felt she now needed something, actually to prevent her fainting. The room was unsteady. She poured out two large brandies and gave one to Nina. Both their hands were shaking horridly.

They drank quickly and shuddered and drank again.

Nanny returned. She took a look at them and said: "I see you know."

"Sort of," said Maggie. "Only what happened. Not how, or why or anything else."

"I saw Mr. Masters. The first anybody knew was the head carried on by Mr. Sears. Mr. Masters said that was absolutely all and he's coming to see you as soon as he can. While we were talking a very distinguished-looking gent came up who said he was the Yard. And that's all *I* know," said Nanny. "Except that Mr. Masters said I could give them your telephone number and after a word with Mr. Masters the gentleman said I could take you home. So we'll go home, love, shan't we?"

"Yes. What about you, Nina? You could ask to go and I could take you."

"I said I'd go with Bruce. I'm on his way and he'll drop me. I've finished my drink, thank you all the same, dear Maggie, and I feel better."

"Come on, then. So do I. I think," said Maggie. "Lock up, Nanny. We'll go home. They want our keys, don't they?"

They left their keys with Mr. Fox. Masters was in deep conference with Alleyn but he saw her and hurried toward her.

"Miss Mannering, I am *so* sorry. I *was* coming. Did Nanny explain? Is your car here? This is appalling, isn't it?"

They fled. Their car was waiting and there was still a small crowd in the alleyway. Maggie turned up her collar but was recognized.

"It's Margaret Mannering," shouted a man. "What's happened? What was the accident? Hi!"

"I don't know," she said. Nanny scrambled in beside her and the driver sounded his horn.

The car began to back down the alleyway. Greedy faces at the windows. Impudent faces. Curious, grinning faces. A prolonged hooting and they were in Wharfingers·Lane and picking up speed.

"Horrible people," she said. "And I thought I loved them." She began, helplessly, to cry.

Gaston Sears walked up the path to his front door and let himself in. He was, by habit, a night owl and a lonely bird, too. Would it have been pleasant to have been welcomed home by a tender little woman who would ask him how the day, or rather, the night, had gone? And would it have been a natural and admirable thing to have told her? He went into his workroom and switched on the light. The armed Japanese warrior, grimacing savagely, leaped up, menacing him, but he was not alarmed. He found, as he expected, the supper tray left by his Chinese housekeeper. Crab salad and a bottle of a good white wine.

He switched on his heater and sat down to it.

He was hungry but worried. What would be done to his claidheamh-mor? The distinguished-looking policeman had assured him that great care would be taken of it but although he called it by its correct name he did not, he could not, understand. After all, he himself did not fully understand. As things had turned out it had fulfilled its true function but there was no telling, really, if it was satisfied.

He had enjoyed playing Macbeth for the police. He had a most phenomenal memory and years ago had understudied the part. And of course, once memorized, it was never forgotten. It struck him, not for the first time, that if they decided to go on they would ask him to play the part. He would have played it well.

By Heaven! he thought. They will offer it to me! It would be a good solution. I could wear my own basic Macbeth clothes for the garments. Any personable extra can go on for Seyton. And I invented and know the fight. It went well in their reconstruction. I would have been a success. But it would not be a gracious thing to do. It would be an error in taste. I shall tell them so.

He fell to with an appetite on his crab salad and filled his Waterford glass to the brim.

Simon Morten lived in Fulham on the borders of Chelsea. He thought he would walk to St. James's and on by way of Westminster where he would probably pick up a cab.

Mentally he went over the fight. Gaston played it all-out

and backed into the O.P. He yelled and fell with a plop. I couldn't have done it, thought Simon. Not in the time. Found the claid-something. Removed the dummy head. Placed it by the body. Two-handed grip on the pommel. Swing it up and what's he doing all the time? Gaston was gone. He walked off and found him standing with Nina Gaythorne and the King and William. He waited for his reentrance. Gaston came down and followed him on.

There was the repeat and then the Yard men with their notes and inaudible discussions and then they were told they could all go home.

In a way Simon was actually sorry. There hadn't been time to think coherently. He went to Maggie's dressing-room but she was gone. He went to his own room and found Bruce Barrabell there, putting on his dreary coat.

"We have to suppose these Yard people think they know what they're doing," he said, "I take leave to doubt it."

Simon got his own coat and put it on. He pulled his brown scarf out of a pocket, wound it about his neck and tucked the ends in.

"Our Mr. Sears had himself a marvelous party, didn't he?"

"I thought he was very good."

"Oh yes. Marvelous. If you were in the mood."

"Of course. Good-night."

"Good-night, Morten," said Barrabell and Simon took himself off.

He was deadly tired. He had thought the fresh air would revive him but he was beyond that point. He walked quickly but his legs were like logs and each stride took an intense mental effort. Not a soul about and St. James's a thousand miles away. Big Ben tolled three. The Thames slapped against the Embankment. A taxi came out of a side street.

"Taxi! Taxi!"

It wasn't going to stop. *"Taxi!"* cried Simon in despair.

He forced himself to run. It pulled into the curb.

"Oh, thank God," he said. He got into it and gave the

address. "I'm stone-cold sober," he said, "but, my God, I'm tired."

Bruce Barrabell fastened his awful coat and pulled on his black beret. He was going to drop Nina on his way home. She was coming to the Red Fellowship meeting next Sunday and would probably become a member. Not much of a catch but he supposed it was something to have a person from the Dolphin company. He must try to keep her off her wretched superstitious rigmaroles, poor girl.

He lit a cigarette and thought of the killing of Dougal Macdougal. Just how good was this Alleyn? A hangover from the old school tie days, of course, but probably efficient in his own way.

We shall see, thought Barrabell. He went along to Nina's dressing-room.

II

THE sun was high and reflected from the river.

"I wonder," said Emily, "what the Smiths are doing."

"The *Smiths*?" asked Crispin. "What Smiths? Oh, you mean William and his mum," he said and returned to his book.

"Yes. He was sent home as soon as they realized what had happened. I think he was just told there'd been an accident. They may have said, to Sir Dougal. There's nothing they could have read in the Sunday papers. It'll be an awful shock for them."

"How old is he?" asked Robin, who lay on his back on the windowseat, vaguely kicking his feet in the air.

"Who? William?"

"Yes."

"Nine."

"Same as me."

"Yes."

"Is he silly and wet?"

"He's certainly not silly and I don't know what you mean by 'wet.' "

"Behind the ears. Like a baby."

"Not at all like that. He can fight. He's learning karate and he's a good gymnast."

"Does he swear?"

"I haven't heard him but I daresay he does."

"I suppose," said Robin, bicycling madly, "he's very busy on Sundays."

"I've no information. Shall I ask him to come to lunch? You could go over in a taxi to Lambeth where he lives and fetch him. Only an idea," said Emily very casually.

"Oh, yes. You could do that, I suppose. Do that," shouted Robin and leaped to his feet. "Ask him. Please," he added. "Thrice three and double three. Two for you and three for me. Please."

"Right you are."

Emily consulted the cast list that Peregrine kept pinned up by the telephone and dialed a number.

"Mrs. Smith? It's Emily Jay. I've got two sons home for half-term and we wondered if by any chance William would like to pay us a visit today. Robin, who's William's age, could come and collect him for luncheon and we'd promise to return him after an early supper here. Yes. Yes, would you?"

She heard Mrs. Smith's cool voice repeating the invitation: "You'd like that, wouldn't you?" she added and William's voice: "I think so. Yes. Thank you."

"Yes, he'd like to come, thank you *very* much."

"Robin will be there in about half an hour depending on a cab. Lovely. Mrs. Smith, I suppose William told you what happened last night at the theatre? Yes, I see. . . . I'm afraid they were all in a great state. It's Sir Dougal. He's died. . . . Yes, a fearful blow to us all. . . . I don't know. They'll tell the company at four this afternoon what's been decided. I don't think William need go down. He'll be here and we'll tell him. Tragic. It's hard to believe, isn't it? . . . Yes. Good-bye."

She hung up and said to Robin: "Go and get ready," and to Crispin: "Do you want to go, Cip? Not if you don't."

"I think I'd like to."

"Sure?"

"Yes. I can see the infant's on his best behavior, can't I?" Robin from the doorway gave a complicated derisory noise and left the room.

"There's always that," said their mother. "There's just one thing, Cip. Do you know what happened last night? Sir Dougal died — yes. But how? What happened? Did you see? Have you thought?"

"I'm not sure. I saw — it. The head. Full-face but only for a split second."

"Yes?"

"Lots of people in the audience saw it but I think they just thought it was an awfully good dummy, and lots didn't. It was so quick."

"Did Robin?"

"I'm not sure. I don't think he's sure either but he doesn't say. He doesn't want to talk about it."

"The thing is, young William didn't see *anything*. He was waiting offstage. He only knows Sir Dougal is dead. So don't say anything to upset that, will you? If you can, keep right off the whole subject. Right?"

"Yes."

"That's fine. Here he comes."

Crispin went out to the hall and Emily thought: He's a nice boy. Old for his years but that's rather nice too. She went up to the ex-nursery and hunted out a game of Chinese Checkers, one of Monopoly, a couple of memo pads.

Then she went downstairs and looked out of the window. No sign of her sons so they must have picked up a cab. She went to the kitchen and found her part-time cook making a horseradish sauce. There was a good smell of beef in the air.

"Richard's spending the day with friends but we've got an extra small boy for lunch, Annie."

"That's okay," said Annie, whose manner was of a free and easy sort.

"I'll lay the table."

"Will the boss be in?" asked Annie.

"If he can make it. We're not to wait."

"Okeydoke," said Annie. "All serene."

Emily couldn't settle to anything. She wandered downstairs and into the living room. Across the river the Dolphin stood out brightly from its setting in the riverside slums. Peregrine was there now, and all the important people in the Dolphin, trying to reach a conclusion on the immediate future.

I hope they decide against carrying on, she thought. It would be horrible. And, remembering a halfhearted remark of Peregrine's to the effect that Gaston would be good: It wouldn't be the same. I hope they won't do it.

She tried to think of a revival. There was Peregrine's own play about the Dark Lady and the delicate little Hamnet and his glove. The original glove was now in the Victoria and Albert Museum. They had discussed a revival, and it seemed to fill the bill. The child they had used in the original production had been, as far as she recollected, an odious little monster. But William would play Hamnet well. She began to cast it from the present company in her mind, leaving herself out. She became excited and got a pencil and paper to write it all down.

It being Sunday, there was very little traffic in their part of the world. The boys decided to walk to the main street. They set out and almost at once a cruising taxi came their way. Crispin held up his first finger as his father always did and Robin pranced, waved his arms and imitated a seagull's cry.

Crispin gave the driver the address and Robin leaped into the taxi.

"Takin 'im to the naughty boys' 'ome" asked the driver, "or is 'e the Bishop of London?"

Crispin laughed and Robin piped down and was quietly thoughtful. They drove through a maze of small streets, coming finally into Lambeth. Robin broke his silence to start an argument about where the Palace could be and was taken aback when they stopped in a narrow lane off Stangate Street in front of a tidy little house.

"Will you wait for us, please?" said Crispin to the driver. "You wait in the car, Rob."

Crispin got out of the taxi and went up the flight of three steps to the front door. Before he could ring, the door opened and William came out.

"I'm Crispin Jay," said Crispin. "That's Robin halfway out of the cab."

"I'm William Smith. Hullo. Hullo, Robin."

"Hullo," Robin muttered.

"Get in, William," Crispin said. And to the driver: "Back to Bankside, please."

They set off. Robin said he bet he knew all the streets they would go through before they got to Bankside. Crispin said he wouldn't and won. William laughed infectiously and got a number of the early ones right. "I walk down them every day when I go to school," he said, "so it's not fair."

"I go to the Blue Caps," said Robin. "When I'm the right age I'll go to Winchester if I pass the entrance exam."

"I went to the Blue Caps when I was six but only for a term. I wanted to be an actor so I got a scholarship to the Royal Southwark Drama School. It's a special school for actors."

"Do you like it?"

"Yes," said William. "I do like it, very much."

"Do you like being in the play?"

"Gosh, yes."

The taxi made a sharp turn to the right. Crispin took the opportunity to kick his brother, who said: "Hi! Watch your great feet where you put them. Oh! Sorry."

[185]

"There's the river," said Crispin. "We're nearly home."

"Gosh, I'm starving. Are you starving, William?" Robin inquired.

"You bet," said William.

They drew up and stopped.

The two little boys tumbled out and ran up the steps. Crispin paid the taxi and gave the driver a fifteen percent tip.

"Much obliged, your reverence," said the driver.

"There's our car," said Crispin. "Pop's come home. Good."

Emily opened the door and the boys went in, Robin loudly asking if it was time for lunch and saying that he and William were rattling-empty. William shook hands and was not talkative. Peregrine came out to the hall and ran his fingers over William's hair. "Hullo, young fellow," he said. "Nice to see you."

"Hullo, sir."

"I'm afraid I've got disturbing news for you. You know Sir Dougal died very unexpectedly last night, don't you?"

"Yes, sir."

"Yes. Well, we've been trying to decide what to do: whether to continue with someone else in the part or close down for a week and then rehearse and reopen with a revival. We have almost decided on the latter policy, in which case the play will have to be chosen. There are signs of a return to popularity of the sophisticated romantic drama. Christopher Fry, for instance. Your immediate future depends, of course, on our choice, which will have to be made tonight. There has been one suggestion of a play we used years ago for the gala opening of this theatre. It's a small cast and one of the characters is a boy. I wrote it. If it's the play, we will suggest you read for the part. You die at the end of Act One but it is an extremely important part while you're with us."

William said: "Could I do it?"

"I think so. But we'd have to try you, of course. You may not suit."

"Of course."

"The character is Hamnet Shakespeare, Shakespeare's son. I thought I might as well tell you what we're thinking about. You're a sensible chap."

"Well," said William dubiously, "I hope I am."

"Luncheon," cried Emily.

Peregrine found in his place at table a sheet of paper and on it in her handwriting a new casting for *The Glove* by Peregrine Jay. He looked from it to her. "Extraordinary," he said. " 'Two minds with but a single thought.' Or something like that. Thank you, darling."

"Do you like the idea? Or have you grown out of your play?"

"We're in such a state I don't know what I think. I've been reading it, and I fancy I still quite like it."

"It wouldn't matter that it was running years ago at the Dolphin, at the same time as that other messy business?"

"Only you and I and Jeremy and Winty would know. It was a long run, which is all the management considers."

"Yes."

Peregrine looked at her notes. "Maggie: The Dark Lady. Yes. Shakespeare — Simon Morten? Do you think?"

"Yes, I do. He's got a highly strung manner, a very quick temper, and a sense of humor. And with a Shakespeare wig he'd look marvelous."

"Better than Barrabell?"

"I think so, but then I don't like Barrabell. What little I've seen of him."

"He'd succumb to the Voice Beautiful, I fear. He doesn't as Banquo but the Bard himself would be too much for him. He'd begin to sing."

"He's a meany."

"Yes."

"I've got a riddle," Robin shouted.

"I'm no good at riddles," William said doubtfully.

"Look —" Crispin began.

"Shut up, Cip. Your mother and I are talking. Pipe down.

[187]

Who wants more beef? Anybody? All right, clear away the plates and tell Annie we're ready for her delicious pudding."

"Annie! Pud!" Robin yelled.

"That's *really* rude," said Emily. "Crispin, go into the kitchen and ask her properly. And if she doesn't throw a pot at you it's because she's got much nicer manners than any of us. Honestly, Perry, I sometimes wonder where these boys were lugged up."

"William, will you have a look at this part and I'll get you to read it for me before I go down to the theatre?"

"Yes, sir."

"You can read it in my study. The boys are not allowed in there."

And so, for about an hour after lunch William read the first act. There were passages he did not understand and other passages which, though clear enough as far as the words went, seemed to convey another meaning from the one that was usually attached to them. But the boy, Hamnet, was plain sailing. He was ill, he was lonely; his mother was too much occupied with a personal resentment to do more than attend impersonally to him, and his father was a star-like, marvelous creature who came and went and was adored and vilified.

He began to read the boy's lines, trying them one way and another until the sound of them seemed right or nearly so.

Peregrine came in, so quietly that William did not hear him. He sat down and listened to the treble voice. Presently he opened his copy of the play and began to feed out the lines. William looked up at him and then returned to his task and they finished the act together.

"Well," said Peregrine, "that was a good beginning. It's three o'clock. Let's go up to the nursery and see what the others are doing."

So they went to the ex-nursery and found Emily and Robin playing with Robin's train and Crispin, oblivious to the noise, deep in his book. It was all about the play of *Macbeth* and the various productions through the past four centuries. There was a chapter on the superstitions.

"You're not going on with this play, are you?" asked Crispin.

"No," said his father. "It's tempting, but I don't think we are."

"Why tempting?"

"I think Gaston would be exciting as Macbeth."

"Yes?"

"But terribly risky."

"Ah."

The telephone rang.

"I'll answer it, Mummy. May I?" asked Robin.

"If you're polite."

"Of course." He ran out of the room, leaving the door open. They all waited to hear what he would say.

"Hello?" said the treble voice. "This is Mr. Peregrine Jay's house. . . . Yes. . . . If you don't mind waiting for a moment, I'll find out if he can speak to you. Hold on, please. Thank you."

He reappeared. "It's Mr. Gaston Sears, Pop," he said. "And he sounds very sonky-polly-lobby."

"I'll speak to him," said Peregrine and went out to the telephone, shutting the door behind him.

Crispin said: "I daresay, William, you are wondering what 'sonky-polly-lobby' means. It's a family thing and it means 'happy with yourself.' And a bit self-conscious, too."

"Oh."

The little boys returned to their train. Emily and Crispin waited. When he came back Peregrine looked disturbed.

"Gaston," he said, "has had the same idea as we have. He thinks that if we did decide to go on with *Macbeth*, he would be good in the name part, but would have to decline, out of feelings of delicacy. He said it would be an error in taste if he accepted. He said he knew we all thought him a heartless kind of fellow, but he was not. He felt we should be told at once of this decision."

[189]

"He — oh, *dear!* He took it as a matter of course he would be cast?"

"Yes. And he was perfectly right. He would have been."

"What did you say?"

"That we have for many reasons almost decided against it but that, had the many reasons not existed, I agreed. I thought he would have been good. So did the management. With reservations that I didn't mention."

"And he took it?"

"He said, 'So be it,' in a grand voice and hung up. Poor old boy. He would be good, I do believe, but an awful nuisance nevertheless."

"I'm sure you're right, Perry."

"Hoo, hoo," shouted William. "Clear the line. The midnight express is coming straight through."

Emily looked at him and then at Peregrine, who gave her a thumbs-up signal. "Very much so," he said.

"Really? That's quite something."

"All aboard. All aboard," said Robin. "All seats, please."

He blew a piercing blast on a tin whistle. William rang the minute station bell and pressed a button. The toy train lit up and moved out of the station.

"Now, I take over till we reach Crewe," said Robin. He and William changed places. The train increased its speed. William answered a toy telephone.

"Midnight express. Urgent call. Yes?" He panted and blew. "Gaston Sears speaks," he gasped. "Stop the train at Crewe. He's hurt and he's due at the theatre at seven."

"Hooooo. Clackity-bang. Coming into Crewe. Clear the line."

William produced a white van with a red cross and placed it on a sideline. "Ready for Mr. Sears," he said.

"Where's Sears?"

William emptied out a box of toy soldiers: army, navy, Highlanders, crusaders. He cried out triumphantly and displayed a battered crusader with an enormous sword and full mask and black cloak. "Look! Perfect," he cried. "In every detail."

"Hooray. Put him in the van."

The game proceeded with the preposterous ill-logic of a child's dream and several changes of plot. The train arrived conveniently at Waterloo Station. "Gaston Sears" was pushed onto a battered car and, remarking that he'd got his "second wind," was sent to the Dolphin Theatre. End of game.

"That was fun," said Robin, "wasn't it?"

"Yes," his father agreed. "Why did you have Gaston Sears in it?"

"Why not?" Robin replied with a shrug. He walked away, no longer interested.

"Because he was breathless?" William suggested vaguely. "He said it was asthma but he pretends it isn't now he's an actor again."

"I see," Peregrine lied. "Show it to me. The toy Sears."

William took the battered little figure out of the car. A shrewd whack in some past contest had disposed of the cross on its cloak. The sword bent but intact, was raised above its shrouded head in gloved hands. It was completely black and in its disreputable way, quite baleful.

"Thank you," said Peregrine. He put it in his pocket.

"Have you finished with the train?" asked Emily.

"We might want it later," said Robin quickly.

"I don't think you will. It's 'The Duke' on telly in a quarter of an hour and then tea-time."

"Oh, *Mummy!*"

The train was carefully put away and the toy soldiers swept into their box pell-mell, all except the "Mr. Sears," which was still in Peregrine's pocket when he looked at his watch and prepared to leave.

"I must be off," he said. "I don't know when I'll get home, my love. Cip says he'll come down with me and walk back so I'll leave you to take William home. Okay? Good evening, William. Come again soon, won't you? We've enjoyed having you here."

"Thank you, sir,' said William, shaking hands. "It's been a lovely day. The nicest day I've ever had."

"Good. Cip! Ready?"

"Coming."

They banged the front door and ran down the steps to the car.

"Pop," said Crispin when they got going, "that book you paid for last night. About *Macbeth*."

"Yes?"

"It's jolly good. It's got quite a lot about the superstitions. If you don't mind I would like just to ask if you *totally* dismiss that aspect of the play."

"I think," said Peregrine very carefully, "that the people that do so put the cart before the horse. Call a play 'unlucky' and take any mishap that befalls the rehearsals or performances, onstage or in the dressing-rooms or offices, and immediately everyone says: 'There you are. Unlucky play.' If the same sort of troubles occur with other plays nobody counts them up or says anything about them. Until, perhaps, there are rather more misfortunes than with other contemporary shows and someone like poor maddening Nina says: 'It's an unlucky piece, you know,' and it's got the label tied round its neck for keeps."

"Yes, I see that. But in this instance — I mean that business with the heads. It's a bit thick, isn't it?"

"There you go! Cart before the horse. They may have been planted to make us believe in the unlucky play story."

"I see what you mean, of course. But you can't say it applies to this final tragedy. Nobody in his right senses is going to cut off a harmless actor's head — that's what happened, Pop, isn't it? — just to support the unlucky play theory?"

"Of course not. No. And the only person who might be described as being a bit dotty, apart from Nina, is old Gaston, who was chatting away to the King and William and Nina and several others at the time the murder was committed."

There was a longish silence. "I see," said Crispin at last.

"I don't want you to — to —"

"Get involved?"

"Certainly not."

"Well, I won't. But I can't help *wondering*," said Crispin. "Seeing you're my father and seeing the book I'm reading. Can I?"

"I suppose not."

"Are you going on with *Macbeth*?"

"I don't think so. I think it'll probably be a revival of my own play."

"*The Glove?*"

"Yes."

"That *will* be fun. With William, of course?"

"He gave a very promising reading."

"A talented child," said Crispin.

They crossed Blackfriars Bridge and turned left and left again into Wharfingers Lane. There were three cars ahead of them.

"Winty's car and two of the board. As usual I don't know when I'll be home. Good-bye, old boy."

" 'Bye, Pop."

Peregrine watched him walk away up Wharfingers Lane. He went in by the stage door.

Most of the cast were there in groups of three or four. The stage had been scrubbed down and looked the same as usual. He wondered what would be its future. The skeleton hung from the gallows and swung in the draft. Bob Masters and Charlie greeted him and so did a number of the actors They gathered around him.

He said at once: "No absolute news but it will, I imagine, be out before long. The pundits are gathering in front-of-house. I think, my dears, it's going to be the end of *Macbeth*. I hope the new play will be announced tonight. I'd like to say now that it will almost certainly be a much, much smaller cast, which means that for a number of you the prospect of a long season comes to an abrupt end. I'd like to thank you from a very full heart for your work and say that, no matter

what may befall in the years to come, you will be known —
every bit-part of you — for having played in, to quote several
of the reviews, the 'Flawless *Macbeth*.' "

"Under flawless direction, Perry," said Maggie and the
others, after a murmured agreement, clapped him: a des-
ultory sound in the empty Dolphin. It died away. A throat
was cleared. Gaston stepped forward.

Somebody said: "Oh, no."

"I may *not*," Gaston proclaimed with an air of infinite
conceit, "be considered the appropriate figure to voice our
corporate approval of the style in which the play has been
presented. However, as no one else has come forward, I
shall attempt to do so." He spread his feet and grasped his
lapels. "I have been glad to offer my assistance in matters
of production and to have been able to provide the replicas
for the weapons used by Macbeth and Macduff. I made
them," he said, with a modest cough. "I do, however, now
frankly deplore the use of the actual, historical claidheamh-
mor. At the time I felt that since no hands but my own would
touch it, there would be no desecration. I was utterly mistaken and take this opportunity of admitting as much. The
claidheamh-mor is possessed of a power —"

"For God's sake, somebody, stop him," muttered Simon.

"— it moves in its own appointed way —"

The doors at the back of the stalls opened and Alleyn
came into the house and walked down the center aisle.

Gaston paused, his mouth open. Peregrine said: "Excuse
me, Gaston. I think Mr. Alleyn wants to speak to me." The
actors, intensely relieved, set up a buzz of affirmation.

"It's to say that we've just about finished our work in the
theatre," Alleyn said, "and the dressing-rooms are now open
for use. I must ask you all to remain at your present addresses
or, if any of you change your address, to let us know. If this
is inconvenient for any of you I am very sorry. It will not,
I hope, be for very long."

He turned to Peregrine. "I think the management would
like a word with you," he said.

Bruce Barrabell said importantly, "I am the union's representative in this production. I will have to ask for a ruling on the situation."

"No doubt," said Alleyn politely, "they will be glad to advise you. There is a telephone in the Prompt corner." And to the company: "Mr. Fox has the keys. He's in the greenroom."

"I suppose," said Barrabell, "you've been through our private possessions like the proverbial fine-tooth comb."

"I'm not sure how proverbial fine-tooth combs work but I expect you're right."

"And retired to your virtuous bed to sleep the sleep of the just, no doubt?"

"I didn't go to bed last night," said Alleyn mildly. He surveyed the company. "The typescripts of your statements are ready," he said. "We'd be grateful if you'd be kind enough to read them and if they're correct, sign them before you go. Thank you all, very much."

In the boardroom, Peregrine faced his fellow guardians and Winter Meyer. Mrs. Abrams was secretary.

"In the appalling situation in which we find ourselves," he said, "the immediate problem is how we conduct our policy. We've been given twenty-four hours in which to decide. One: we can go dark and advertise that money for advance bookings will be refunded at the box office. Two: we can continue with the presentation. Simon Morten would take the lead and his understudy play Macduff. The fight at the end will be replaced by a much simpler routine. *Or,* and this is an unorthodox suggestion, Gaston Sears would play the lead. He tells me he is in a fair way to being word-perfect and of course he knows the fight, but he adds that he feels he would have to decline.

"Three: we can take a fortnight off and reopen with the revival of one of our past successes. *The Glove* has been mentioned. As the author I feel I can't speak for or against the play. I can, however, say that I have heard William Smith read the very important part of the young Hamnet Shakespeare and he promised extremely well. We can cast it from the present company. Maggie would be splendid as the Dark Lady and I fancy Simon as the Bard and Nina as Ann."

He was silent for a second or two and then said: "This is a terrible thing that has happened. One would have said that our dear Sir Dougal had no enemies — I still can't get myself around to — to — to facing it and I daresay you can't either Of one thing we may all be sure, he would have wanted us to do what is best for the Dolphin."

He sat down.

For a time nobody spoke. Then one bald and stout guardian whispered to another and a little pantomime of nodding and portentous frowns passed around the table. The senior guardian, who was thin and had a gentle air, stood up.

"I move," he said, "that we leave the decision in Mr. Peregrine Jay's hands and do so with our complete trust in his decision."

"Second that," said another guardian.

"Those in favor? Unanimous," said the chairman.

8
DEVELOPMENT

I

"I SUPPOSE I ought to be feeling all glowing and grateful," said Peregrine, "but I'm afraid I don't. They are nice old boys, all of them, but they're dab hands at passing the buck and making it look like a compliment."

"You've been given a completely free hand and if it turns out a dead failure you'll find yourself out on a limb and all of them saying, ever so delicately, that they felt at the time the decision was a mistaken one," Alleyn observed.

"That's right."

"If it's any comfort, which it isn't, I'm familiar with these tactics."

"Why don't we leave them to make the decision? Why don't I say I feel it would be better, under the circumstances, for somebody less intimately concerned with the Dolphin to produce the next show? God knows it'd be true."

"Yes?"

"But I'd feel I was ratting." He dug his hands into his pockets. "I'm fond of them. We've taken a journey together and come out on the golden sands. We've found *Macbeth*. It's a marvelous feeling. Or was. Are *you* any further on?"

"A little, I think. Not enough, not anything like enough to even think of an arrest."

Peregrine's fingers had been playing with something in h

pocket. They closed around it and fetched it out, a dilapidated little figure, jet black, flourishing a bent weapon.

"Where did you find that?" Alleyn asked.

"It's one of my boy's toy soldiers — a crusader. William found it."

"William?"

"Smith. He spent the day with us. He's the same age as young Robin. They got on like a house on fire playing with the boys' electric train. This thing was a passenger, picked up at Crewe. He said he was hurt but he had to get to the theatre at seven. It gave me quite a shock — all black and with a claymorish thing — like Sir Dougal. Only they called him Sears. Extraordinary, how children behave. You know? William didn't know what had happened in the theatre, only that Sir Dougal was dead. Robin didn't know or wasn't certain about the decapitation, but he'd been very much upset when it happened. I'd realized that, but he didn't ask any questions and now there he was, making a sort of game of it."

"Extraordinary," said Alleyn. "May I have it? The crusader? I'll take great care of him."

"All right," said Peregrine and handed it over. "It might be Sir Dougal or Barrabell or Sears or nobody," he said. "It doesn't look tall enough for Simon Morten. It's masked, of course."

"*He* wasn't masked. And in any case —"

"No. In any case the whole thing's a muddle and a coincidence. William fished this thing out of a box full of battered toys."

"And called it — what? Sears?"

"Not exactly. I mean, it became Sears. They picked him up at Crewe. Before that, William — being Sears at the moment when he used the telephone — rang up the station for an emergency stop. He said — what the hell *did* he say? That he was hurt and had to get to the Dolphin by seven. That's when William took this thing from the box and they put it in the train. It was a muddle. They hooted and whistled and shouted and changed the plot. William gasped and panted a lot."

"Panted? As if he'd been running?" Alleyn asked.

"Yes. Sort of. I think he said something about trying not to. I'm not sure. He said it was asthma but Sears wouldn't let on because he was an actor. One thing I am sure about, though."

"What's that?"

"They got rid of whatever feelings they had about the real event by turning it all into a game."

"That sounds like good psychology to me," said Alleyn. "But then I'm not a psychologist. I can understand Robin calling this thing Sears, though."

"Why?"

"He was here, wasn't he? In the theatre. He saw the real Sears carry the head on. Associated images."

"I *think* I see what you mean," said Peregrine doubtfully. "Well. I had better go back to the offices and tell them my decision and get audition notices typed out. What about you?"

"We'll see them out of here," said Alleyn.

"Good luck to you," said Peregrine. He vaulted down into the orchestra well and walked away up the center aisle. The doors opened and shut behind him.

Alleyn went over his notes.

"Is there a connection or isn't there?" he asked himself. "Did the perpetrator of these nasty practical jokes have anything to do with the beheading of an apparently harmless star actor or was he practicing along his own beastly self indulgent lines? Who is he? Bruce Barrabell? Why are his fellow actors and — well, Peregrine Jay — so sure he's the trickster? Simply because they don't like him and he seems to be the only person in the company capable of such murky actions? But *why* would he do it? I'd better take a potshot and try to find out." He looked at his notes. "Red Fellowship. Hmm. Silly little outfit, but they're on the lists and so's he. Here goes."

He walked down the dressing-room corridor until he came to the one shared by Barrabell and Morten. He paused and listened. Not a sound. He knocked and a splendid voice said, "Come." They always make such a histrionic thing of it when they leave out the "in," Alleyn thought.

Bruce Barrabell was seated in front of his looking-glass. The lights were switched on and provided an unmotivated brilliance to the dead room. The makeup had all been laid by in an old cigar box fastened by two rubber bands. The dirty grease-cloths were neatly rolled up in a paper bag, which was next to a battered suitcase with Russian labels stuck on it. On the top of his belongings was a programme, several review pages, and a small collection of cards and telegrams. Crumpled tissues lay about the dressing-table.

Simon Morten's possessions were all packed away in his heavily labeled suitcase, which was shut and waited on the floor, inside the door. The indescribable smell of greasepaint still hung on the air and the room was desolate.

"Ah. Mr. Alleyn!" said Barrabell expansively. "Good evening to you. Can I be of any help? I'm just tidying up, as you see." He waved his hand at the disconsolate room. "Do sit down," he invited.

"Thank you," said Alleyn. He took the other chair and opened his file. "I'm checking all your statements," he said.

"Ah yes. Mine is quite in order, I hope?"

"I hope so, too," Alleyn said. He turned the papers slowly until he came to Mr. Barrabell's statement. He looked at his man and saw two men. The silver-voiced Banquo saying, so beautifully: *"There's husbandry in Heaven; their candles are all out,"* and the unnaturally pale actor, with light eyes, whose hands trembled a little as he lit a cigarette.

"'I'm sorry. Do you?" Barrabell asked winningly and offered his cigarettes.

"No, thank you. I don't. About these tricks that have been played during the rehearsal period. I see you called them 'schoolboy hoaxes' when we asked you about them."

"Did I? I don't remember. It's what they were, I suppose. Isn't it?"

"Two extremely realistic severed heads? A pretty case-hardened schoolboy. Had you one in mind?"

"Oh no. No."

"Not the one in Mr. Winter Meyer's 'co,' for instance?"

There was a pause. Barrabell's lips moved, repeating the words, but no sound came from them. He slightly shook his head. "There was somebody," Alleyn went on, "a victim, in the Harcourt-Smith case. Her name was Muriel Barrabell, a bank clerk." He waited. Somewhere along the corridor a door banged and man's voice called out. "In the greenroom, dear."

"Was she your sister?"

Silence.

"Your wife?"

"No comment."

"Did you want the boy to get the sack?"

"No comment."

"He was supposed to have perpetrated these tricks. And all to do with severed heads. Like his father's crimes. Even the rat's head. A mad boy, we were meant to think. Like his father. Get rid of him, he's mad, like his father. It's inherited."

There was another long silence.

"She was my wife," said Barrabell. "I never knew at the time what happened. I didn't get their letter. He was charged with another woman's murder. Caught red-handed. I was doing a long tour of Russia with the Leftist Players. It was all over when I got back. She was so beautiful, you can't think. And he did that to her. I made them tell me. They didn't want to but I kept on and on until they did."

"And you took it out on this perfectly sane small boy?"

"How do you know he's perfectly sane? Could you expect me to be in the same company with him? I wanted this part. I wanted to work for the Dolphin. But do you imagine I could do so with that murderer's brat in the cast? Not bloody likely," said Barrabell and contrived a sort of laugh.

"So you came to the crisis. All the elaborate attempts to incriminate young William came to nothing. And then, suddenly, inexplicably, there is the real, the horrible crime of Sir Dougal's decapitation. How do you explain that?"

"I don't," he said at once. "I know nothing about it. Nothing. Apart from his vanity and his accepting that silly title, he was harmless enough. A typical bourgeois hero, which maybe is why he excelled as Macbeth."

"You see the play as an antiheroic exposure of the bourgeois way of life, do you? Is that it? *Can* that be it?"

"Certainly. If you choose to put it like that. It's the Macbeths' motive. Their final desperate gesture. And they both break under the strain."

"You really believe that, don't you?"

"Certainly," he repeated. "Of course, our reading was, as usual, idiotic. Take the ending: *Hail, King of Scotland!* In other words, 'Hail to the old acceptable standards. The old rewards and the old dishing out of cash and titles.' We cut all that, of course. And the bloody head of Macbeth stared the young Malcolm in the face. Curtain," said Barrabell.

"Have you discussed the play with your political chums at the Red Fellowship meetings?"

"Yes. Not in detail. More as a joke, really."

"A *joke*," Alleyn exclaimed. "Did you say a *joke*?"

"A bit on the macabre side, certainly. There's a meeting every Sunday morning. You ought to come. I'll bring you in on my ticket."

"Did you talk about the murder?"

"Oh yes. Whodunit talk. You know."

"Who *did* do it?"

"Don't ask me. *I* don't know, do I?"

Alleyn thought: He's not so frightened, now. He's being impudent.

"Have you thought about the future, Mr. Barrabell? What do you think of doing?"

"I haven't considered it. There's talk of another Leftist Players tour but of course I thought I was settled for a long season here."

"Of course. Would you read this statement and if it's correct, sign it? Pay particular attention to this point, will you?"

The forefinger pointed to the typescript.

"You were asked where you were between Macbeth's last speech and Old Siward's epitaph for his son. It just says, 'Dressing-room and O.P. center waiting for a call.' Could you be a little more specific?" Alleyn asked.

"I really don't see quite how."

"When did you leave the dressing-room?"

"Oh. We were called on the tannoy. They'll give you the time. I pulled on my ghost's head and the cloak and went out."

"Did you meet anybody in the passage?'

"*Meet* anyone? Not precisely. I followed the old King and the Macduffs, mother and son, I remember. I don't know if anyone followed me. Any of the other 'corpses.' "

"And you were alone in the dressing-room?"

"Yes, my dear Chief Superintendent. Absolutely alone."

"Thank you." Alleyn made an addition and offered his own pen. "Will you read and sign it, please? There."

Barrabell read it. Alleyn had written: "Corroborative evidence. None."

He signed it.

"Thank you," Alleyn said and left him.

In the passage he ran into Rangi. "Hullo," he said, "I'm getting statements signed. Would it suit you to do yours now?"

"Good as gold."

"Where's your room?"

"Along here."

He led the way to where the passage turned left and the rooms were larger.

"I've got Ross and Lennox and Angus in with me," Rangi said. He came to the correct door and opened it. "Nobody here. It's a bit of a muddle, I'm afraid," he said.

"Doesn't matter. You've packed up, I see."

He cleared a chair for Alleyn and took one himself.

"Yours was a wonderful performance," said Alleyn. "It was a brilliant decision to use those antipodean postures: the whole body working evil."

"I've been wondering if I should have done it. I don't know what my elders would say: the strict ones. It seemed to be right for the play. Mr. Sears approved of it. I thought maybe he would think it all nonsense but he said there are strong links throughout the world in esoteric beliefs. He said all or anyway most of the ingredients in the spell are correct."

"I'm sure you're right," Alleyn said. He saw that around his neck on a flax cord Rangi wore a *tiki,* a greenstone effigy of a human fetus. "Is that a protection?" Alleyn asked.

"In my family for generations." The brown fingers caressed it.

"Really? You're a Christian, aren't you? Forgive me; it's rather confusing —"

"It is, really. Yes. I suppose I am. The Mormon Church. It's very popular with my people. They don't 'mormonize,' you know, only one wife at a time, and they're not all that fussy about our old beliefs. I suppose I'm more *pakeha* than Maori in ordinary day-to-day things. But when it comes to this — what's happened here — it — well, it all comes rolling in, like the Pacific, in huge waves, and I'm Maori, through and through."

"That I understand. Well, all I want is your signature to this statement. You weren't asked many questions but I wonder if you can give me any help over this one. The actual killing took place between Macbeth's exit fighting and Malcolm's entrance. Those of you who were not onstage came out of your dressing-rooms. There were you three witches and the dead Macduffs and the King and the Banquo under his ghost mask and cloak. Is that correct?"

Rangi shut his large eyes. "Yes," he said. "That's right. And Mr. Sears. He was with the rest of us but as the cue got nearer he moved away into the O.P. corner with Macduff, ready for their final entrance."

"Was anyone following you?"

"The other two witches. We were in a bunch."

"Anyone else?"

"I don't think so."

"Sure?"

"Yes," said Rangi firmly. "Quite sure. We were last."

He read it carefully and signed it. As he returned it to Alleyn he said: "It doesn't do to meddle with these things. They are wasps' nests that are better left alone."

"We can't leave a murder alone, Rangi."

"I suppose not. All the same. He made fun of things that are *tapu* — forbidden. My great-grandfather knew how to deal with that."

"Oh?"

"He cut off the man's head," said Rangi cheerfully. "And ate him."

The tannoy broke the silence that followed. "Members of the company are requested to assemble in the greenroom for a managerial announcement. Thank you," it said.

II

ALLEYN found Fox in the greenroom. "Finished?" he asked.

"I've got all the statements. Except, of course, your lot. They're not conspicuously helpful. There's one item that the King noticed. He says — hold on a jiffy — here we are. He says he noticed that Sears was wheezing while he waited with them before the final entry. He said something about it and Sears tapped his own chest and frowned. He made a solemn thing with his eyebrows. 'Asthma, dear boy, asthma. No matter.' Can't you see him doing it?"

"Yes. Vincent Crummles stuff. He must have found that massive claidheamh-mor a bit of a burden lumping it around with him.'

"What I thought. Poor devil. Here comes the management. We'll hand over."

They put the statements in a briefcase and settled themselves inconspicuously at the back of the room.

The management came through the auditorium and on-stage by way of the Prompt box and from thence to the greenroom. They looked preternaturally solemn. The senior guardian was in the middle and Winter Meyer at the far end. They sat down behind the table, watching the company file in.

"I'm afraid," said the senior guardian, "there are not enough chairs for everybody but please use the ones that are available. Oh, here are some more."

Stagehands brought chairs from the dressing-rooms. There was a certain amount of politeness. Three ladies occupied the sofa. Simon Morten stood behind Maggie. She turned to speak to him. He put his hand on her shoulder and leaned over her with a possessive air. Gaston Sears stood apart with folded arms and pale face and dark suit, like a phony figurehead got up for the occasion. Bruce Barrabell occupied an armchair. Rangi and his girls were together by the doorway.

And in the back of the room, quietly, side by side, sat Alleyn and Fox, who sooner or later, it must be assumed, would remove one of the company, having charged him with the murder by decapitation of their leading man.

The senior guardian said his piece. He would not keep them long. They were all deeply shocked. It was right that they should know as soon as possible what had been decided by the management. The usual procedure of the understudy taking over the leading role would not be followed. It was felt that the continued presentation of the play would be too great a strain on actors and on audiences. This was a difficult decision to take when the production was such a wonderful success. However, after much anxious consideration it had been decided to revive *The Glove*. The principals had been cast. If they looked at the board they would see the names of the actors. There were four good parts still uncast and Mr. Jay would be pleased to audition anyone who wished to apply. Rehearsals would begin next week. Mr. Meyer would be glad to settle *Macbeth* salaries tomorrow morning if the actors would kindly call at the office. He thanked them all for being so patient and said he would ask them to stand in silence for one minute in remembrance of Sir Dougal Macdougal.

They stood. Winter Meyer looked at his watch. The minute seemed interminable. Strange little sounds — sighs, a muffled thump; a telephone bell; a voice, instantly silenced — came and went and nobody really thought of Sir Dougal except Maggie, who fought off tears. Winter Meyer made a definitive movement and there was no more silence.

"Excuse me, Mr. Chairman. Before we break up."

It was Bruce Barrabell.

"As representative of Equity I would just like to convey the usual messages of sympathy and to say that I will make suitable enquiries on your behalf as to the correct action to be taken in these very unusual circumstances. Thank you."

"Thank you, Mr. Barrabell," replied the flustered senior guardian.

He and his colleagues left in a discreet procession by the stage door.

III

MACBETH
All Personnel
Announcement Extraordinary

Owing to unforeseen and most tragic circumstances this play will, as from now, be closed. The
play *The Glove* by Peregrine Jay will replace it.
Four of the leading parts are cast from the existing
company. The remainder are open for auditions.

The management thanks the company for its out-
standing success and deeply regrets the necessity to
close.

Samuel Goodbody, Chairman
Dolphin Enterprises

At a respectable distance was a second announcement:

Current Production
The Glove. Auditions: Today and two following days,
11 A.M.–1 P.M., 2 P.M.–5 P.M.

Shakespeare	Mr. Simon Morten
Ann Shakespeare	Miss Nina Gaythorne
Hamnet Shakespeare	Master William Smith
The Dark Lady	Miss Margaret Mannering
Dr. Hall	
Joan Hart	
Mr. W.H.	
Burbage	

Books of the play obtainable at office.

Peregrine came in and looked at the notices. Then he began to move chairs onto the stage, placing them facing back to back to mark the doorways into Shakespeare's parlor and leaving a group of six as working props. He brushed against the skeleton still swinging from the gallows and pushed it offstage. Then he went into the stalls and sat down.

I must pull myself together, he thought. I must go on as usual and I must whip up, from somewhere, enthusiasm for my own play.

Bob Masters came onstage and peered into the auditorium.

"Bob," Peregrine said. "We'll hold the auditions here in the usual way when everyone comes. Oh, and do put that skeleton somewhere else."

"Right," said Bob. "Will do. People will be down in half an hour — Winty is settling the treasury."

"Okay." ·

From the shadows a lonely couple emerged and appeared onstage. William and his mother: she, tidy in a dark gray suit and white blouse, he, also in dark gray — a trouser suit — with white shirt and dark blue tie. He walked over to the board, looked at the notices, and turned to his mother. She joined him and put her hands on his shoulders. "I'm not sure," he said clearly. "Don't I have to audition?"

"Hullo, William," Peregrine called out. "You don't, really. We're taking a gamble on you. But I see you've got your book. Go and collect your treasury and come back here and we'll see how you shape up. All right?"

"Yes, thank you, sir."

"I'll come back and wait for you outside," said his mother. She had gone out by the stage door before Peregrine realized what she was up to.

William went through the house to the offices and, for a short time, Peregrine was quite alone. He sat in the stalls and supposed that people like Nina had begun to say that the Dolphin was an unlucky theatre. And suddenly time contracted and the first production of his play seemed to have scarcely completed its run. He could almost hear the voices of the actors . . .

William came back. He went through the opening scene and Peregrine thought: I was right. The boy's an actor.

"You'll do," he said. "Go home and learn your lines and come down for rehearsals in a week's time."

"Thank you, sir," said William and went out by the stage door.

" 'Yes, sir. No, sir. Three bags full, sir,' " said an unmistakable voice. It was Bruce Barrabell, at the back.

Peregrine peered at him. "Barrabell?" he said. "Are you going to audition?"

"I thought so. For Burbage."

He doesn't come on until the second act, Peregrine thought. He would be good. And he felt a sudden violent dislike of Barrabell. I don't want him in the cast, he thought. I can't have him. I don't want to hear him audition. I don't want to speak to him. He thought of what Alleyn had told him the evening before, of Barabell's confession, if such it could be called.

The part of Burbage was of a frantically busy man of affairs and an accomplished actor in the supposed Elizabethan manner. Silver-tongued, blast it, thought Peregrine. He's ideal of course. Oh, damn and blast!

There was a bustle as the actors began to trickle in from the offices and Mrs. Abrams came down to take notes for Peregrine and say, "Thank you, darling. We'll let you know." The Ross auditioned for Dr. Hall. He read it nicely with a good appreciation of the medical man of his day and his anxious and lethal treatment of young Hamnet. The Gentlewoman tried for Joan Hart, the sister who was closest to the poet. That had been Emily's part and Peregrine tried not to let himself be influenced by this. If he suggested she come back and play it she would say she was too old now.

They plodded on.

IV

At the Yard, Alleyn was going through the statements. He put the regulation conclusion before himself and Mr. Fox, who remained, as it were, anonymous.

"If all reasonable explanations fail, the investigation must consider the explanation which, however outlandish, is not contradicted?"

"And what in this case is the outlandish explanation that is not contradicted?"

"There is not enough time for the murder to be accomplished between the end of the fight and the appearance of Macbeth's head on the claidheamh-mor, so it must have been done before the fight. But Macbeth spoke during the fight. True, his voice was hoarse and breathless."

Alleyn took his head in his hands and did his best to listen to the past. ". . . *get thee back, my soul is too much charged with blood of thine already.*" Sir Dougal had the slight but unmistakable burr of Scots in his voice. He had given it a little more room for the Thane: "*too much charrged.*" A grievous sound. It drifted through his memory but his recollection held no personality behind it. Just the broken despair of any breathless, beaten fighter.

He must look for a new place in the play where the murder could have been committed. It was Sir Dougal who fought and killed Young Siward. He wore his vizor pushed up, displaying his full face. His speech ended with his desperate recollection of the last of the witches' equivocal pronouncements:

"*. . . weapons laugh to scorn*
Brandish'd by man that's of a woman born"

and there, suddenly, in his imagination, stood the actor. Up went the gauntleted hand and down came the vizor. He went off into the O.P. corner — and was murdered? Macduff came on. He had a soliloquy, broken by skirmishes and determined searches. Outbursts of fighting occurred, now here, now there. The Macbeth faction was dressed alike: black, gauntleted, some masked, others not. The effect was nightmarish. What if Macduff encountered a man uniformed like Macbeth — but not Macbeth? Pipes. Malcolm, with a group of soldiers, marched on. Old Siward greeted him and welcomed him to the castle. He made a ceremonial entry with pipes and drums. Cheering within. The masked "Macbeth" entered. Macduff came on. Saw him. Challenged him. They fought.

"Yes," Alleyn said, "It's possible. It's perfectly possible but does it throw a spanner in all our calculations and alibis? None of the 'corpses' are in position for the curtain call then. The Macduff, Simon Morten, could *just,* I suppose, have done it, but he'd have got a nasty shock when the dead man turned up to fight him. On the other hand, as Macbeth's understudy he would know the fight. But he was already engaged in the fight himself. Damn. Barrabell? Gaston? Props? Rangi? All possible. But, wait a bit; all but one *im*possible. Unless we entertain the idea of a collaborator who understood the fight. Hold on. Let's take any one of them regardless and see how it works out. Rangi."

"Rangi," said Fox without enthusiasm.

"He would do the murder at the earlier time. He'd wait till the last minute, then rush around to Gaston and say Sir Dougal's fainted and he, Gaston, will have to go on for the fight with Macduff. All right so far?"

"It's all right." said Fox, "as far as you've got. Motive, though?"

"Ah. Motive. His great-grandfather knew how to deal with this sort of nonsense. He told me in the nicest way imaginable. He cut off the other chap's head and ate him."

"Really!" said Fox primly. "How very unpleasant. But I suppose he could have done a return to his great-grandfather's state of mind and killed Macbeth. You know, reverted to the Stone Age, sort of."

"Any of the others could have done the same thing."

"You don't mean —"

"I don't mean the chopper and cooking-pot bit, and I'll thank you not to be silly. I mean, could have gone to Gaston at the last moment and asked him to fight. The catch in that is, it'd be a damnable bit of evidence against him, later on."

"Yerse," said Mr. Fox. "And whoever he was, he didn't do it."

"I *know* he didn't do it. I'm simply trying to find a way out, Fox. I'm trying to eliminate and I *have* eliminated."

"Yes, Mr. Alleyn. You have. When do we book the gentleman?"

"I doubt if we've got a tight enough case, you know."

"Do you?"

"Blast the whole boiling of them," said Alleyn. He got up and walked about the room. "Do you know what they're doing now? At this precise moment? Holding auditions for the replacement. A good play by Jay built around the death of Shakespeare's young son and the arrival of the Dark Lady. So far they haven't cast the murderer but there's no guarantee they won't. What's more it's the play they were doing with great success when this theatre reopened. There was a mess then. Remember?"

"I remember," said Fox. "Proper turn-up for the books, that one was."

"And a right proper young monster the boy was. This is altogether a different story. D'you know who this kid is?"

"No. Ought I to? Not anything in our line of business, I suppose."

"No — well, that's not quite true. He's a nice, well-brought-up little chap and he's the son of the Hampstead Chopper. He doesn't know that and I'm extremely anxious that he won't find out, Fox."

"Harcourt-Smith, wasn't it?"

"It was. His mother dropped the Harcourt. He knows his father's in a loony-bin but not why."

"Broadmoor?"

"Yes. A lifer."

"Fancy that, now," Fox said shaking his head.

"One of his father's earlier victims was a Mrs. Barrabell."

"You're not telling me —"

"Yes, I am. Wife. Barrabell put those practical jokes together. He hoped the management would think the boy was responsible and give him the sack."

"Has he told you? Barrabell?"

"Not in so many words but as-good-as."

"He's a member of some potty little way-out group, isn't he?"

"The Red Fellowship. Yes."

"What do we know about them?"

"The usual. Meeting once a week on Sunday mornings. Genuine enough. No real understanding of the extraordinary and extremely complicated in-fighting that goes on at sub-diplomatic levels. A bit dotty. He and his mates iron everything out to a few axioms and turn a blind eye to all that doesn't fit. The terrible reality of Bruce Barrabell rests in the fact that his wife was beheaded by a maniac. I think he believes, or has brooded himself into believing, that the child has inherited the father's madness and that sooner or later it'll emerge and then it'll be too late."

"I still don't know where Sir Dougal fits in. If he does."

"Nor do I. Except that he was a far from subtle funster and Bruce came in for his share of the ragging. He was forever making snide references to leftish groups and so on."

"Hardly enough to make Bruce cut his head off."

"Not if we were dealing with anything like normal people. I'm beginning to believe there's a stepped-up abnormality about the whole thing, Fox. As if the actors had become motivated by the play. That leads one to the proposition that no play should be as compulsive as *Macbeth*. Which is ridiculous."

"All right. So what, to get down to our weekly pay packet, do we do to earn it?"

"Find a conclusive reason that will give us the time as

being immediately after *Brandish'd by man that's of a woman born*. Find alibis for all but one of the company at that time and then face him with it. That's the ideal, of course. Let's tackle the alibis and see if we can do it with both feet on the ground. Now, the troops and all the extras and doubles are already engaged in battle. All the thanes; the doctor, disguised as one of Macbeth's soldiers; Malcolm; Siward. Macduff's out. That leaves Rangi, Gaston, and Banquo. The King. Props."

"He was in and out of the O.P. corner fixing the clai-dheamh-mor. And that's all," said Fox.

"And we can cut out the King, I imagine."

'Why?"

"Too silly," said Alleyn. "And too elderly."

"All right. No King. How about Props? Any motive at all?"

"Not unless something turns up. In a way he's tempting, though. Nobody would pay any attention to him slipping into or out of the O.P. corner. He'd be there with the naked claidheamh-mor when Macbeth came off and could kill him and put his head on it."

"He'd have to give the phony message to Gaston, but I think it would hold up," said Fox. "Gaston's hanging about there and Props says to him, 'For Gawd's sake, sir, he's fainted. You've got this one speech and the fight. You know it. You can do it.' And later on when the body's found he says it was so dark he just saw it lying there and realizing there was only a matter of minutes before Macbeth's entrance for the fight he rushed out, found Gaston, and asked him. It hangs together. Except —"

"No motive? Bloody hell, Fox," shouted Alleyn, "we've lost our touch. We've gone to pieces. Gaston being told Macbeth's fainted doesn't work. It doesn't work with anyone asking him to do it. He'd have told us. Of course he would. Back to square one."

There was a long silence.

"No," said Alleyn at last. "There's only one answer."

"I suppose so," said Fox heavily.

V

THE auditions were nearly over and the play almost fully cast from the present company. In the office, announcements for the press were being telephoned and Peregrine actually felt better. Whatever the outcome and whoever was arrested, they were doing their own thing. In their own theatre. They were doing what they were meant to do: getting on with a new piece.

The discordant note was sounded, needless to say, by Gaston. He had not, of course, auditioned but there he was at the theatre. No sooner had an audition finished than he began. He buttonholed one nervous actor after another and his subject was the claidheamh-mor. He wanted it back. Urgently. They tried to shut him up, but he kept recurring like a decimal and complaining in an audible rumble that he would not be held responsible for anything that happened to anyone into whose care it had been consigned.

He asked to see Alleyn and was told he and Fox were not at the theatre. Where had they gone? Nobody knew.

At last Peregrine stopped Rangi's audition and said he could not allow Gaston into the auditorium while they were working. What did he want?

"My claidheamh-mor," he roared. "How often must I say it! Are you an idiot, have you not been given sufficient evidence of what it can do if a desecrating hand is laid upon it? It is my fault," he shouted. "I allowed it to become involved in this sanguinary play. I released its power. You have only to study its history to realize —"

"Gaston! Stop! We are busy and it is no affair of ours. We have no time to listen to your diatribe and it is not within my sphere of activities to demand the thing's return. In any case I wouldn't get it. Do pipe down like a good chap. The weapon is perfectly safe in police custody and will be returned in due course."

"Safe!" he cried swinging his arms about alarmingly. "Safe! You will drive me demented."

"Not far to go," remarked a splendid voice in the back stalls.

"Who made that repulsive observation?"

"I did," said Barrabell. "In my opinion you're certifiable. In any correctly ordered state —"

"Shut up, both of you," Peregrine cried. "Good Lord! Haven't we had enough to put up with! If you can't pipe down both of you go out of earshot and get on with it in the yard."

"I shall bring this up with Equity. It is not the first time I have been insulted in this theatre —"

"— my claidheamh-mor. I implore you to consider —"

"Gaston! Answer me. Are you here to audition? Yes or no."

"I am here . . . no."

"Barrabell, are you here to audition?"

"I was. I now see that it would be useless."

"In that case neither of you has any right to stay. I must ask you both to go. Go, for pity's sake, both of you."

The doors into the foyer opened. Winty Meyer's voice said: "Oh, sorry. I didn't realize —"

"Mr. Meyer, wait! I must speak with you. My claidheamh-mor! Mr. Meyer! Please!"

Gaston hurried down the aisle and out into the foyer. The doors swung to behind him and he became a distant rumpus.

Peregrine said: "I'm extremely sorry, Rangi. We'll go on when I've settled this idiotic affair. Now then, Bruce."

He took Barrabell's elbow and led him aside. "My dear chap," he said and forced his voice into a warmth he did not feel. "Alleyn has told me of your tragedy. I couldn't be sorrier for you. But I must ask you this. Don't you feel that with young William in the company you would be most un-happy? I do. I —"

Barrabell turned deadly white. He stared at Peregrine.

"You little rat," he said. He turned on his heel and left the theatre.

"Whew!" said Peregrine. "Okay, Rangi. We'll have an audition."

9

FINIS

AND now the theatre was almost rid of *Macbeth*. The units that from the audience had seemed solid but had silently revolved, showing different aspects of the scenery, had been taken apart and stacked against the walls.

The stage, every inch of it, was scrubbed and smelled of disinfectant. In front-of-house, advertisements for the new play replaced the old *Macbeth* posters and in the foyer the giant photograph frames were empty. The life-size photograph of Sir Dougal was rolled up and slid into a cardboard cylinder. It disappeared into the basement.

The bookstall had its display for the most part taken down and stacked in cartons; the programmes had been cleared out and stuffed into rubbish bags that awaited the collectors.

Going, going, gone, thought Winter Meyer. It was a lovely show.

The dressing-rooms were empty and scrubbed. All except the star room, which was locked and untouched, except by the police, since Sir Dougal Macdougal had walked out of it for the last time. His solicitors had given notice of sending persons in to collect his possessions. His name had been removed from the door.

Nina in her diminutive flat told herself that the malign influence of *Macbeth* was now satisfied and made a solemn promise to herself that she would not talk about it inside the theatre. She was greatly distressed, of course, and she wondered avidly who had done the murder, but she was sustained and even excited by being so overwhelmingly right in all her pronouncements.

They've not got a leg to stand on, she thought triumphantly.

Simon Morten rang up Maggie Mannering and asked her to lunch with him at the Wig and Piglet. She said she would and invited him to come early for her so that they could have a good talk in private. He arrived at noon.

"Maggie," he said holding her hands. "I wanted to ask you last night but you've been so *remote,* darling. I thought perhaps — I didn't know how you felt or — well, I even thought you might have your doubts about me. And I thought that I'd better find out, one way or another. And so — here I am."

Maggie stared at him. "Do you mean," she said, "that you thought I wondered if you decapitated Dougal? Is that it?"

"Well — I know it's idiotic but — well, yes. Don't laugh at me, Maggie, *please.* I've been in hell."

"I'll try not to," she said. "I'm sure you have. But why? Why would I think you'd done it? What motive could you have had for it?"

"I was still so horribly jealous," he muttered, turning dark red. "And you did the sex thing with him so awfully well. Just looking at you and listening — I — well, I'm sorry."

"Now, just you look here, Simon," said Maggie vigorously. "We're both going to play in *The Glove.* You're going to be tormented by me and it is not going to be all muddled up with the real thing: that way it'll go wrong. The audience will sense there's another reality intruding on the dramatic reality and they'll feel uncomfortable. Won't they?"

"I know how *you* feel about the mask an actor wears," he said.

"Yes, I do. And you take yours off at your peril. Right?"

"All right."

"Shake?" she said holding out her hand.

"All right, shake," he said and took it.

"Now we can go and have our blameless luncheon," said Maggie. "Come on. For the first time since it happened, I'm nervous. Let's talk about The Bard in love."

So they went to the Wig and Piglet.

To everyone's relief Gaston retired to his own premises, presumably to lick his incomprehensible wounds. But he renewed his assault on the Yard. Mr. Fox was called to the telephone, which was switched through to Alleyn's room. "Hullo?" he said.

"First of all," roared the intemperate man, "I intimated that I wished to communicate with Chief Superintendent Alleyn. You do not sound like the Chief Superintendent."

"This is his room, sir, but I am not the Chief Superintendent. He is unable to come to the telephone and authorizes me to speak for him. What seems to be the trouble, sir?"

"Nothing *seems* to be the trouble. The trouble *is*. I *demand* — repeat *demand* — the instant return of my claidheamh-mor under police armed guard, to my personal address. Today. Now."

"If you'll hold on for a minute, sir, I'll just write a note to that effect and leave it here in a prominent position on his desk."

Fox clapped his enormous paw over the receiver and said: "Sears."

"So I supposed."

"Here we are, sir. What was the message?"

"Odds bodkins, fellow —"

"I beg your pardon, sir?"

A stream of abuse, or what seemed to be abuse, followed by a deathly silence and then a high-pitched female voice.

"Master not velly well, please. Sank you. Good-bye," and the telephone was disconnected.

The Jay boys were returning to school. Crispin left by train in a dignified manner with a number of young men of equal status, an array of noisy smaller boys, and a little group of white-faced new ones. Robin and Richard behaved with the eccentricity that the household had come to expect of them on these occasions, even though they frequently returned home on Sundays and gorged themselves. Peregrine came to bid them good-bye. Fishing in his pocket for some coins to give them for spending money, he found the toy crusader, which Alleyn had returned to him.

"I forgot about you," he said and took it out and stared at it for a moment.

"May I have him back?" asked Robin. He took the mannikin and went to the telephone.

"Whom are you ringing up?" asked Peregrine.

"A boy."

He consulted the list and dialed the number. "Hullo, Horrible," he said. "What d'you think I've got? Three guesses. No . . . No. . . . Yes. Hooray. Clever old you. What are you doing? . . . Oh, *Daddy's* play? Well, I thought you'd like to know we're going back to school today so we'll be half-starved. Oh, well. Bung-ho."

He hung up and immediately dialed again.

"It's me again," he said. "I forgot to mention that I knew all along the fighter wasn't Macbeth. I'll give you three guesses who. . . . One. No. . . . Two. No. . . . Three. No. I'll give you till next Sunday." He replaced the receiver.

"Out of the mouths of babes and sucklings," muttered Peregrine. "Robin! Come here. You must tell me. How did you know?"

Robin looked at his father and saw that he meant business. He adopted a defiant attitude: feet apart, hands on hips, slightly nervous smile. "Three guesses?" he invited.

But Peregrine needed only one.

He rang up Alleyn at the Yard.

II

THE company of Dolphins at the Swan was diminished but Rangi and Ross and Lennox were still regulars and they met there for lunch. Rangi was quiet and withdrawn. His dark eyes and brilliant teeth dominated his face and it struck the others that he looked more "native" than he had before. But he was pleased with his new part, Mr. W.H., an ambiguous gentleman from Italy, overdressed and wearing a single earring.

"We start rehearsals tomorrow," said Ross. "Thank God, without the ineffable Sears *or* dreary old Banquo. The whole tragedy as far as the Dolphin's concerned is finished." He made a dismissive gesture with both hands.

"It won't be finished, my dear chap," said Lennox, "until somebody's under lock and key. Well, ask yourself. Will it?"

"*No*," said Rangi. "The stigma remains. It must."

"I looked in this morning. It's as clean as a whistle and smells of disinfectant everywhere."

"No policemen?"

"Not then, no. Just the offices clicking over merrily. There's a big notice out in front saying people can use their tickets for the new play or get their money back at the box office. And a board with nothing but rave notices from the former production of *The Glove*."

"Any reasons given?"

"There's a piece in the papers. I suppose you saw."

Lennox said yes, he had read it.

"I haven't seen the papers," said Rangi.

"It just says that Dougal died on Saturday night very suddenly in the theatre. And there's the usual obituary: half a column and photographs. The Macbeth one's very good," said Ross.

"It said that 'as a mark of respect' the theatre would be dark for three weeks," Ross added.

"It's been an honor to play in it. It'll be remembered," said Lennox.

"Yes," said Ross.

Rangi said, as if the words were dragged out of him, "It's *tapu*. We are all *tapu* and will be until the murderer is found. And who will *whakamana*?"

There was an awkward silence.

"I don't know what you mean," Lennox said.

"Better that you don't," said Rangi. "You wouldn't understand."

"Understand what?" asked Lennox.

"*Maoritanga.*"

"Maori how much?"

"Shut up, old boy," said Ross and kicked him underneath the table.

"Why?" Lennox looked at Rangi and found something in his face that made him say hurriedly: "Sorry. Didn't mean to pry."

"Not at all," said Rangi. He stood up. "I must get back. I'm late. Excuse me."

He went to the counter, paid his bill, and left.

"What's biting him?" Lennox said.

"Lord knows. Something to do with the case, I imagine. He'll get over it, whatever it is."

After a pause Lennox muttered, "I didn't mean to be rude or anything. Well, I wasn't, was I? I apologized."

"Perhaps you said something that upset his *mana*."

"Oh, to hell with him and his *mana*. Where did you pick up that word, anyway?"

"In conversation with him. It means all sorts of things but pride is the principal one."

They ate their lunch in silence. Rangi had left a copy of *The Stage* on the bench. Ross looked at it. A small paragraph at the bottom of the page caught his eye. "Hi," he said. "This would interest Barrabell. This is the lot he went abroad with. Take a look."

Lennox bent over the table. He read:

"The Leftist Players are repeating their successful tour of

Soviet Russia. They are now about to go into rehearsal with three contemporary plays. Ring club number for auditions."

"That's the gang he went with before," said Ross.

"He wouldn't be let go. Not while nobody's been caught."

"I suppose not."

"I wonder if he's seen this," said Ross without interest.

They finished their lunch without much conversation.

Barrabell had seen it. He read it carefully and consulted his notebook for the club number.

His bed-sitting room carried the absolute negation of any personal characteristics whatever. It was on the large side, tidy and clean. Its two windows looked across an alley at the third-story shutters of an equally anonymous building.

He opened his wardrobe and took out the battered suitcase with the old Russian airways labels on it. Opened, some tidily folded garments — pajamas, underclothes and shirts — were revealed and under these a package of press cuttings and the glossy photograph of a good-looking young woman.

The press cuttings were mainly of productions that he had appeared in, but there were also relics of the trial of Harcourt-Smith. A photograph of the man himself, handcuffed between two policemen, entering the Old Bailey and looking blankly at nothing. Another, of Mr. Justice Swithering, and a third, of William and his mother, taken in the street. There were accounts of the trial.

Barrabell read the cuttings and looked at the photographs. He then put them one by one into the dead fireplace and burned them to ashes. He went to the bathroom on his landing and washed his hands. Then he replaced all the theatrical reviews in the suitcase and looked for a long time at the glossy photograph, which was signed "Muriel." His hands trembled. He put it under the reviews and shut and locked the case.

Now he consulted his copy of *The Stage* and rang the number given for inquiries about auditions.

He made a quick calculation, arrived at the amount he

owed his landlady, and put it in a used envelope with a cellophane window. He wrote her name on the front and added: "Called away very unexpectedly. B.B."

Whistling almost inaudibly, he reopened the case and packed into it everything else in the room that he owned. He double-checked every drawer and shelf, put his passport in the breast pocket of his jacket, and, after a final look around, picked up his case and left the room. The landlady's office was locked. He pushed the envelope under the door and walked out.

He was on a direct route for his destination and waited at the bus stop, dumping his case on the ground until the right bus came along. He climbed aboard, sat near the door, tucked his case under his legs, and paid his fare.

The man who had been behind him in the queue heard him give the address and gave the same one.

Shortly thereafter a message came through to Alleyn.

"Subject left lodging-house carrying suitcase with old Russian labels. Followed to address suggested and is still there."

To which he replied: "Keep obbo. No arrest but don't lose him."

III

"It's one thing," said Alleyn, "to have the whole case wrapped up in the copper's mind and to be absolutely sure, as I am, who's responsible; and it's an entirely different cup of tea to get a jury to believe it. God knows it's a tangle and can't you hear counsel for the defense? 'Ladies and gentlemen of the jury, you have listened very patiently to this impudent tarradiddle — ' and so on and so on. I've been hoping for something more to break — the man himself, perhaps — but nothing — nothing."

Fox made a long sympathetic rumbling sound.

"I've read and reread the whole case from the beginning, and to me it's as plain as the nose on your old face, Br'er Fox, but I'm damned if it will be for anybody else. It's too far removed from simple, short statements, although, God

knows, they *are* there. *I* don't know. You've got the warrant.
Shall we walk in and feel his collar or shan't we?"

"We're not likely to pick up anything else if we don't."

"No. No, we're not, I suppose."

His telephone rang. It was Peregrine.

As Alleyn listened and made notes, his face cleared.

"Thank you," he said, "I think so. I freely confess I didn't
notice. . . . It may be considerable. . . . I see. Thank you,
Peregrine," he said again and hung up, pushing the paper
over to Fox, who had assumed his spectacles in preparation.
"This helps," he said.

"Certainly does," Fox agreed.

"I never noticed," said Alleyn.

"You didn't know there was going to be a murder."

"Well, no. All the same — nor did young Robin. Lay on
a car and a couple of coppers, will you, Fox?"

He took a pair of handcuffs from a drawer in his desk.

"Think he'll turn ugly?" asked Fox.

"I don't know. He might. Come on."

They went down in the lift.

It was a warm early summer evening. The car was waiting
for them and Alleyn gave the address to the driver. He and
Fox sat in front and the two uniformed police in the back.

"It's an arrest," Alleyn said. "I don't expect much trouble
but you never know. The *Macbeth* murder."

The traffic streamed past in a world of lights, hurrying
figures, incalculable urgencies proclaiming the warmth and
excitability of London at night. In the suburbs the traffic
thinned out and presently they slowed down and pulled up.
It was a dark entry with no lights in the front of the house.
A man was waiting for them and came up to the car.

"Hullo," said Alleyn. "Nobody stirring?"

"He hasn't left the place, sir. There's another of our chaps
by the back entrance."

"Right. Ready?"

"Yes, sir." The other three men spread out behind him.

Alleyn pressed a bell. Footsteps. A dim light behind glass

panels and a fine voice, actor-trained, called out: "I'll go."
Footsteps sounded and the clank of a chain and turn of a
key.

The door opened. The tall figure was silhouetted against
the dimly lit hall.

"I was expecting you," the man said. 'Come in."

Alleyn went in, followed by Fox. The two constables followed. One of them locked the door and pocketed the key.

"Gaston Sears," said Alleyn, "I am about to charge you
with the murder of Dougal Macdougal. Do you wish to say
anything? You are not obliged to say anything unless you
wish to do so but whatever you say will be taken down and
may be given in evidence."

"Thank you. I wish to say a great deal."

Fox took out his notebook and uncapped his pen. Alleyn
said: "I will search you, if you please, before you begin."

Gaston turned and placed his hands against the wall.

He wore his black cloak. There were letters and papers
of all kinds in every pocket. Alleyn handed them to Fox,
who noted their contents and tied them together. They seemed
for the most part to be concerned with ancient weaponry
and in particular with the claidheamh-mor.

"Please do not lose them," Gaston said. "They are extremely valuable."

"They will be perfectly safe."

"I am relieved to receive your assurance, sir. Where is my
claidheamh-mor?"

"Locked up at the Yard."

"Locked up? *Locked up?* Do you know what you are
saying? Do you realize that I, I who know more about the
latent power of the claidheamh-mor than anyone living, have
so disastrously aroused it and am brought to this pass by its
ferocity alone? Do you know —"

On and on went the great voice. Ancient documents, the
rune on the hilt, the history of bloodshed, formal executions,
decapitation in battle, what happened to the thief of the
sixteenth century (decapitation), its effect on people who

handled it (lunacy). "I, in my pride, in my arrogance, supposed myself exempt. Then came the fool, Macdougal, and his idiot remarks. I felt it swell in my hands.

"And what, do you suppose, inspired the practical joker? Decapitated heads. How do you account for them? You cannot. I could not until I discovered Barrabell's wife had suffered decapitation at the hands of the so-called Hampstead Chopper. Wherever the claidheamh-mor turns up, it is associated with decapitation. And I, its demented agent, I, in my vanity —"

Gaston stopped, wiped his brow, said he was rather warm, and asked for a glass of water, which the Chinese woman brought.

"Before you go on again," said Alleyn, "You have just said" — he consulted his notes —" 'I, its demented agent. I, in my vanity.' What were you about to say?"

"Let me think. 'Demented agent,' did I say? 'In my vanity.' But it's as clear as may be, surely. It came alive in my hands. I was the appointed man."

"You mean you killed Dougal Macdougal?"

"Certainly. If holding the claidheamh-mor can be *called* 'killing,' I killed him." He drew himself up. He might have been an eccentric professor about to address his class. He grasped the lapels of his cloak, raised his chin, and pitched his voice on a declamatory level.

"It was after the servant put the false head on my claidheamh-mor. He carried it into the appointed corner and left it there and went away. I went in. I removed the head and laid it aside on the floor. I removed my belt. I held the claidheamh-mor in my hands and it was alive and hot and desirous of blood.

"I stood there in the shadows. Very still. I heard him declaim:

. . . *weapons laugh to scorn*
Brandish'd by man that's of a woman born.

I heard him cross the stage. I raised the claidheamh-mor. He came in, shielding his eyes in the comparative dark. He said. 'Who's there?' I said, 'Sir Dougal, there's a thong loose on your left foot. You will trip,' and he said, 'Oh, it's you, is it? Thank you.' He stooped down and the claidheamh-mor leaped in my hands and decapitated him. I put the head on it and left it in the corner. The coronet had fallen off and I put it on my own head. I could hear Macduff's soliloquy and his encounters with the other figures that he mistook for Macbeth and I was ready. I heard Old Siward say, *Enter, sir, the castle,* and I pulled down my vizor and adjusted my cloak and I went on and fought and Macduff chased me off and he ran on past me. I replaced my belt. That is how it was. I was the avenger. I was proud as Lucifer."

IV

A SUNNY May Sunday and sightseers' craft plied up and down the Thames on their trips to the Tower. The Jays with Alleyn were drinking their after-luncheon coffee on the terrace outside their house. Across the river the Dolphin, having had its outside washed down, sparkled in the sunshine. William, whose Sunday visit had become a fixture, was being noisily entertained upstairs in the ex-nursery by Robin and Richard.

"Gaston's saved us a lot of trouble," said Alleyn, "by confessing. Though I can't think of a more *mot injuste* for his manner of doing it. He sticks to his story and I can't make up my mind, to my own satisfaction, whether the plea's altogether genuine. Luckily I don't have to. The defense, if he allows it, will be guilty but insane. His back history will support it but he'll fight it tooth and nail. But he was very cunning, you know. He managed an alibi for himself by committing the crime earlier. He was talking away to the covey of 'corpses' when the murder was supposed to be done, and alleging he suffered from asthma, which he kept quiet about for professional reasons. He's as strong as an ox with the wind of a bellows. There's no question of its being an unrehearsed impulse. All the same —"

"All the same?" said Emily.

"Whatever the verdict is, I've an idea it won't upset him.

as much as it would anyone else. He'll write a book, I dare-say. And he'll adore the trial."

"What about Barrabell?"

"Horrid little man with his tricks and manners and anony-mous messages. But we won't let him go to Russia. He's wanted to give evidence. I shouldn't talk like this about him, he's had an appalling experience, God knows, but it's not fair to be such a good actor and such a crawler. In a way he s a link in the whole business. He started the decapitation business and he got Gaston thinking about it and about the claidheamh-mor. Upon my word, I wouldn't be surprised if he planted the idea in Gaston's wild imagination. How's your play going? You've started rehearsals, haven't you?"

"Yes. All right. Too early to predict. Young William's an actor. Maggie's shaping well. And — good Lord, I've for-gotten. It's why I asked you to lunch in the first place. Wait a moment."

He went indoors. There was a wild shriek from above and the three little boys came tumbling downstairs. They fell into a scrum and out of it and rushed round the house, William shouting, *"The devil damn thee black, thou cream-fac'd loon!"*

Alleyn called out: "Robin. May I interrupt?"

"Yes, sir?" said Robin warily.

"It's about you knowing the fighter wasn't Macbeth."

"Did you guess?" said Robin, rallying.

"Only after you gave the hint. Macbeth and all his men wore black lambskin tunics, didn't they?"

"Yes."

"And Seyton wore a heavy belt to support the claidheamh-mor?"

"That's right."

"And when he took it off it showed the wear — lambskin all flattened and worn?"

"Yes. Only when his cloak-thing shifted."

"I should have noticed and I didn't. You've been a great help, Robin."

"Whangee! Will I have to give evidence?"

"No. I just wanted to thank you."

"You didn't notice at the time, sir. I expect you would have," said Robin kindly, "when you got around to it."

"I hope so," said Alleyn meekly.

"Hi!" Robin shouted. "William!" and tore off round the house.

Peregrine reappeared. He carried a long package carefully wrapped in brown paper. "Do you know what's in here?" he asked.

Alleyn took it, passed his hands over it, and weighed it. "Dummy swords?" he asked.

"Right. The wooden swords used for rehearsing the fight while Gaston made the steel ones. Being Gaston's, they are needlessly ornate and highly finished. Now read this."

He gave Alleyn an open envelope addressed to "Master William Smith." "Read it," he said.

Alleyn took it out.

> *Master William Smith.*
> *I regret that I, having been much engaged of late, forgot the promise I made you at the beginning of the season. I have, as some compensation, included both weapons. You will be anxious to learn their correct usage. Treat them with the utmost care and respect. Regrettably, I shall not be at liberty to teach you but Mr. Simon Morten will, no doubt, be glad to do so. You will be a good actor.*
> > *I remain,*
> > *Your obedient servant,*
> > *Gaston Sears*

"Shall I give them to the boy? And the letter?"

After a long pause, Alleyn said: "I don't know William. If he is a sensible boy and respects the tools of his trade — yes. I think you should."